My Fair Marchioness

by
Christi Caldwell

Other Titles by Christi Caldwell

Five Days with a Duke

Lords of Honor
Seduced by a Lady's Heart
Captivated by a Lady's Charm
Rescued by a Lady's Love
Tempted by a Lady's Smile
Courting Poppy Tidemore

Scandalous Seasons
Forever Betrothed, Never the Bride
Never Courted, Suddenly Wed
Always Proper, Suddenly Scandalous
Always a Rogue, Forever Her Love
A Marquess for Christmas
Once a Wallflower, at Last His Love

Sinful Brides
The Rogue's Wager
The Scoundrel's Honor
The Lady's Guard
The Heiress's Deception

The Wicked Wallflowers
The Hellion
The Vixen
The Governess
The Bluestocking
The Spitfire

The Theodosia Sword
Only For His Lady
Only For Her Honor
Only For Their Love

For more information about the author:
www.christicaldwellauthor.com
christicaldwellauthor@gmail.com
Twitter: @ChristiCaldwell
Or on Facebook at: Christi Caldwell Author

About the Book

Miss Julia Smith peddles flowers for her daily bread, but lands in the Duchess of Arlington's household when selling blooms becomes unexpectedly hazardous. To Julia's surprise, Her Grace offers not only safety, but also a chance at a new, fancier life—a life Julia isn't sure she wants.

Harris Clarendale, Marquess of Ruthven, has seen his dear godmother taken in by one charlatan after another as Her Grace has searched in vain for a missing niece. Harris determines to charm his way past Julia's defenses, and expose her for the schemer she is. Instead, he finds a woman of wit, honor, and integrity, and more than a little passion, and Julia learns that a fancy lord can also be a decent man with a loyal heart.

When secrets are revealed, will love be enough for Julia and Harris to forge a future together?

Chapter 1

Covent Garden
London, England
1828

There was no understanding a toff.

Those fancy lords, who had everything under God's sun, seemed determined to amass it all, and then once they had it, they were content to squander it.

This time, what this gent appeared ready to squander was... flowers.

And a whole lot of them at that.

Waiting in the wings, hovering in the shadows, along with every other flower seller in Covent Garden, Julia Smith intended to make their waste her riches.

"... and it says she is a duchess," said Adairia, her friend, sister in all but blood, and the only person Julia trusted.

"Imagine that," Julia murmured, and it was all the other woman needed to hear to continue on with... whatever she was on about.

Not that Adairia needed any encouragement.

She'd been a prattler since they'd found each other as girls on the street outside of a Drury Lane theater. Alone, wearing tattered garments, the girl had been lost and crying, her piteous wailing ignored by all. Except Julia and her mother. Julia's mother had urged Julia to go collect the lost little girl. Together they'd brought Adairia back to the hovel they'd called home, and there the girl had stayed.

Adairia had always been whimsical.

Hell, when they'd first met, the other young woman had insisted she was a princess and wanted to find the way back to her castle.

Which was why Adairia was the absolute worst person to whom Oswyn, that bloody street tough, could have approached with all this nonsense about Adairia being a 'lost lady'.

Adairia, who was no princess.

Adairia, who, like Julia, had no father or family… beyond Julia.

The gentleman was speaking to one of the drivers, directing the distribution of those flowers. As he checked the glimmering fob that dangled from his perfectly cut black trousers, there clearly wasn't a place the fellow cared to be less.

But then, what person in their right mind would prefer these parts, compared to the ones a bloke like him was accustomed to?

"Oswyn said Rand Graham has information about me…and that he wishes to speak with me about…things he knows about my abduction," Adairia ventured, and Julia abruptly stopped. Adairia halted beside her.

Rand Graham. The evil leader of the Rookeries. Younger and more deadly than even Diggory. And that was saying something about his evil. Before he'd been taken down by the head proprietor of the Hell and Sin Club, the late Mac Diggory had ruled the streets of East London—and he'd done so with a viciousness that lived on in the memories of him that still haunted these cobblestones.

"First, you aren't a viscount's long lost daughter," Julia started.

"An earl's," Adairia swiftly amended.

Innocent as the London day was unforgiving, Julia's sister was too-naïve-for-her-own-good. "And you were *not* abducted, Adairia," she continued. "My mother and I found you. You were lost," she said bluntly, reminding her sister of that forgotten details. "Do you remember that?"

Adairia's features fell. "Yes, but—"

"And third of all, are you really suggesting we answer a summons from Rand Graham, the most ruthless gang leader in the Dials since Mac Diggory, and discuss your supposed abduction from these parts?" Rand Graham who now controlled these parts.

After a beat of silence, Adairia beamed. "Yes!"

Oh, good Lord in heaven. Julia took her sister-from-the-streets by the arm and marched her toward more important matters—the fellow passing out flowers.

Except, Adairia wasn't done.

"I don't understand what the harm is in speaking with him. Oswyn said Graham knows information that no one else knows. He says I have an aunt, and she is a duchess, and—"

"You really don't understand the danger?" Julia snapped, fighting to maintain her patience and realizing for the first time just how much she'd failed Adairia while trying to preserve her joyful spirit and innocence. "Since Diggory's death, Graham's openly fought for control of St. Giles and the Dials, and you really have no idea about his reputation?"

"But—"

"Let us assume that this farcical story is true. Let us assume you were abducted, which you absolutely were not," Julia took care to remind Adairia. "The ones behind that evil would have been people Rand Graham is even now seeking to protect."

Her eyes tortured, Adairia troubled at her lower lip, and for the span of a heartbeat Julia believed she'd managed to get through to her sister.

And then, Adairia lifted her palms. "But I have to know, Julia. I *have* to."

"Aren't we enough?" Julia implored. "Do you really need to go chasing dreams of bigger"—better—"families?"

That managed to cut through her friend's jabbering.

Briefly. "Of course you are. But, Julia…" Adairia gripped her by the shoulders, turning Julia away from the street and forcing her to meet her eyes. "This is our chance."

"Aye, it's our chance."

The other woman's gaze lit.

"Our chance to get ourselves a windfall." And they had to act before they were beaten to it. Julia pointed past her friend's shoulder, directing her focus and attention precisely where it should be… on the crates upon crates overflowing with the whitest, most-silken-looking flowers she'd seen in all her years as a flower peddler.

Which, given that she'd been doing it since she was a small girl and had continued doing it all these years later, was saying a good deal indeed.

Adairia frowned, that downturn slip of the woman's lips as rare as her silence. "I'm not talking about the flowers."

"I know," she said. "But you should be."

The tall, golden-haired fellow headed to one of those carriages, and Julia instantly strained. He was leaving, which meant they had to act now.

Wait...

The servant collected another small case of white flowers.

No... there were more blooms, was all. So many. Why, at that amount, she and Adairia would be selling for days. There were so many, it would be impossible to keep up. They'd have to dry some of them out.

Fingers tugged at her sleeve.

"Julia."

Dried flowers fetched less.

"Julia."

But with this many of them, they could string together even more when the fresh buds weren't plentiful.

"Julia!" There came another frantic tug on her tattered sleeve, and Julia ripped her attention her friend's way.

"What?"

"What? Haven't you been listening to a word I've said, Julia? I'm pointing out that if we pursue this," Adairia said, "then we can put all of this behind us."

Bloody hell.

The swarms had already converged upon the gent, and he and his servants were handing out cases of flowers to the waiting girls around him.

"Let's go!" Julia muttered. Taking her friend by the

hand, she began dragging her forward.

At her side, Adairia smiled. "Splendid. I—"

"I'm talking about the flowers. They're going to be all gone." Blast and hell. She maneuvered herself through the collection of smallish children and young women. "Flowers, please, sir," she called, lifting her palms up to the liveried footman who was accepting offerings from another ridiculously bewigged fellow inside the coach.

The man gave her a once-over and frowned.

"Those ones are a bit old to be flower sellers, don't you think, my lord?" he called, and Julia followed his stare to the person to whom he'd directed that question. Tall, attired in an elegant cloak, the man was already retreating, indicating how little he cared about this. "Probably one of the whore sorts."

The whore sorts.

Of course, because everyone knew there were two types of flower sellers—the youngest of girls, who hawked their blooms from baskets outside of Covent Garden theaters, and the older girls, who were no longer children and who coupled the sale of a flower with a coupling.

The gentleman didn't bother to glance back. But why should he? It was a wonder he was involved in any way in the common task before him. "Distribute the rest as you see fit," the young lord said, heading for his grand carriage.

"He don't care," she said, unable to keep a frantic note from creeping in. "And I'm not a whore," she felt compelled to add. Because a pompous one like him who'd mentioned it would care.

Sniffing at the air, he bypassed her, ignoring her assurances and handing the offering over to—

"You," she spat.

Meg Silvers, the most notorious seller of both flowers and her body and now also a notorious sellout to Rand Graham, smirked. "Step aside."

That bastard had come and solicited help from those who'd grown up and still lived in these parts. For their fealty and information he found useful, he gave them protection in the form of safety and monies.

Several of the children who stood in wait assessed the arrival of Meg Silvers. Knowing the threat they faced now if they secured flowers over her, a favored hand of Rand Graham, those children scattered.

Fury licked at Julia's insides. She'd be cursed to hell and back before she ceded these flowers to this sellout. Edging Meg Silvers out with a swift elbow, she angled herself in front of the other woman and held her arms up to the servant. "Give me a bloody case."

"Phew, the mouth on you," the man spat as he drew that offering back.

No!

Everything in Julia cried out at the loss of that gift, one that would have seen them fed and the rent paid and without worries for at least two months.

"You can keep your damned flowers," she shouted, waving a fist.

She dimly registered someone tugging at her sleeve.

"We are, and we'll give them to more thankful, more grateful people than the likes of you." The nasally nosed bastard flicked a glance over Julia before handing that crate and then another and another to Meg and the children and other women who'd resumed swarming them.

Desperation nearly brought her doubling over as she surged forward. "She's not more grateful. She's a liar. She is the wh—"

"Julia. Julia," Adairia said more insistently. "Come."

She allowed herself to be dragged away, her gaze locked on the dwindling supply and the cheering children until the mirth faded, and the carriages rolled away. The streets returned to their usual bustling activity, devoid of charity and filled with the cries of the piteous hawking their wares.

Julia sank down onto the slight stoop where the pavement met the cobblestones and stared forlornly out.

Gone.

It was all gone.

"We didn't need their flowers anyway," Adairia said with her usual sunny optimism.

Something snapped. "Actually, we did, Adairia," she exclaimed. "We needed every single one of those damned flowers. To sell. To dry and then sell."

"But we can have more than flowers." The younger woman withdrew a small official-looking sheet and waggled it under Julia's nose. "Oswyn gave me this. It is from a detective whose been sending queries around St.—"

Cursing, Julia ripped the page from her friend's hand hard and fast enough that it shredded at the corner, leaving a remnant of the damning scrap in Adairia's fingers. "Have a care," Julia ordered the younger woman. "Lest someone discover you with this."

Julia should be kinder, and she should be more patient

and understanding, but the other woman didn't know the level of danger she played with. If anyone How could she not realize that? And worse, how could she believe this shite?

But they all did what they had to to cope in these parts. Her friend had opted to live a life of make-believe, where she wasn't just some fatherless bastard whelped by a whore and turned into a flower seller.

Adairia frowned. "You don't believe it."

Julia stole a frantic look about. "I believe you should put this away," she muttered, and hopping to her feet, she promptly folded and stuffed the ivory page inside the front of her dress.

All that fucking Graham had brought to their step was potential peril. She damned that ruthless bastard to hell.

"But there's this detective and Graham who are both saying—"

"To hell with Graham," Julia interrupted. "Graham is consolidating power and flushing out people who might have been disloyal to Diggory so he can purge people he deems traitors."

Adairia proved as persistent in this as she did in that fanciful dream she'd allowed herself to believe since she'd been all but a babe. "But—"

"How have you still not learned that a person doesn't bring attention to themselves in the Rookeries?" *Or claim that you are a rightful lady taken from a noble family by the ruthless people who still dwell in these parts?*

Her friend smiled. "Because sometimes there are things too wonderful to turn away from. Because fear should not chase away chance and hope and truth."

Why, that rumor alone that her friend spoke so freely of was enough to see a woman with the hilt of a dagger buried in her throat. Because the ones who'd supposedly had a hand in the disappearance of a child, were also the ones who'd pay for those crimes.

She'd failed the other woman. There was nothing else for it. Julia shuddered.

Understanding dawned in Adairia's eyes. "Ahhh…"

Do not say more. She's only put that soft little utterance there to get you to say more. Do not. Do—

Julia hopped to her feet. "What?" she snapped.

With all the grace and aplomb of the princess she'd professed to be, Adairia sailed to her feet. "You're scared," the other woman murmured in her soft, lyrical speech. "But you don't have to be. This woman who is looking for me is my aunt."

"Aye, I'm scared. I'm scared that we don't have enough money to fill our bellies. I'm scared we'll have to turn ourselves to whoring." Which, by the grace of God—nay, to hell with that fake figure. Which, by the grace of Adairia's songbirdlike voice, which she employed at the start of and end of every Coven Garden production, they'd been spared. "And you know what else I'm scared of?" she demanded, taking a furious step closer and angling her head back to meet the taller, willowier woman's gaze. "I'm scared that you don't have the sense God gave a damned flea to know this is a ploy of Graham's, one where you end up dead or worse." A test that Adairia was failing mightily.

"What kind of ploy could it possibly be?" Adairia asked with all the exasperation only one of her innocence could manage.

"I don't...know," Julia said. "Perhaps he'll use you to get money from the peerage. Or perhaps he wants to see if you would point fingers of blame at people from these streets. All I know is I can't get it through your goddamned head,"— Julia jammed a finger into her own forehead—"there isn't a damned way out for you or me. We do not have time for children's games and bloody fairy tales. You aren't the damned princess you claimed to be the day we met, and you certainly aren't one now. My mum went where you said you were from and asked whether they'd lost a child. There was no lost daughter. There was no earl. Now, if you could just... let this rest, before Graham's people get wind of it and nick the both of us." Cursing herself for saying all those damning words as loudly as she had, Julia lowered her voice to a whisper. "Please, Adairia."

Adairia's stricken eyes stared back, ravaging even Julia's life-hardened breast with guilt.

Hell. Fear made a person do shite things in life. But yelling at one's only family? That was the worst. "Oi don't want ye to feel bad," she said gruffly, slipping briefly from the proper King's English to the coarse cockney her mother had abhorred and had gone to efforts to instruct her out of. Julia looked about and moved closer to her sister. "It is just the more you spin this yarn, the more likely it is we're going to find ourselves... in a bad way."

Nay, there was only one fate that awaited them were Adairia's wishful imaginings about being the niece of a duke overheard. Gooseflesh climbed along her arms. Dead. They'd find themselves dead, and likely raped, beaten, and bloodied bad enough beforehand that they'd be grateful when that blade was last stuck inside them, ending their misery. Because those who'd been involved with the children being taken and sold to Mac Diggory wanted nothing more than their role in those abductions to go away.

Even so, she didn't want to hurt the other woman. "I'm sorry they've filled your head with this, Adairia," she said with all the gentleness she could. "I truly am." A pained laugh spilled from her lips. "Do you truly think I wouldn't, more than anything in the world, want this to be real? But it's not." She held the younger woman's eyes, trying to will her to see the truth. "It's not, Adairia," she said, this time infusing a greater emphasis meant to puncture the fantasies her friend had let herself believe these past years.

"It is," Adairia whispered, touching a hand to her heart. Such intensity radiated from within the blue depths of Adairia's irises that Julia shivered. "I know it. I believe it. And this is our path out."

Our path out.

As if there was such a thing. How did a person even come to believe such a thing in these parts?

Because that was what kept her sane.

"There's no path out, Adairia," she said quietly. "There's just work and more work. There isn't the happily-ever-afters of the stories you used to tell. And then we die. I'll head to Colvill's for their day's refuse," she said, of the exotic nursery near Sloane Square. "You head to Knight's." Because as it stood now? They didn't have a damned bloom to sell.

Adairia beamed. "We'll be fine. You'll see!"

With that, Julia wheeled around and went in search of

the hothouse-flower shops' waste. "Stupid, silly magic," she muttered as she trudged onward to Hillier's Flower Shop.

Stepping quick, Julia headed westward toward the florist. She should have gone there first. But she, like all the other peddlers, had seen that handsome toff raining flowers down on them.

She should have known better. Julia did know better. She'd gotten careless.

It was all Adairia's talk of magic and easy living and—

Two figures stepped into her path, bringing her up short.

Oh, bloody hell.

She eyed the hulking pair warily.

Both bald, both toothless, and both attired in matching crimson garments, they might as well have been twins. The similar look of them, however, marked them as members of Rand Graham's gang.

"We got questions for ye."

Julia eyed the pair and the path behind her. "Step aside," she demanded. "I've a place to be."

One of the fellows took a step forward, and she instinctively backed away.

"Ye were given a cloak. 'Ad some dealings ye did with a lady?" he asked. "Or was that the other one?"

Oh, God. No.

"It was me," she said quickly. That damned cloak. A gift given to her by some benevolent lady on the street. She'd said she'd be wise to sell it. She'd known it made her and Adairia a mark of some sort, but Adairia had desperately wanted it.

Both brutes peered more closely at her.

"You wouldn't just be saying that now, would ye?"

Calm. Be calm. Revealing too much in these parts was perilous. "I wouldn't," she said evenly. "I have an affinity for living."

Both men chuckled.

"Graham's got some questions for ye. About that lady." They were already reaching for her.

She evaded their grip. "I don't know who she is," she protested, her heart hammering. "She was just a stranger."

"Yea. Sure. Either way, ye can tell that to Graham."

Gasping, she turned and tried to run.

Too late.

One of the men caught her plait, yanking her back hard, pulling a scream from her.

Her assailant immediately clamped a hand over her mouth, stifling the remainder of that cry, burying it with the stench of sweat and grease.

He cursed, tightening his hold.

Julia bit down hard on his palm, gagging on the taste of his blood. His grip slackened, and she fought her way out of his arms.

She made it a pace before one of the men slammed into her, knocking her forward onto the pavement, sucking the breath from her lungs and sending stars dancing in her eyes.

Julia blinked back those slight flecks of light.

"Ye're makin' this 'ard when ye don't need to," he panted against her ear, his breath as uneven as her own from the fight she'd given him.

Good. The bastard.

Finding another burst of energy, the kind that could

come only from the desperate need to survive, Julia bucked, and then she felt something hard prod her lower back and instantly stopped, recoiling as she realized he was aroused by her struggles.

"If ye choose to not cooperate, we can enjoy ourselves first." He pressed a sloppy kiss against her cheek.

Terror and horror all rolled together inside as he shoved her face down onto the pavement. The cobblestones scraped her cheek.

She whimpered, choking with desperation.

And then, suddenly, the weight was gone.

Julia lay motionless, registering the absence of that pressure on her chest, and then, scrambling up onto her knees and then her feet, she faced the tableau behind her.

Like some Arthurian warrior Adairia had told her tales of, he stood there, braced over the two men he'd felled. One of the brutes was unconscious, the other dazed.

His slightly long golden hair was loosely tousled, his body as broad and powerful as the pair at his feet.

"That isn't the way to treat a lady," he said coolly, his voice as even as if he'd casually commented on the weather and not as though he'd impressively beaten two large grown men.

"That one ain't a lady," her assailant stammered. "Got something that belongs to me, she does."

"I didn't take anything that belongs to him," she spat.

"No, I rather trust your word. It seems a good deal more reliable than that of a man who'd put his hands upon a woman."

With that, he brought his arm back in a quick right hook

and hit her assailant.

The man's eyes rolled in his head, and then his form went limp.

The gentleman glanced briefly back, and her breath caught as his gaze locked with hers. Blue. As blue as the skies Adairia whispered of that she recalled from the English countryside, a color so vibrant she'd doubted her sister's telling. The hue of his irises managed to suck the thoughts clear of Julia's head.

"Well done, my lord." A servant came rushing forward, shattering the connection, but the gentleman held a hand up, dismissing him, and started for Julia.

She immediately tensed, the cloud of wonder now gone.

He reached into his jacket, and she took a hasty step back.

"It is fine," he murmured in tones better suited for the fractious mouser she and Adairia kept. He withdrew a crisp handkerchief embroidered with three initials and snapped it open. Once. Twice. And then ever so slowly, he reached out. "May I?" he murmured, and it took a moment for her to gather that he was asking permission for… something, and it didn't make sense, because people didn't speak to her in those gentle tones, or worry after her.

She told herself to nod, even as she wasn't certain what she was agreeing to, and then he tenderly brushed away the small stones that clung to her cheek.

"Are you hurt?" he asked quietly.

She didn't feel a thing. She felt as light as air, with her feet five feet above the earth.

Julia lowered her lashes and peered up at him. "I—?"

"Darling, do hurry along."

And just like that, the moment was again shattered, and she was reminded all over again that she was a poor peddler girl. And he? Why, he might as well have been the prince she secretly—and never dared admit aloud to Adairia—dreamed of. She followed his focus over to a grand black conveyance. A flaxen-haired beauty hung partially out of the carriage, impatience stamped upon her features. Never had the sorry state of her appearance, and very existence, been starker than it was in this very moment with that fair princess waiting for him.

"I'll be along shortly," he called, and the woman frowned, but then she ducked back inside the carriage.

The driver pushed the door shut, bringing Julia's gaze to the familiar crest, and she froze.

He returned his attention to Julia. "Patience has never been one of her virtues," he said with a wink.

With the threat of danger having receded, she registered his identity. The affable, and detached, flower distributor.

"Thank you, sir," Julia said gruffly.

"I recognized you."

Oh, God. Her stomach churned. "Forgive me. I didn't mean—" Julia's speech dissolved, wavering between the coarse cockney she'd been born with and the proper English she'd learned at Adairia's hand.

"No. No," he said, brushing off her apology, and then he started for the carriage.

Julia stared after him as he said something to the driver, who handed down a crate.

She stared on in wide-eyed disbelief as the gentleman

made his way back. "Here," he said, placing the case of flowers at her feet.

Struck silent, she moved her gaze between the offering of roses and the gentleman.

"Hardly seemed fair that my godmother's servant got to make the determination as to who was worthy or not of the flowers."

Words… failed. She attempted to get them out.

He reached inside his fine wool coat and removed a purse. "Here," he said, handing that sleek sack out.

Of their own volition, her hand immediately shot up, claiming that most precious of gifts, and her fingers brushed his.

Heat. And warmth. Fingers that were not stained with dirt and grime as hers were, but yet somehow, the long, golden digits evinced strength.

She hurriedly snatched her palm back. "Thank you," she said quickly. The weight and clink of coins within indicated he'd proffered a small fortune.

The carriage door opened once more. "Darling," the stunning creature called out. Impatience lent her voice a whine.

The gentleman, whose name was nothing other than "darling" to Julia, winked. "As I said, patience is a virtue." He cast a glance to where her assailants lay motionless on the ground, and she followed his stare.

They'd begun to stir.

"I've had the constable fetched."

Her stomach lurched. Oh, God. No. What had he done? He'd meant well.

As if on cue, a pair of constables came rushing over and proceeded to drag the pair to their feet and off.

"You needn't worry about them any longer," the handsome stranger said, with the assurance and confidence of a man who had absolutely no idea how these streets worked.

"Come, darling. We shall be late."

He sighed, lingering still, and for a moment, Julia thought he intended to stay. That he, at the very least, intended to say something more.

But then, with a bow, he tipped the brim of his high hat and left.

He'd bowed?

And tipped his hat?

At her?

They were peculiar details to fixate on, considering the stranger had left her with a veritable fortune, or at least enough to see her and Adairia's rent paid and to more than match a month's work of peddling flowers.

Gathering up the crate, Julia stood there, staring half dazed as the gentleman drew himself inside the conveyance. A servant pushed the door shut, and after he climbed back atop the box alongside the driver, the carriage lurched into motion.

For the first time in Julia's life, her heart fluttered, and her thoughts were in disarray, and as the carriage drove off, she thought mayhap Adairia wasn't altogether wrong. Perhaps magic truly did exist for people like her after all.

Chapter 2

Over the years, there were any number of emergencies Harris Clarendale, the sixth Marquess of Ruthven, had solved for his godmother and her two friends.

Said emergencies had included rescuing a cat who'd climbed a tree on the junglelike grounds she called gardens at her Mayfair home. Granted, there had been any number of footmen and servants closer at hand of similar height and frame, but who, according to the eccentric duchess, didn't have his prowess in climbing trees.

For her latest crisis, the servants had chosen the wrong shade of flower to adorn one of her elaborate balls, and he'd been needed to scour hothouses all over London to acquire all the white blooms he could.

Only to arrive with his carriage full and his servants unloading the flowers before discovering she'd opted for pink.

Which had then resulted in the next emergency of finding a purpose and home for those blooms so they wouldn't go to waste. Which, of course, had led to her next catastrophe—finding the most proper home.

"You can say no to her," the naked beauty sprawled on her side reminded Harris as he shook free the remnants of water from his hair. "And yes to this." Lady Sarah Windermere let her legs part in invitation, revealing a bare, shaved apex.

Seeing his attention on that place between her thighs, she smiled and slid a palm over her mon and slipped a finger inside. "I'm ready for you, darling. Come feel."

She'd been ready every time they met for their monthlong arrangement. However, her shrewish displays last week, when he'd been handing out those flowers for his godmother and when he'd come upon the young woman being assaulted in the streets, had marked the moment he'd known their time together was at an end. Yes, the auburn-haired woman had been lovely, but that certainly hadn't merited Sarah's coldness or impatience. There was no place in Harris's life for a woman so clingy as to have taken offense at his aiding another woman.

"I'm afraid I have to leave, sweet," he said, reaching for his trousers.

Her eyes grew slightly hazy and her breathing labored as she stroked herself, her efforts a carnal feast for the eyes that proved too much even to him with his growing ennui toward the lady.

Drawn to that bed, Harris padded across the room and perched himself on the edge of the mattress.

The countess immediately lifted her mouth to his, and he claimed it in the kiss she craved. Moaning, she grabbed his hand, putting it to that place she'd been petting herself moments ago, and he obliged.

"Feel how wet I am for you, Ruthven," she panted.

Knock, knock, knock.

"My Ladyship, an envoy is waiting downstairs for your guest." The announcement came muffled by the carved oak slab, but the impatience of the speaker was as clear as the light of day.

"It is your godmother and her friends again. Oh, stuff those old busybodies," Lady Sarah breathed against his mouth, and tenacious like English ivy, she switched positions so she straddled his waist and thrust her generous bosom forward in his face. "They can wait. I cannot." She trailed a path of kisses down his cheek, biting him as she went. "And neither can you." She wrapped her fingers around his swollen cock and squeezed.

Old busybodies. Those old busybodies had been like a trio of mothers, looking after him since his own mother died when he was a boy of five.

Harris drew back. "Alas, I'm afraid we're finished, sweet," he said, setting her off of him.

"Just like that, you'll stop, darling?" She wrapped a determined arm about his waist and took him again in her more-than-capable hand.

"Just like that," he said, effortlessly disentangling her cloying grip from his person.

With a pout, she immediately flopped onto her back, bouncing on the mattress, her breasts bobbing. "You are as cold as they say."

Colder. But then, being trapped in marriage at eighteen by a mercenary, title-grasping woman and then left a widower at nineteen had that effect upon a fellow.

Harris shoved his right foot through the pantleg of his breeches and then the next.

She rolled onto her stomach and kicked her legs up behind her. "When will you return?"

Never. "I cannot say." He offered that vaguest of answers meant to put off what flowers and a note would ease the way of.

Scowling, she sat up and swung her legs over the side of the bed. "You're breaking it off with me, aren't you?"

Knock, knock, knock.

"I'll be there shortly," he called to the impatient servant, sharing in the fellow's frustration.

"I could have chosen Rothesby," Lady Sarah said, her tone creeping up a fraction. "He is a duke, but I chose you."

Bloody hell, she'd not make this parting clean.

Harris grabbed for his shirt and gave it several snaps before tugging it over his head. He joined her at the side of the mattress. "We've had a good time, love."

Lady Sarah immediately twined her arms about his neck. "The best," she whispered, kissing his neck and suckling that flesh.

There was no *best*. Hell, there wasn't even a *better*.

All these encounters, all these exchanges, were the same. Based on gratification and satiating a physical urging.

Like a cat in heat, she rubbed herself against him. "I let myself get too clingy, didn't I? They say that is the rule. Never get clingy."

Harris leaned down and kissed her mouth, once more giving her some of what she sought until a breathy sigh slipped out. "It was good," he said, infusing a parting into those three words.

This time, as she sank back on her naked haunches, she

gave a sigh of resignation grounded in the reality of the end of their agreement. As a rule, he preferred to keep company with those women who had absolutely zero expectations of anything more than a sexual relationship. Every single woman—the innocent, the debutantes, the bluestockings—was to be avoided at all costs.

He'd learned his lesson the hardest of ways.

Harris made quick work of tying his cravat.

"Someday, you are going to meet the woman who thaws your jaded heart and makes you forget your heartbreak," she said.

His heartbreak.

He stared off as memories slipped in of Clarisse's cries and screams as they'd grown weaker and weaker. He gave his head a hard shake, thrusting back those memories. There'd been no love between him and his late wife, but the horrors of her passing would haunt him forever.

It still stunned him that the whole of Polite Society had made his marriage into something that it wasn't.

Harris tugged the chair out from the lady's vanity and sat to draw his boots on.

But then, the only thing more titillating than gossip to the *ton* was a perceived aggrieved widower. Everyone wished to craft those fellows into tragic figures in need of saving.

"If you ever change your mind, Ruthven—"

He wouldn't.

"—and are looking for a bed to warm…" She smoothed a palm over the rumpled satin sheets, her meaning clear.

There was no doubt he'd be looking for a bed to warm, but it would not, however, be hers.

"I thank you, my lady, for these wonderful weeks."

She'd taken the news of their breakup amicably. Better than he could have expected, given her recent clinginess.

Without a backward look, Harris quit the lady's private suites and greeted the servant standing at the entry "Stebbins."

His godmother's favorite footman sprang to attention.

The young man held over a folded note. "Her Grace has—"

"An emergency?" he asked, taking the sheet, the words on it dashed in a flourishing scrawl that could belong only to a self-possessed woman confident in her rank and place in this world.

They started through the narrow halls.

"Indeed," Stebbins said as they walked. "I took the liberty of calling for your carriage."

"Thank—"

"Because you know how Her Grace quite detests being kept waiting." The other man gave him a pointed look.

The moment Lady Sarah's butler spied them, the fellow, one arm tucked behind his back, drew the door open.

Harris would wager his favorite mount that the duchess' favorite footman had also ordered the head of this household to remain at the door, prepared for when Harris and he came so they might make a quicker escape.

Bounding down the steps, Harris headed to his carriage.

A short ride later, he found himself inside a different household.

"What took you, boy?" his godmother, the Duchess of Arlington, demanded as soon as he entered the parlor.

She paused in the middle of snipping away at a peculiar, potted tree.

"I came as soon as I could, dear Duchess," he greeted. Crossing over, he bent and dropped a kiss on her smooth, impressively unwrinkled-for-her-years cheek.

She grunted, waving her scissors about. "Trying to butter me up."

"With a woman, he was," his godmother's closest and dearest friend called over from around the gossip sheet held up before her face.

Harris swiftly shifted course. "Ah, it is ever a joy to see you, my ladies," he greeted.

As one, the identical twins, Lady Medeira, the Countess of Cowpen and Lady Astrid, the Countess of Cavendish, told apart by only the favorite turbans they wore, lowered their newspapers a fraction, eyed him up and down, and then, with matching grunts, they raised those scandal sheets back up.

"With a woman indeed."

He bristled. "I'm perfectly groomed, not even a bit rumpled. One might say it is scandalous for you to assume—"

Lady Cavendish patted her cheek, directing his kiss there.

At age seven, he'd learned the lesson that it was always better to comply than to face a vicious cheek-pinching from the unrepentantly ruthless countess.

"When I was widowed, I wasn't out and about bedding anyone and everyone, which, given you men and that itch you can never get properly scratched, is saying something."

Harris briefly closed his eyes.

His godmother leaned forward, peering at him, particularly at his face and neck. "Hmph. He's still capable of a blush, so mayhap there's hope for him yet. Here." She thrust a page at him. "Read this.'

Collecting the source of her latest crisis, Harris read the page aloud. "We have every reason to believe your niece, Miss Adairia…" His words immediately trailed off.

Well, this was indeed a real emergency.

"We need your help," Lady Cowpen said, wringing her hands.

Yes, someone was preying upon them once more.

Measuring his response, Harris helped himself to a seat across from the trio. After all, having grown up with the three of them as de facto mothers, he knew better than anyone how many hours they'd spent searching. How many papers and files they'd pored over. All in the hope of Adairia being one day returned. In time, however, they'd come to realize the deception played out in the hopes of attaining the wealth the duchess might afford them.

They stared expectantly back.

"Well?" his godmother urged.

And then horror settled in his brain as he realized what united them in their usual contrary opinions. "You… aren't seriously believing this is really her?" he asked, his voice strained. Praying.

"We are," his godmother announced.

Lady Cowpen leaned forward. "Deadly so."

That was enough to give him pause, and he edged back in his seat. When the mood suited them, there wasn't a more ruthless trio than the one assembled before him.

"But you said yourselves it was time to set aside the

dream."

"This isn't a dream, Harris," the duchess said brusquely. She pointed at the page. "This time, it is the real thing."

Here they went. Again. Harris looked hopefully to the greatest cynic of the ladies. "Not you, too, Lady Cowpen. Surely you aren't intending to go along with this?"

"Harumph, dear boy," she said, thumping her orchid-headed gold cane upon the hardwood floor. "I don't go along with anything. I make my own mind."

He latched on to that. Certainly he could appeal to one of them, who could in turn make the others see reason. "And surely you're not trusting that this girl is somehow... out there?"

"Have a care," his godmother snapped. "First, that girl is my niece. Second, you were the one who suggested we hire the investigator Steele."

Yes, because he'd expected and hoped that famed gentleman investigator would put an end to this once and for all. Harris resisted the urge to jam his fingertips against his temples. "Your Grace," he began gently, "Adairia... she wandered away from her family outside a ballet. She was five."

"Five."

"That was thirteen," going on fourteen. "years ago," he said over her interruption.

"And it was inevitable that she'd be found," she said calmly. "She's been identified by individuals who live in East London."

Harris jumped up. "But not by Steele." The investigator whom Harris had hired on his godmother's behalf. "Steele put out inquiries all over East London. If this was real, he would have brought this to you not some," He slashed a hand about. "cryptic note delivered by who knows?" And yet, it wasn't his godmother's fault that she was desperate. Harris forced himself to take a calming breath. "The girl is a damned charlatan. A fake. Someone who is taking advantage of a wo—"

Pale blonde eyebrows came sliding together, forming a hard, warning line that dared him to finish the remainder of his sentence.

Harris wisely corrected course.

"Someone who is taking advantage of an old story about an earl and countess' missing daughter."

Lady Cowpen leaned in, directing her hushed words at her sister's ear. "That was clearly not what he was intending to say." She grunted. "You were going to say 'woman'."

"It wasn't even a good attempt at covering it up," the lady's twin whispered none too discreetly around her hand.

This time, he didn't fight it. Harris pressed his fingertips into his temples. He let his hands fall and trained his efforts on the person here who mattered most in this exchange. The one who stood to lose the most. "I know you want your brother's daughter to be found. Through the years, you've shared stories about the girl." Catching the edge of his King Louis XIV chair, he dragged it closer. "But it's not her. She's gone."

"Your cynicism will be the ruin of you," his godmother said in pitying tones that sent a rush of heat up his neck.

"I was ruined long ago." The moment he'd heard a scream and gone running to the rescue of a damsel in distress, only to find himself damned by the lady's trickery. His stomach muscles seized. And then he'd stood by, watching that same woman suffer the most painstakingly slow death. He'd not loved her. He'd not even liked her. He'd not, however, have wished that pain on anyone. "I cannot be ruined any more than I was," he said quietly to himself.

"Says all dark, cynical rogues," Lady Cavendish added proudly.

"I personally think the dear boy likes to be dark and cynical," her sister lamented.

"I'm not dark and cynical," he called over their chattering. "I'm a realist."

"Not all women are bad, you know, Harris," his godmother said with a frown.

Three sets of eyes swiveled his way, and he resisted the urge to squirm the way he had when he'd been a boy caught putting on a production with her then-beloved pugs in costume. "I know that because I have sterling examples seated before me of just how wonderful women can be."

"Good answer."

"Because he's not stupid." Lady Cavendish paused. "That is, not entirely."

"Thank you," he said dryly. "I appreciate that great show of love and affection." It was also true. Even having their own lives and responsibilities, they'd stepped forward to raise him the moment his mother had died.

"Oh, hush, Harris." The duchess clapped once, commanding the room to silence with the brusque method she'd employed over the years with servants and family and loved ones alike. Chin elevated, she passed a glance over the loved ones she'd assembled before ultimately settling that terrifying focus on Harris. "The fact remains, Harris, you are quite the clever boy. Like your mother. Not your father. God rot him."

"God rot him." The other two icons of Polite Society raised imagined glasses as if in toast.

God rot his father indeed.

The late marquess had been obsessed with their family's reputation and had also played a hand in the trap Harris had inadvertently stepped into. In so doing, he had ruined the grasping lady's life, and Harris'.

"You see life in black and white, however, failing to see the world is one great prism of color," his godmother said. "My niece has been found, and we intend to see that she's restored... whether you'll be supportive or not."

Harris scrubbed a hand over his forehead.

Whether he'd be supportive or not.

Except... she knew. Just as he knew that she knew, he knew. There was nothing he would not do for her or her two eccentric friends.

"I'll be most supportive," he finally pledged, earning smiles from the twins.

His godmother, however, focused a narrow-eyed gaze oozing with suspicion on his person. "I know you, dear boy. That capitulation comes entirely too easy."

"No games. I wouldn't dare think of it, Your Grace." And were the lady restored, as his godmother said, Harris *would* be supportive... of his godmother and her two magnanimous friends, and he'd ensure that they didn't fall prey to the same grasping he had all those years ago.

Chapter 3

S he had no right to go.

In fact, of all the people in Covent Garden, Julia had less right to go than anyone else who dwelled in these parts.

After all, she'd been the one who'd resisted this very move from the start. Julia hadn't believed her, and because of that lack of faith Andaira was gone. It had been days since Julia's windfall, and in those days the flowers given her by some dashing gentleman in the streets had withered and died. The once vibrant silken-petaled blooms had wilted and faded, becoming dried husks.

Seated on the floor of the hovel she'd called home with her sister, Julia stared blankly at the basket of dying and dead flowers from that once hopeful day.

All along, Julia had been the one to call the tale of Adairia being an earl's lost daughter false. Her mother after all had said it was the imagination of a girl who could no longer cope.

And nothing had changed in that regard. Julia no more believed Adairia to be a Lost Lady, the cherished niece of a duke and duchess, than she took herself to be the Lord and Savior, Jesus Christ. Both were fictional stories. Both were dangerous to believe.

But what proved even more dangerous was remaining in Covent Garden with Rand Graham's people out to silence Julia.

Silence her, as they'd silenced Adairia.

Just as Julia had expected they'd try to do. Because she knew they'd...killed Adairia. Adairia who must have met with Graham and said no to his ploy. The fancily-spoken, ethereal young woman was after all the only young woman in the Rookeries who could have pulled off his planned deceit. To Graham it had always been a deceit to garner a windfall, but Adairia? She'd actually believed that drivel.

Oh, God.

Julia sucked in a ragged breath; her entire body aching and hurting from the loss.

It was her fault.

She'd gotten Adairia killed.

She was responsible for her disappearance.

If Julia had allowed her the opportunity to pursue her dream, Adairia would have gone to Mayfair. She would have presented herself as a duchess' niece. And she would have possibly been here now.

Possibly.

Huddling in the folds of the cloak she'd been given months earlier because of the random kindness shown her by a lady in the street, Julia burrowed deeper within the velvet folds, seeking warmth. Finding none.

Adairia had loved this garment. After Julia had received it, she'd reluctantly handed it over to her friend, because she was still the dreamer of their pair.

Mayhap if she hadn't allowed that whimsy, then Adairia

wouldn't have been such easy prey in terms of the loyalty test, one that had used her dreams against her. That blasted scrap had brought back all of the old wants of what Adairia had believed was her true identity.

Julia knocked the back of her head against the wall. So many mishaps.

None of those regrets she'd sit here lamenting, however, since Adairia's disappearance hadn't changed anything. Nor would it. Nay, the longer she sat here, she was a duck ready to have her feathers plucked before she was tossed atop a skillet and roasted.

And perhaps it spoke to the selfishness in her soul that she didn't want to go. She didn't want to be kidnapped as Adairia had been and face whatever wretched fate she'd endured at the hands of Rand Graham's brutal henchmen.

Julia stopped hitting her head and yanked the well-read page from the bodice of her dress. She'd done it many times, considering a traitorous act so many times she'd lost count. Unfolding the letter, she read the words there, ones she'd already committed to memory.

Dearest Adairia,

You have been gone years from our lives, but you've not truly been gone. You have a home here, with me, your aunt. You were so very loved and beloved. There has been a void with your absence. I implore you to come home and claim your rightful place as the earl's daughter and a duke and duchess's niece that you are. The world awaits. I await.

Ever yours,

The Duchess of Arlington

Numb inside, Julia trailed her fingers along the words upon the page that were the most faded, indicating another fingertip had run most frequently over them.

You were so very loved and beloved. There has been a void with your absence.

That would have been the part that her whimsical, fanciful, head-in-the-clouds Adairia would have focused first and foremost upon. Not about claiming her rightful place. Not about being an earl's daughter or a duke's niece. Rather, she'd focused on the romantic words of a relative who missed her and wanted her back.

Hugging her arms around her middle, Julia inadvertently crushed the note in her hand. She immediately relaxed her palm, sparing the page that had given her friend such hope, this only real piece she had that belonged to Adairia.

Nay, that was why she couldn't go. She'd encouraged Adairia to give up that dream and stay here. And if she'd gone, she would have been safe. At least for a while. Who knew? Perhaps she could have fulfilled a dream that this duchess had, and in so doing, she could have found a place of security and happiness among the ranks of the princes and princesses she'd always imagined belonging to.

Her entire being aching at the loss, a loss that was her fault, Julia rolled onto her side. Her hood flopped, and she lay with her cheek upon the dirt and stone floor. Rocks bit painfully into her face, and she welcomed the sting of pain for the distraction it provided from the agony of Adairia's death. Reaching inside her cloak, she fished out the heavy purse she'd been given by the gent in the streets. How excited and relieved Adairia would have been. Not when all the money that fine lord had given Julia couldn't bring her sister back.

Noisy footfalls sounded outside, the clumsy sounds hinting at a drunken man unstable on his feet.

Unblinking, Julia stared at the narrow one-foot-by-one-foot window that revealed a pair of tattered trousers on a man outside.

Then those trousers disappeared from sight, and the handle of her door jiggled.

This was whom he'd sent for her? A drunken, slurring lout?

With a sigh, Julia stared overhead at the cracked plaster ceiling.

Just let it happen.

Get it over with.

Rand Graham knew her to be as disloyal as Adairia and deserving of a swift end for it. They wouldn't rest until she was offed.

And she shouldn't rest in peace as long as Adairia was gone.

Graham's henchman fought with the handle once more. "Oi know ye're in there. Open the door. Wouldn't be locked if ye wasn't."

Well, that was a surprisingly cognizant conclusion, given his inebriated state.

"Open up so Oi can get this done with."

Get this done with.

As in kill her.

And perhaps rape her first. That was, after all, the way of

the streets. The gang leaders, and the men who answered to them, brought as much suffering as they could to the unlucky ones on the receiving end of their wrath.

Muttering and cursing to himself, the stranger finally abandoned the handle. A moment later, his legs reappeared in the window.

He dropped down on his knees, and resting his palms on the ground, he pressed his face against the panel.

Adairia had insisted upon keeping their window clean. To let the light in, she'd always said.

Leering eyes met hers, and the moment that bloodshot gaze landed on her, a smile split the bearded stranger's face, revealing a mouth bare of all teeth but for the front four, brittle and yellow and surely to fall from his rotted mouth soon.

He waved. "Let me in, Princess. Wait… that was the other one." He chortled, his corpulent frame shaking like he'd told the most hilarious jest and not as though he'd spoken about Adairia. "Sent to have a talk with ye," he called. "An' give ye a gift, too." He cupped himself between the legs.

Her teeth chattered, and while he proceeded to cajole her into letting him inside, Julia let her gaze slip to the elegant scrawl and the fine, fancy words written there. It was likely a trap. There was, as she'd said to Adairia, little chance that any of this was real and that when she got there, she'd be met by one of Rand Graham's many brutes. That it was nothing more than a trap.

I deserve the same fate.

"Now, open up now… because Oi'm startin' to get angry…"

She didn't deserve to run and hide, and yet… God help her. She wasn't ready to go. Certainly not like this, curled up on the floor like a beaten dog.

Fueled by a sudden and selfish determination to live, Julia stuffed the purse inside her cloak and scrambled to her feet; the heavy cloak fell in a whoosh about her ankles. She stuffed the suddenly even more precious page inside her dress and fetched the fireplace poker.

Brandishing it close, she hovered at the side of the door. "Get the hell out of here," she called.

"Ye're as brave as yer friend was stupid. Or maybe ye're just stupid, too." He guffawed, and then he heaved his broad frame into the panel, shaking the wood.

She drew in a shaky breath and let him continue to batter the panel. Then, swiftly turning the lock, she yanked the door open.

The man cried out, his forward momentum sending him flying, and his head collided with the edge of the hearth.

His big frame stiffened and then went limp. He lay there… motionless.

A rocklike pressure cutting off her air flow, Julia stared dumbly at Rand Graham's felled henchman, taken down by his own impatience and size.

Julia's skin went clammy. Her chest rose and fell as she struggled to get a breath in through the fear.

This was a doubly unforgivable grievance. One didn't take down Rand Graham's henchmen. They were a protected class, that security afforded them by the dirty work they did for that bastard. Backing away from the felled stranger, she edged toward the door.

This bastard might have failed, but there would be others behind him. There might even be another one out there right now.

Julia proved a faithless friend, choosing life when death had chosen Adairia.

She scrambled to the opposite side of the one-room abode she'd shared these years with her sister. All the while, she kept her gaze averted from the little puddle of blood that had formed around the brute's head. His face, buried down in the stone floor as it was, concealed the extent of the gruesome, fatal injury he'd suffered.

Dropping to her knees beside the bed Adairia had once slept in, she fished out the small treasure trove the other woman had kept through the years. Julia clutched the case to her chest, and with the cherished items cradled close, she bolted.

Julia ran, stretching her legs and strides as long and fast as they could go.

The moment she turned the corner of Aldridge Street, she forced a moderation to her cadence. Drawing attention to oneself in these parts was dangerous. Doing so after causing the death of Rand Graham's minions would be a fatal folly.

Her lungs burning from the earlier pace she'd set, Julia kept her gaze forward, heading straight for a hackney.

The man gave her a dismissive once-over. "You got coin?"

Aye, he'd read the financial state of his potential passenger quite well. Fishing coin from the purse she'd been given days? A lifetime ago, Julia shoved them at the driver, and gave the Duchess of Arlington's address. "Now, if you please, Mayfair." As she spoke, she scoured the streets behind him for any hint that Graham's men had found her out and were looking for her.

Apparently, the world wasn't all out of miracles where she was concerned. There was a placid calm, a mundanity to the everyday bustle of Covent Garden.

Climbing inside the hack, Julia rapped once on the roof.

A moment later, the driver shut the door, the carriage dipped, rocked forward, and she headed onward to perhaps an even greater danger—meeting with one of London's most powerful peeresses.

Chapter 4

H arris had imagined there wasn't anything worse than agreeing to accompany his godmother and her two friends to Almack's...and right on the heels of her ball, at that.

He'd been wrong.

At least Almack's wasn't capable of killing him. At least with anything beyond boredom.

"Can they not drive faster?" his godmother called, knocking hard and loud on the roof of her enormous, and in that moment also cramped carriage.

There came the crack of reins, and a moment later, the conveyance hitched forward before resuming a breakneck speed, at a curve no less.

Cursing, Harris braced his feet upon the floor to keep himself from flying sideways into the carriage wall. Packed on the bench as they were, the three matrons barely moved a smidge from the erratic driving.

"You are determined to throw sand upon her arrival," his godmother said with the same grace and aplomb as if they rolled in a curricle at a sedate pace along Rotten Row and not as though, with every turn of the wheels, they ran the risk that the Marquess of Ruthven line would pass to the next sorry gent.

The carriage rocked precariously to the right, throwing Harris against the opposite side of the conveyance. He grunted, pain exploding along his arm where his elbow caught the side.

The twin countesses, on the other hand, yawned.

Shooting a hand up, he banged hard on the ceiling. "I'm determined to infuse some logic and calm into it," he gritted out, and the carriage came to a slower, safer pace.

The duchess was already countering Harris' unspoken command to the servant atop that box. "Do not go dictating the speed of my carriage, Harris."

Once again, the spacious carriage picked up speed.

He cursed, and again planted his feet on the floor to keep himself from being pitched about. "I daresay risking death to see *the lady* runs very much counter to a happy reunion." Harris grunted as Lady Cavendish managed to wiggle her cane free and knock him hard in the shin. "What—?"

"I do not like your tone, dear boy."

Her own crisp, angry tone was hardly befitting the term of endearment the duchess had affixed to him since he'd been just a child.

"I agree. I'm also displeased with your sarcastic use of the term 'lady.' As though we aren't quick-witted enough to pick up on your insults." Lady Cavendish took a shot at his left shin this time.

Wincing, Harris leaned over and rubbed the latest injury he'd sustained. "Of course I didn't mean to cast aspersions upon your intelligence." At this rate, he was going to be sporting black and blues down his limbs. And that was if he survived the damned erratic carriage ride his godmother had set them on.

Bending over proved the wrong thing to do.

The carriage jolted, sending him pitching forward.

The three ladies reached as one and shoved him back into his seat.

"What I'm merely pointing out—"

"This time," the friends said in unison.

"—is that you are going to get all of us killed. And while you might be quite content with the years you've lived, I am far less eager to die in this conveyance." And certainly not while racing off to meet who was surely yet another charlatan intending to pass herself off as the duchess' niece.

Her Grace tossed her head back and laughed. Hers was the practiced, careful nature of measured mirth. "Oh, come. You, who are notorious for racing curricles and horses to win some wager or another, has grown squeamish when it comes to speeding about?"

"I haven't raced a curricle in some years now," he muttered.

"He's grown into a fogey with age," Lady Cowpen whispered.

"A good deal less fun, he is," her sister returned in not-at-all-hushed tones.

"I can hear you, you know," he said dryly.

The twins nodded. "Then that is good. You can do something about your fogey-ness."

His... This was really enough. "I'll have you know, the last thing I'm known for is... is..."

"Being a fogey," his godmother snorted. "No. You're known for womanizing and wagering and indulging in spirits."

His neck went hot, and shock of all shocks, his cheeks flushed with a warmth that felt remarkably like a blush.

At last, as the carriage approached the duchess' palatial, detached residence, he sent a prayer upward at having survived both the hazardous ride and the razor-sharp lecture and insults. "Why do I continue to dance attendance on you?" he muttered.

Lady Cavendish patted his hand and smiled. "Because you love us, and you are a good boy." She paused. "Just a good boy who's lost his way."

The carriage finally stopped, and he sat there in silence with those words of Lady Cavendish.

Lost his way. Had he ever been... found? He, who'd gone from one miserable existence as the son of a man who'd had no need or want of him after the death of his wife, to a marriage with a mercenary woman who'd trapped him more neatly and surely than the late Boney could have.

Cursing, the duchess yanked the curtains back and looked out, angling her head back and forth. "Blasted servants. If a woman wants something done, she need do it herself," she muttered, and before Harris realized what she intended to do, she pressed the handle, opened the door, and jumped out.

"You're going to injure yourself," he called after her. Scrambling down, he hurriedly reached back to help the twins.

"You really are a fogey. The twins are right," his god-mother drawled, taking the steps of her home with about the same caution as she'd made the descent from her garish pink-lacquer conveyance.

Chapter 5

The duchess' servants hadn't sent Julia away.

Why, they hadn't even mistaken her for a beggar girl and directed her round back for handouts.

The butler hadn't summoned the constable, as he would have been wise to do.

Rather, he had attempted to help her out of the cloak that she was decidedly not parting with, shown her to a parlor that was finer than any castle for a queen, fetched her a tray that she'd promptly devoured, and set her by a warm fire…

Where she'd sat for nearly an hour, huddled in her cloak, periodically stealing glances at the silent maid embroidering on a fancy upholstered bench across the room.

They'd been expecting Adairia.

That was the only way to explain why Julia had been ushered through the front door.

That was all that explained it.

It hadn't been a trap by Graham. This was…real. *How* could it be real?

And yet, the longer she sat, the more she kicked herself for coming here. For coming to tell the duchess about the girl named Adairia who'd believed herself the lady's niece and who'd believed it so much she'd been willing to die for the dream.

As soon as the fantastical thought slid in, she quashed it.

Even if by some far-fetched, magical chance Adairia had been who she'd professed to be, there'd hardly be forgiveness for Julia, the one who'd let the other woman be slaughtered.

It didn't matter that Julia had helped keep Adairia safe for years. What had transpired in the span of these past days mattered the most, her greatest of failings.

I *am so sorry, Adairia. So very sorry.*

What was she doing?

When she'd fled Covent Garden, she'd had only one thought in mind—escape. She'd run as fast as she could to the place where even Rand Graham's reach was thin and his ability to extricate her would be a struggle.

Now she found herself seated in a duchess' fine parlor and not knowing what in hell she actually planned to say.

I had a dear friend who was like a sister and who believed she was a princess and that she was the daughter of nobility. Oh, and I also deterred her from coming to see you and didn't safeguard her enough, so she's no more.

Julia squeezed her eyes shut. A pike might as well have been run through her chest for the pain there. Adairia... was gone.

And Julia? Didn't have so much as a body to bury or eyes to slide closed. She'd nothing more than eternal regrets and an empty void that could never, ever be filled.

She needed to leave.

Now.

Julia flew to her feet.

Just as the pounding of footfalls filled the corridor and reached into the grand parlor.

The doors were thrown open, and as one, there stumbled into the room a trio of ladies somewhere in their fortieth years. Two of the women were identical pictures of each other. However, with the loud silks and turbans they all wore, they might as well have been triplets.

Gasping and out of breath, they hunched over, each pair of enormously rounded eyes on Julia.

Her toes curling into the worn soles of her boots, Julie tensed.

Tick.

Tock.

Tick.

Tock.

The clock continued to mark the never-ending stretch of silence while they studied Julia, an oddity on display like those parrots and monkeys employed by people in Covent Garden to attract a crowd and earn a coin.

And then one of the women straightened and sailed forward.

And Julia realized just how wrong she had been about them being triplets. This woman was different from the others. With a regal bearing suited for a queen, she had an aura of authority and power that clung to her person like a tangible trait that could be seen and touched.

This was the duchess.

Upon her approach, Julia's spine reflexively drew straighter.

The blonde-haired woman reached Julia and then

stopped. Shrewd eyes smarter than a fox's narrowed and then moved in a methodical glide over Julia's features.

Tell her. Just blurt out why you've come and make your apologies... and go find someplace to hide, where you can be safe.

At worst, she'd be turned out fast and hard on her arse, which might not be the worst of things, as that would ensure her speediest departure from this place.

At best, the woman might take mercy and offer some coin for coming, which between that and the purse given her by the gentleman would provide Julia cover from having to hawk her flowers at Covent Garden for time enough to remain hidden.

But that wouldn't last forever. Ultimately, she'd have to return to peddling her wares.

They're going to find you anyway.

Which is what you deserve. Adairia is dead because of you.

Through the powerful peer's scrutiny, she made herself go as still as possible. Odd how, just a short while ago, she'd attempted to make herself motionless in much the same way, feeling that same breathless sense of terror and anticipation. Both the last man she'd faced and this powerful peeress before her had the power to end Julia. Only, this one was draped in striking orange silk and dripping with diamond and rubies.

The woman was flanked by the pair of noblewomen, though the duchess had still not spoken. They set themselves up like ladies-in-waiting to the queen, dutifully and obsequiously silent as they also took up the study of Julia.

They slid their eyes up and down her person. Their scrutiny landed on the quality cloak she wore that showed its wear. Ultimately, they raised their eyes in an unnerving synchrony and settled that probing examination upon her face.

Reflexively, she huddled in the velvet-lined garment, seeking warmth, seeking a place to hide.

Suddenly, the duchess moved closer. Stepping away from the group, she closed the remaining distance between them.

From the corner of her eye, Julia caught movement as another figure joined the gathering.

The man was as big and as finely muscled as the greatest warriors who sparred at Savage's fight club. His angular features were arranged in a mask that marked him as hardened and cynical as any man of the streets. Only, his golden strands, loosely arranged, gave him the look of an angel.

Julia drew back, reeling as recognition set in.

She gasped. "You." Her savior from the streets. That one moment of hope when someone had come to her aid.

"She recognizes Harris," Lady Cavendish whispered.

Except, she must have imagined that moment on the streets between them, for this emotionless stranger bore no resemblance to that gentleman. His cerulean blue eyes narrowed. Ice dripped from his gaze, colder than any winter's night she'd been forced to work while cloakless. She couldn't suppress another little shiver.

"Of course she does! How many times did she come round when Harris was here?" the duchess asked the room at large.

Those words registered, and she forced her gaze away

from the gentleman. "No. I... He... looked familiar," she finished weakly. Clearing her throat, she reached inside her bag and fished out the pendant Adairia had squirreled away. She made to press the cherished piece into the duchess' hand.

The gentleman lunged forward.

Another gasp exploded from Julia's lips, and her entire body tensed, her muscles coiling tight as she eyed the path around him.

Her flight was cut off by the unlikeliest savior.

The duchess slid herself between Julia and the fierce man and quelled him with a look. "Harris, step aside." There was an exasperated quality to her voice.

"Your Grace," he said through gritted teeth.

"I said step aside, Harris," Her Grace snapped in a tone that brooked no room for being gainsaid.

Still, the man—Harris—revealed a greater obstinacy, glowering darkly at Julia.

"Do you truly believe the girl has come to do me harm?"

The girl...

Julia hadn't been a girl in a long time.

Mayhap forever. Children of the streets weren't ever really born innocent. They came into the world hungry and crying for help... that never came.

"Listen to your godmother, Harris," one of the ladies flanking the duchess advised.

So he was the lady's godson.

She eyed him warily.

He was protective of the duchess. He'd not tolerate one such as Julia darkening this household.

More than ever, she needed to leave. That much was

true, and it couldn't have been any clearer than now with the cynical stranger watching her every move.

Broad shoulders tense, the gentleman gave Julia another frosty once-over and then stepped aside.

"You needn't worry about him, dear," one of the ladies murmured, jerking Julia's attention away from the menacing figure, who looked ready to take Julia apart should she make one wrong move. "He's as gentle as they come."

The man who'd tenderly brushed the dirt and small rocks from her cheek on that London street? Yes. This frosty figure who eyed her with the suspicion he should? Far less so.

Avoiding his eyes, Julia stepped forward once more and gave that precious necklace Adairia had so loved over to the duchess.

The regal lady, stared at the piece for a long while, and then she drew in a quick, noisy breath. She exhaled slowly through her nose as though any show of emotion were alien to her, and she sought to suppress that hint of weakness.

It was a surprising connection to find between her and the duchess. The two of them might as well have been born to foreign planets.

Oh, God. It hit Julia with all the force of a basket that had been tossed out a window, catching her in the back as she walked and stealing the breath from her lungs and the thoughts from her head but for one: The duchess recognized the necklace.

It was familiar to her.

Which meant Adairia… had been right after all?

Surely not. Surely…

"Adairia," the woman whispered, pressing a fist to her

mouth, and then on an exuberant laugh, she did the most unduchesslike thing. She threw her arms about Julia's shoulders and drew her in.

Julia's body tensed, and she stood there stiffly as the woman hugged her. There were so many things she should say in this moment:

I'm not Adairia. Adairia is gone. Dead. Kidnapped and made to suffer the most brutal of deaths because I did not protect her.

All those words were the ones she should speak, but she was incapable of focusing on anything but the oddest thing—a hug.

Not even her own ma had hugged her.

Working all day and well into the night selling flowers as they had, the moment she and Adairia had returned to the cramped quarters they shared, their hadn't been much time for maternal warmth. Julia's mum had been exhausted from the long days they'd spent peddling their goods, and had gone to sleep almost the moment they entered their home.

While she'd slept, Julia and Adairia would all but collapse on a thin mat that served as a mattress. In all those times, she and Adairia had sat there, whispering and talking and imagining the very life Adairia had dreamed herself a part of. Adairia had ultimately come to relinquish those fantasies and had finally grasped the reality that existed for people like her. Mums who'd had time to hug their babes and where stability that was forever.

Now, Julia found herself seduced once more by the whisper of delusions that, at the most unexpected of moments, inserted themselves with a startling tenacity.

Julia briefly closed her eyes. Folded as she was in that warmth, with affection and love spilling from the other woman into her, Julia raised her arms and hugged the woman back.

But this is also a lie, that voice taunted at the back of her mind.

Do you think she'd be hugging you, the stranger and street rat, in place of the one whom she truly wishes?

At last, the woman released her, and Julia immediately backed away from that display... and the guilt... and the man glaring at her.

Aye, that was the correct sentiment. He had the right of it.

Julia breathed deep and forced herself to reveal the true reason she'd come. "I'm afraid—"

Another one of the women stepped closer and wrapped her arms about her shoulders. "There, there, my dear. No need to be afraid any longer."

As the three surrounded her, talking all at once, Julia tried—and failed—to get a word in edgewise.

"A bath. I am sure the dear girl would enjoy a bath, and a meal, and a warm bed," the woman's twin was saying.

"Yes, but that isn't why—"

"You're here," the duchess said. "That's all that matters. We can speak of everything else after."

They were a whirlwind, sweeping her off, steering her around the menacing stranger, and coward that she was, Julia went.

Chapter 6

Nearly three hours after the departure of the duchess' friends, Harris remained in the same parlor where the Great Reunion, as his godmother and her dearest friends had taken to referring to the night's event, had taken place.

Arms folded, he stood sentry at the door, assessing the hall. Even at this late-night hour, the footmen remained at their usual, daytime posts, on guard, as he'd instructed the moment the duchess and Ladies Cavendish and Cowpen had whisked Lady Adairia abovestairs.

Perhaps he'd be better served in the foyer?

Or mayhap outside the young woman's room? Yes, that made the most sense.

At that moment, the duchess came sweeping down the hall, speaking a quick, curt word to the footmen as she passed. Each servant bowed and then backed away, abandoning their posts.

Harris' eyebrows came flying together.

She was dismissing them.

"What are you doing?" he asked the moment she reached his side.

"You are relieved," Her Grace advised the final servant, who bent low at the waist.

"Why are you sending them away?" Harris demanded as she swept into the room. He followed behind her.

"I am letting my servants sleep," she drawled. Heading to the sideboard, she made herself a claret. "As good mistresses of households do." She looked him over. "And I take it you're staying."

"Of course I'm staying." As though he intended to vacate this household as long as that bloody charlatan remained.

His godmother sipped her claret. "I do welcome you staying here. However, I assure you, dear boy, I've survived these forty-five years without your assistance, and I shall continue to carry on just fine without you," she said dryly.

Joining her at the liquor cabinet, Harris helped himself to a brandy. Nay, there was no way in hell that he intended to let his godmother remain in this household alone with that woman. "You're not naïve," he said. "You're not one to have the wool pulled over your eyes." He held his glass out, gesturing her way. "You're quite logical and rational, and one might even say ruthless, in the way you conduct yourself in matters."

In fact, many did.

A smile graced her lips, and she elevated her chin, like one taking the most generous of compliments. "Why, thank you—"

"You are not, however, able to think clearly on the matter of your niece," he interrupted. "From the moment the Lost Lords of London began *reappearing*—"

"They weren't reappearing, Harris. They were found." She set the dainty, etched crystal glass down. "They were found."

"Since they were found…" He allowed that concession. He wasn't going to get hung up debating her on semantics when there were far more pressing points to win with her. "Male children were taken. There were no girls."

She scoffed. "Of course there were. Why should a criminal overlord obsessed with having connections to the peerage steal only male children and not girls, hmm?" She lifted a white eyebrow.

There was a warning there.

Abandoning his drink, Harris faced his godmother. "I don't presume to know how or what a madman rumored to take noble children would think, Your Grace," he admitted.

He also didn't believe it. Not beyond the one gent whose family had tried to rid themselves of him when he'd been a boy so they could take his title and lands. What Harris *did* believe was that any number of men were now foisting themselves off on lords and ladies who were desperate to believe their missing family members had been found. "What I do know is that there's been no hint of the girl for years. There was never an indication that she lived."

His godmother took him by the shoulders. "Adairia *lived*. The pendant proves it."

He scoffed. "A small girl born to the comfortable, luxurious life of the peerage and then lost in London's streets would have never survived, Your Grace," he said with the bluntness his godmother needed, while still sparing her the ugly reality. Lady Adairia would have met a fate undoubtedly too agonizing for his godmother to wrap her brain around.

"There was a time when you came to visit, while Adairia was here," his godmother said, altering their discussion enough to briefly knock him off-balance. "She was just four. You didn't like to be tasked with playing with a little girl. You were ten years older. But you were always a good, dutiful boy, and you would entertain her for us anyway." That earned his shoulder a pat. "One day, you were playing hide-and-go-seek with Adairia. You were, of course, so much older and more adept. You always easily found her. Until one turn, do you remember what she did?"

He'd barely a recollection beyond a child's annoyance he'd felt as a boy at having to occupy his godmother's cherished niece. He searched his mind, distantly recalling some of that day.

The duchess' eyes twinkled. "You remember." Yes, he remembered, but she continued with her telling, reminding him anyway. "She slipped outside and scaled one of my trees. We searched all day for her. And it wasn't until night that we visited the gardens and found her, sleeping there." She gave his arm a squeeze. "And that, Harris, is how we know she survived. She would have found her way. Found a place..."

He bit his tongue to keep from pointing out that she spoke of a child hiding in walled-in, meticulously tended gardens and not the rough and ruthless streets of London.

"Go home," she said, managing to meld gentleness with a no-nonsense firmness that Harris normally wouldn't have dared defy.

This time, however, was different.

"I said I am staying, Your Grace."

He didn't trust the interloper who'd come here clutching that heart-shaped necklace. Not for a damned moment.

Since the first time a London street tough had shown up,

promising information about his godmother's lost niece if she paid a hefty sum, he'd learned to not trust a single person who'd arrived with word of the duchess's nieces. Not when that time and all the ones to follow earned her nothing more than a statement of promise that the girl—now a woman—was alive and selling flowers in Covent Garden.

The duchess gave him a long look and then sighed. "How long?"

Until the woman was gone. "Long enough to ensure that you are safe and that she can be trusted."

"She can," she said before that last word had fully left his mouth.

"Splendid if she can." But she couldn't. "Then there is no harm in me remaining and ensuring that you are looked after."

His godmother joined her fingertips in a steeple, staring at him over the top. "Do you know, I cannot imagine anything more splendid than you remaining and renewing your acquaintance with the lady and making her time here more comfortable."

Oh, bloody hell. That was decidedly not what he had a damned intention of doing.

He called after her retreating form, "I did not say I intended to make her time more comfortable."

"You could and should and will." The duchess' was a decree that she didn't so much as deign to turn back to give. She spoke it as the command it was, one that brooked zero room for dispute or challenge.

With his godmother gone, Harris let free a stream of dark curses that would have gotten his ear snagged and twisted by any one of the women his dearly departed mother called best friend.

When the duchess had her mind on something, there was no swaying her from her course. There was no reasoning with her. She was determined to take in this charlatan.

She'd intended to tell the duchess everything.

Julia had meant to correct the erroneous conclusion the woman had come to about her identity and that necklace, but everything had happened so quickly. She'd been surrounded by the trio of ladies and a small contingent of servants who'd put her in a bath and brought forth new garments, the finest, softest, most luxuriant articles she'd ever seen, let alone worn. A quality suited to the patrons milling outside Covent Garden theaters when she was hawking her flowers.

And then there'd been a tray of food. Roast beef, its scent wafting on the air, and roasted carrots and potatoes and bread.

She'd, of course, eaten, swearing she'd tell them afterward. Just as soon as her mouth wasn't stuffed with food.

Then they'd brought her over to the bed, and she'd sat on the mattress, as soft and light as she imagined a cloud to be.

And she'd not told them.

She'd watched them whirl off, like the same dervishes they'd been when they'd entered, until Julia was alone, with nothing more than the hum of quiet left in their wake.

She lived in the loudest end of London, where one could always count on falling asleep to the shouts and cries of its unluckiest inhabitants. There wasn't anything more dangerous, darker, or evil than the din to be found in East London. Life had proven to Julia that invariably coupled with that ruckus were knives and assaults and various other ruthless attacks.

That was what Julia had believed anyway.

But the moment the duchess and her not-so-small entourage had taken their collective leave, ushering in a heavy silence, Julia had discovered just how very wrong she'd been over the years. Evil didn't spring from the noise.

It slipped forward into the quiet when one was left alone with only one's thoughts. From there, Satan slithered in, whispering with ideas a person shouldn't have. Dangling forth seductive gifts. Like security. And safety. And food and a warm home.

What if Julia stayed?

She didn't have to leave. At least not right away.

Eventually, she would.

But for now, they'd mistaken her for Adairia.

It would be wrong to deceive the family that had so missed Adairia. And yet, perhaps if she remained, she could share with them how Adairia had spent these past years.

That thought did little to ease her guilt at the deception she intended to carry out, one born of desperation and rooted in a fear of a future that was far more uncertain and perilous than lying to a woman who was so determined to take her under her wing.

Restless, Julia gathered the cotton wrapper and drew it

on. Belting it at the waist, she headed for the doorway.

It should be Adairia.

It should be Adairia.

With every step she took that put her farther from her borrowed chambers and through the duchess' carpet-clad halls, those four words were an echo in her mind, a litany that played over and over.

She peered into rooms as she raced through the Grosvenor Square mansion, the brightly colored parlors passing so quickly as she flew by they were like a kaleidoscope she'd once found—and then had stolen from her on the streets.

All of these grand spaces were ones Adairia should have explored through the years. She should have been rediscovering them now. If only Julia had listened. If only she'd trusted and believed.

Guilt and shame and pain, together with the pace she'd set, robbed her lungs of their proper function. Those organs ached, strained, and threatened to burst, and she wished they would. Because then she wouldn't have to confront all the mistakes she'd made and the lie she'd resolved to perpetuate against the family Adairia had lost.

Julia continued running and then skidded to a sudden halt, her cotton chemise whirling about her. Gasping for air, she caught a hand against the wall, bracing herself against a bold silk bird.

She immediately drew her hand back, realizing the quality of the painted wallpaper she touched.

Not the chipped and broken brick walls and plaster that had served as her and Adairia's four walls and a roof.

It was not that magnificently peculiar bird, with its wings spread in an array of blues and purples and yellows, that held her riveted. She was drawn back to the last room she'd passed, not one of an endless sea of parlors, retracing her steps and then stopping before the open doorway.

Doused in darkness, without so much as a sconce lit, the room, done in wood flooring and wood paneling, received a natural glow from the full moon that hung in the sky outside.

I remember a music room with so very many instruments, and I was allowed to play with them all.

Wetting her lips, Julia ventured into the room. The floorboards dipped and groaned under the slight weight of her footsteps as she walked.

She passed a harpsichord of gold, so blindingly bright she had to blink to accustom her eyes to its shine.

As she went, Julia glided her fingers along the curve of that instrument that would have fed her forevermore. She continued on through the Music Room, grazing a palm over the cello and violin before coming to a stop beside the pianoforte situated between two floor-to-ceiling windows.

At the time, Julia had listened indulgently to the younger girl, whose telling of that story had persisted through the years. That myth, made up by a girl who loved song and music as she had, fit so very well with what she'd been known as—the Covent Garden songbird; a skill that had brought in coin, even during desperate times. A skill that Julia's mother, a once-great opera singer had helped to perfect.

Only, it hadn't been some fantasy Adairia had clung to

in a bid to survive the cold, miserable world they'd been born to.

So much of it made sense now.

Adairia's ability to read and write and her fine, cultured English tones. The same manner and speech Julia's mother had her learn to earn more coin in the hopes that she and Julia might one day find a well-heeled protector. Yet where Julia's was an act, Adairia was born into the life of culture and grace. Adairia had conducted herself like the finest lady, whom the grime of the London streets had never been able to erase the shine from.

Julia depressed a single key, and the high, thin echo pierced the quiet.

"It is unsurprising to find you in this of all the duchess' rooms, my lady."

Julia gasped and whirled around.

Heart hammering, she squinted into the dark, her gaze landing on the tall figure in the entranceway. Casually lounging as he was, with a broad right shoulder propped against the doorjamb and his stance relaxed, his body's positioning should have calmed her.

It *should* have.

Julia, however, had lived on the streets of the Rookeries long enough to identify a predator.

And then, with the sleekness of one of those dangerous jungle cats Adairia had told her about, the gentleman pushed himself away from the doorway and walked closer with sleek, pantherlike steps. The pace he set was deliberately slow and one he no doubt used to unnerve her. And... his efforts worked.

Her already racing heart pounded all the harder, rattling against her rib cage, the beat increasing with every step he took.

And, God help her, not for the reasons her pulse should have behaved so erratically.

Yet, as he stalked her like that primitive panther she took him for, Julia was hopeless to take her eyes from his approach, and just one word slipped through the cacophony of her disordered thoughts. Beautiful.

The gentleman was all chiseled perfection and gloriously hard angles. His jaw was broad and slightly clefted, his cheeks high, firm slashes, his nose aquiline. And with that body, broad of muscle and barrel-chested with enormous thighs, he didn't have the look of a gentleman's stuffed and soft physique, but of a flesh-and-blood fairy-tale prince come to life.

He reached her, keeping two paces between them, a barrier she was grateful for, as she didn't have to arch her neck back so far to meet his flinty gaze.

With more of that deceptive insouciance, he rested his hip upon the edge of the pianoforte. "Do you find yourself unable to sleep, my lady?"

My God, even the blue of his eyes was a stunning masterpiece of artistic perfection assembled by the Lord Himself. Blue like the skies Adairia had spoken of, a painting of pale shades so clear that Julia had longed to see them. They were here, before her now. "I am," she brought herself to murmur through her appreciation. "It is… all foreign, this."

His lips formed a hard smile. "Oh, I expect it is."

That frosty cynicism had a sobering effect.

Blue like the skies?

A form like a prince?

Her mouth pulled in a grimace.

What madness was this, noting his beauty? When she was the last person to ever have her head turned. Though, in fairness, she'd never seen a male specimen like him. Even so, she'd be wise to focus on the threat he posed.

He'd said something and expected a reply.

What had he said? Something about it making sense that she'd found her way to the music room. It hadn't really been a question he'd put to her, but a statement, and as such, she'd no reason to trip herself up by saying more than she ought, more than was wise. So instead, Julia opted for the course that had always proven the wisest and gave him her silence.

Lord Ruthven lifted a tawny eyebrow, and she fought to push back the daze cast on her already muddled thoughts. "Well?"

"Yours wasn't really a question, was it, my lord?"

His long gold lashes swept low as he peered through the thin, menacing slits they formed, and then he closed the last bit of distance that existed between them. "No, you are correct. You always had a fondness for this room, did you not?" he murmured, reassembling his earlier words into the query they hadn't been, forcing her hand. "But you remember that, do you not, Adairia?"

Hearing her sister's name applied to Julia hit her like a punch to the stomach. Guilt and pain and so much regret roiled in her breast. "I…" She eyed him warily.

He stared directly at Julia, his gaze locked on her face,

awaiting her response so he could pick out lies, no doubt.

Her pulse kicked up its cadence once more. "I am afraid I don't remember, Lord Ruthven. It has been years. There is much I don't"—know—"remember. And if you would...call me Julia. It is the name I've been known by these past years." That request would surely only further rouse his suspicions, and yet, she couldn't allow him and the duchess to refer to her by that name.

He flicked that icy stare up and down her person, his gaze lingering briefly upon the gap in the garment that put her bosom on display. "How unfortunate, *Julia*... or... mayhap it is something else." He straightened, abandoning his place at the instrument and slid close; he stopped before her.

Heat rolled off his powerful frame, touching her with an unexpected warmth and stealing her breath. "Or what, my lord?" she challenged. "Fortuitous?" Her voice emerged breathless and husky to her own ears.

His body froze. He remained motionless, like a man riveted. Captivated. By her? Surely not.

"Ah, but then, you are the one who uttered that word, my lady." Then his eyes fell to her mouth. "Not I." There was a distracted afterthought quality to those latter words. His hand came up, and he brushed his thumb along the seam of her plump lower lip.

The flesh quivered and trembled under his gentle caress. He toyed with that flesh, and there was a gentleness to his exploration.

A delicious warmth stole through her breast, slipping and twisting around inside.

As close as he stood and the tone of his questioning screamed danger, and yet, her body knew nothing about prudence and caution as her breath caught from his nearness and his touch. Heat pooled in her belly.

Suddenly, he lowered his arm, letting it fall to his side, and took a step back. His deep mask of suspicion was firmly back in place.

And then, it hit her.

Why... he'd not been captivated by her mouth. He'd been studying her features. He'd been searching out some hint or sign of proof of her identity.

Julia shivered, drawing the folds of her night wrapper closed and belting it tighter. She resisted the urge to wrap her arms about her middle and hug herself to keep the secrets in.

He no more trusted her than she trusted him.

"How many years it has been," he murmured, confirming that supposition.

"Thirteen," she said, and the harsh slashes of his eyebrows went up. "It's been thirteen, almost fourteen, years." Everything with this man would be a test, and the only way to survive and succeed in the temporary role she played was by throwing him off-balance with the truths she did possess.

But then he had his surprise under control. "Yes. The papers wrote much about that, did they not?"

"I'm afraid I didn't pay attention to the gossip sheets or columns you were afforded over the years, my lord," she said coolly, annoyed that she'd been so muddleheaded moments ago.

He pounced. "Which begs the question, what have you been doing all these years before finding yourself back in the comfortable folds of the duchess' generosity?"

At last, he'd cease toying with her like a cat did the mouse he'd cornered. Good. She'd have their battle up front and honest. Julia lifted her chin. "You needn't beg, Lord Ruthven," she taunted. "I'll happily regale you with how I spent my years."

"Yes, do that. What were you doing?" He peered at her, that piercing gaze threatening to cut through her and her lies. "Where have you been?"

Julia kept herself still, finding herself and her way. She'd faced far greater opponents than a fancy London toff. "I've spent my life selling flowers on Covent Garden to lords and ladies benevolent enough to give me their time and a ha'penny to survive on." And he'd given her more with that one purse and basketful of flowers than all the peers before him combined.

"How have you survived?" he asked quietly.

Her heart squeezed tightly. He was...different than the prince she'd made him out to be that day in the alley. "In other words, am I a whore?" she asked with a bluntness that brought a flush to his high, noble cheeks.

"No!" he spoke with an automaticity only truth could yield, and yet she'd been treated by a whore, called a whore so many times before, that believing this man should be the one who was different, left her unnerved. Rattled.

"That isn't what I was saying, Julia," he stammered.

"If we've reached the point of blunt honesty, then let's both of us be truly honest, my lord."—A muscle twitched at the corner of his left eye.—"Are you hoping that I have sold myself?" she jeered. "So you could tup me for the right amount of coin?" Never knowing there wasn't an amount she'd sell her virtue for.

He flushed even more. "I wouldn't dare," he sputtered.

Because she was a common woman, and he didn't deal with the common. God, how she despised men of his station. Men of every station, really.

"Well, I'm not a harlot. I've sold scraps and petals and full blooms and dried flowers and dead ones, but I've never sold my body." Julia stared curiously at him. "But tell me, though, if I had been one of those women forced to barter my flesh in the name of survival, would that make me somehow duplicitous? Evil and bad? What of the women you surely take to your bed? I'm sure there are fancy mistresses and actresses to whom you give coin for the privilege of your *protection*."

The color deepened on his cheeks, and she smiled. "I see I am on the mark, am I not?" She let that mirthless grin instantly fade. "You don't trust me, do you, Lord Ruthven?" Julia said, getting to the heart of it.

"Do you think I should?" he countered.

"No," she replied quietly. The rub of it was, he wasn't wrong for his suspicions or his resentment and anger. She'd no place to be offended. He was right. She *was* an impostor. Her insides knotted under that truth. But she was also a woman hell-bent on surviving, and this ruse was but temporary.

He sharpened his gaze on her face.

Julia immediately assembled her features, lest she reveal any more hint of wavering. "Why should you believe that I, a common woman, have any place being here? And yet..." She moved closer to him. "Here I am, Lord Ruthven."

"You're right," he said in steely tones. "I don't trust you. I don't believe you. I think you are here to take advantage of a desperate woman's hope."

Trembling so hard her knees knocked together, Julia smoothed her palms over the front of her stomach. "Well, then, I should be fortunate that it isn't your trust I require, but Her Grace's. Now, if you'll excuse me…" She headed for the doorway.

All the while, she felt Lord Ruthven's intense stare, one that saw too much, following her every movement. The sooner he was gone, and she'd only the kindly duchess and her warmhearted friends to worry about, the better off she would be.

Chapter 7

The following morning, before the sun had even crept into the sky, Harris took up a seat at the duchess' breakfast table... and waited.

He waited for the arrival of his godmother's guest. The Lost Lady.

Adairia.

Adairia, who insisted on going by the name of Julia.

Nay, there wasn't anything at all suspicious about that. Not even given her ridiculous reasoning behind it.

He didn't trust her. He didn't believe for one damned moment she was who she said she was, or that her intentions were in any way honorable.

And yet, he'd also said too much last evening. He'd tipped his hand about the reservations he carried, and in so doing, he had alerted the *lady* of his suspicions, thereby affording her the opportunity to dissemble. He'd put her on alert, and it would therefore be that much harder to trick her into revealing the underhanded nature of her being here.

His coffee cup cradled between his hands, he stared at the still-empty doorway.

Waiting as he'd been, Harris had also been afforded the time and opportunity to prepare a plan of attack for his next meeting with Julia. If he was going to fish out the truth of her motives, he was going to have to do a thoroughly better job than outright attacking and accusing.

That hadn't gotten him anything. Nor would it. That was aside from a more difficult task.

After she'd left the music room, he'd resolved to shift course and unleash a charm offensive. Given the roguish existence he'd lived these past years, it should have been the first path he'd set himself on where Lady Julia-Adairia-Whatever-the-Hell-Her-Real-Name-Was was concerned. But it hadn't been. Not when she'd entered the household of one of the three women who'd been like a mother to him. The lady had, however, conducted herself… like a queen. She'd been boldly challenging and spirited in her fury.

So much so that he'd had a moment of doubt. What if she was who she, in fact, claimed and who his godmother desperately wished her to be?

Unlikely.

Every part of his cynical self screamed fraud and caution. But there was a chance, and as such, he was determined to get to the bottom of whomever or whatever the young woman, in fact, was.

Delicate footfalls sounded outside the breakfast room, and he glanced up from his newspaper.

The young woman stopped in the doorway. Her gaze landed on his.

Resolved to get the answers he sought, Harris climbed to his feet, sketching a respectful bow.

"Ugh," she muttered under her breath, briefly considering the path behind her.

He planned to unleash a charm offensive, and yet... "Did you just groan at seeing me?" Harris frowned.

"It wasn't at seeing the sideboard or the staff," she mumbled, stomping over to that mahogany piece of furniture and accepting a porcelain dish handed to her by a grinning Stebbins. With a word of thanks, she proceeded to fill herself a plate.

"My goodness, I daresay I've never seen a chocolate biscuit that looks like this." The lady spoke in awestruck tones. "You really must try it."

Harris opened his mouth to indicate he'd already availed himself, but Julia slid her plate closer to Stebbins.

Harris scowled. He couldn't coax so much as a smile from her, but Stebbins could earn both a smile and a biscuit? And something in that intimate exchange between the pair set Harris' teeth on edge.

"I could not, my lady," the servant demurred.

"Are you certain?" Julia made another attempt to push the treat off on the footman.

"He's certain," Harris snapped.

His ears went hot as multiple sets of gazes swung toward him.

Turning back, revealing a dish heaping with eggs and sausage and toast, Julia assessed the table, and then, dish in hand, she marched with the regal bearing of a princess to the farthest end of the table away from Harris.

With that, she grabbed a fork and knife and began slicing into her food with a speed that should have horrified him, but instead stirred his curiosity. Reclaiming his seat, Harris studied the woman across from him.

The enthusiasm with which she shoveled entirely too big bites of food into her mouth was certainly a clue as to how she'd lived. The quickness with which she ate, coupled with her almost gaunt figure, revealed a woman who'd been hungry. His stomach tightened under the evidence of that.

Suddenly, she looked up, her silver fork poised halfway to her mouth, that same mouth that had so intrigued him and distracted… and tempted last evening.

And he recalled how very close he'd come to taking those lips under his.

Desire coursed through him.

Suspicion deepened in her eyes.

Harris was grateful that she had no idea the wicked path his thoughts had once again slipped down where she was concerned.

"I fear we were off to a bad start, my lady," he murmured.

"To which part do you refer, Lord Ruthven?" she called loudly, her voice carrying. "When you called me a whore? Or the part where you accused me of being a liar?"

His ears burned for a second time that morn.

God, she was prickly. At least where Harris was concerned. With Stebbins, the lady was perfectly amenable. Of course, this was always going to be difficult. He'd made it near impossible for himself. And he certainly wasn't going to try to charm the suspicious lady all the way across his godmother's eternally long dining table.

Standing, Harris collected his plate in one hand and his cup of coffee in the other and headed over to Julia's side.

She watched his approach with a wariness to match the

unease he carried where she was concerned.

They were of like opinion on that, then.

When he reached her side, Harris smiled. "May I?"

Her auburn eyebrows came together. "May you what?"

"Join you, my lady."

"Do I have a choice?"

"Ah, a person always has a choice," he said, waiting and ultimately allowing her control over the decision. If she wished for him to leave, he would. Because forcing his presence upon her would serve him no good, and it would certainly not break down the walls he'd inadvertently fortified last evening through his mistrust.

"And you, with that opinion, my lord, show the privilege of your rank." Julia slowly lowered her fork and nodded her chin to the seat on the other side of the table. With that, she refocused all her attention on her plate and promptly and thoroughly dismissed him.

The privilege of his rank.

That was something he'd not given much thought to. He'd been born to his station and had known from his earliest memories that his obligations included the vast Ruthven estates and the people he was responsible for.

While she ate, Harris picked up his coffee and drank. All the while, he watched her over the rim of his cup. He should be studying her for signs of deception. He should be putting questions to her more subtly than he had last evening so he could ascertain once and for all the truth of her identity. What he should not be singularly focused on was how the sun's morning rays played with her hair, forming a halo about her and drawing his gaze to the luxuriant strands, which had been brought back into a serviceable chignon. Close as he was, he admired the shades of her hair that nighttime light had concealed. Endless hues of color—browns and golds streaked with reds—created the most luxuriant, silken, auburn tresses. Why, in the light, he appreciated just how hasty he'd been in the judgment he'd formed of the lady's beauty. From the delicate point to her chin, to the dusting of freckles along a pert nose, there was a siren's quality to her that compelled a man to—

She looked up. "What?" she snapped.

She'd noted his scrutiny, then. Harris's neck went hot. Unnerved by his inability to look away, he made a clearing sound with his throat. "It is my hope we might… start over," he said, extending that olive branch.

"Why? Because you think it easier to butter me up so you might search out nefarious motives? Ones that I do not have, Lord Ruthven," she said coolly.

My God, she was clever and very much on the mark. And here he'd never before believed there to be a person more cynical and distrustful than himself. "That is not it." Not entirely. "It is my hope that we can start anew, because I was boorish last evening." That wasn't untrue. "Because it was not my intention to be rude. What do you say, Julia?" he pressed. "A new beginning?" He flashed a grin, the same, uneven one he donned when he was charming London's most notorious widows. It was a smile that had never failed him.

"What are you doing with your eyes?" She leaned in and peered closely at his face. "Is that a smolder?"

"Is it perhaps improving your disposition towards me?"

Dropping his elbow on the table, Harris matched her movements, bringing their faces so close her breath, tinged with the hint of mint, wafted over his lips, stirring that earlier awareness.

She snorted. "Decidedly not."

This time, his neck heated for an altogether different reason—the lady's complete lack of awareness where he was concerned.

Across the table, he caught the smiles of the footmen, grins they unsuccessfully attempted to control.

Holding his eye, Julia winked, softening her earlier blow, and then she resumed eating.

She did so with her usual gusto, again revealing a hint of how she was accustomed to living.

And through the haze of suspicion surrounding her and the determination to get to the bottom of whether or not she was who she claimed to be, he removed himself, stepping back to see her life had not been the comfortable one he and those of the peerage knew. He slipped his study lower to the fingers clutching her fork. Her hands were red, callused on the tops, chapped so badly there was the hint of blood within those cracks.

She followed his stare, daring him with fiery eyes to say something.

Harris sat back in his chair and took another sip of coffee. "You mentioned you sold flowers at Covent Garden," he said. Oddly, it was the first time that this desire to learn about her had nothing to do with his suspicions, but rather, a very real desire to know her. For some ungodly reason he didn't understand, her fiery nature only added to her charm.

My God, he must be going as mad as a hatter.

"I do." She paused, staring down at her plate. "I did."

What accounted for the trace of regret he heard in that correction?

"Did you enjoy it?"

"Did I enjoy it?" she echoed. Then Julia laughed, a full, almost musical sound different than the tittering practiced by ladies of the peerage. He found himself preferring the realness and richness of Julia's amusement.

Dusting the mirth from her eyes, Julia shook her head. "My days began while it was still dark. I arose before even the cock crowed the day's start so that I could pilfer hothouse waste to try to find suitable scraps to sell benevolent lords and ladies who'd passed the first time on those flowers."

All enjoyment of her instantly vanished as her revelation knocked him square in the stomach, like a fist he'd taken to the belly at Gentleman Jackson's the first time he'd stepped into that ring years earlier. But she wasn't done with him.

"A flower seller's day doesn't end. You've got passersby to try and sell your goods to. But the real earnings come at night, when lords and ladies are milling outside the theaters, waiting to go in. And then you hang around and wait until they finish their fun and come out once more, and hopefully, if you still have anything left to sell, you reach some other gents and ladies on their way out." With that matter-of-fact telling complete, Julia resumed eating, and this time, he didn't interrupt with more questions.

He left her to her meal and sat in the discomfort of his own thoughts.

He'd been one of those gents she'd spoken so casually of. How many times had he entered a Covent Garden production or a Drury Lane theater, invariably to meet a mistress at the end of a performance, while failing to properly think of the flower sellers and beggars he'd passed on the way in? The extent of his consideration had been to press a purse or coin into their hands, but he'd not studied those fingers, as he did Julia's, to see their life's toil etched upon the palms they'd turned up. It was humbling to confront the reality of one's self-absorption, to acknowledge how very blind he'd been to the luxuries he was afforded and the struggles Julia and so many others had known. Just like so many others, he'd ignored the suffering around him. He'd done so unknowingly; in an unwitting decision born of ease; coming from the simple fact that it was easier to remain blind than acknowledge the wealth of suffering all around.

He didn't trust her, but that didn't mean he wasn't capable of self-reflection on the type of suffering she'd spoken of.

They sat there in silence for the remainder of breakfast, and then Julia took to her feet and left without so much as another glance his way.

He stared at the doorway.

He should let her go.

That would be decidedly better than any of this pathetic weakening she'd managed to inflict with a telling that had been all too real.

Prickly as she was, however, he found himself drawn to her...and her spirit.

And for reasons that had nothing to do with wheedling out her lies or secrets, he went in search of the flower-peddler woman named Julia.

Chapter 8

Seated on a gilded bench in the duchess' sculpture room, Julia stared up at the trio in the painting—a mother, a father, and between them, a bright-eyed, golden-curled angel with the chubbiest cheeks and widest smile. That smile stood in stark contrast to the reserved pair, who'd coaxed their lips into careful lines, as though it had been ingrained into them that any show of emotion was a sin and to reveal it would cost them a place in paradise.

Julia angled her head, studying the husband and wife, the marble room a perfect place for such cool-looking figures.

Only one figure was out of place.

Adairia.

Not even the streets had managed to erase her smile.

Had she been raised as the beloved, cherished daughter of a noble pair and the niece of a duchess, she would have radiated an even greater light.

Tears pricked her lashes, and she blinked them back. One fell, making a mockery of her attempts to stifle them, reminding her of how little control she had over absolutely everything in her life. Julia swiped an angry hand across her cheek.

And yet, it wasn't her deception that held her motionless

in this space. It wasn't a fear of being caught and called out for the impostor she was. Nay, it was a bereft feeling at the fact that Adairia, who'd carried the dream in her heart and been sustained in the darkest of times by the belief that she was, in fact, a princess, should be forever memorialized in this place among her noble ancestors.

Julia hugged herself tightly around the middle and stared blankly out. Despite the vibrant flash of light Adairia had been in the cold world they lived in, she would have hated this room. It would have been too dark and chilly and cheerless for the girl who'd managed to retain a sunny optimism and hope.

But even if she would have hated this room, she'd still belonged here. She'd deserved to be remembered the way her noble ancestors had been.

Julia sucked in a shaky breath.

"They said I might find you here." That deep baritone echoed around the spacious room. The absence of furniture made that greeting boom all the louder.

Oh, bloody hell.

She tensed and didn't face him.

He was... unrelenting.

He'd never come 'round to trusting her. And worse, one such as him? She'd no doubt he could pull the lies from her lips.

He was the last person she wished to see, and bloody crying, no less.

Turning her damp cheek against her satin skirts, she rubbed her face in a bid to discreetly wipe away that moisture, refusing to let him see those crystal drops and implicitly knowing if he did, he'd assume they were just more lies.

He came to a stop before her, blocking her study of that portrait, his long, breeches-encased legs directly in her line of vision. Julia lifted her gaze up his tall, powerful form until her gaze locked with his. "Is there somewhere else I should be? Did you think to find me sneaking about the silver closets and filling my pockets?" She turned her face away. She might be a liar, but her lies were based on her hungering to live. For all the opinions he carried of her, she was no thief. Or whore. She'd managed to retain some sense of self and her worth.

"May I?" he murmured.

She braced for him to take that seat anyway, taking as all men and noblemen were wont to do, and yet, he didn't. He waited there, allowing the decision to lie with her.

Julia edged sideways on the upholstered bench, making room for him and hugging the arm of the bench. Even so, his thighs, the size of some stone pillars on the streets of London, swallowed up most of the space, bringing their legs touching.

From the corner of her eye, she caught him fishing something from his pocket, and then a slip of white cloth fell before her.

"Here," he said, and she hesitated before taking the monogrammed handkerchief and wiping at her face.

He didn't ask questions about her tears or call her out as deceptive once more. Instead, he just sat there, allowing her that quiet and space.

That was, an emotional space. Physically, they sat as

close as two lovers.

Her belly danced wildly, his nearness, his masculinity dizzying distractions that she certainly did not need. With his dashing looks, she found herself enthralled by him. It was a distraction she could ill-afford to indulge in.

"What do you think of Her Grace's marble room?" he asked, the casualness of his tones, ones so very conversational, at odds with her racing heart.

Unlike last evening and breakfast a short while ago, Lord Ruthven's focus when he spoke was not trained with a detective's intensity upon her, but rather, on a nearby bust, a rendering in white so flawlessly done, the sculptor had captured the likeness of the man seated beside her.

"It is icy," she said before she could call the words back. As cold as the man himself. "I think this room is cold." She glanced up just as he angled his head close to hers, and her breath caught on a quick intake.

"A secret?" he whispered, his breath caressing her ear.

Her belly fluttered again, and she gave an uneven nod.

"I have always hated this room. It is one of her favorites, but it is like a cold mausoleum." A glimmer lit his eyes, a mischievous twinkle that... softened him. "One day when I was a boy—perhaps five? mayhap six?—I found sketch paper and drew bodies upon them, and with the help of the servants, we attached the missing parts to the 'poor body-less family members.'"

A startled laugh escaped her. That image of the child bent on fixing the sculptures was so endearing, so adorable that her heart melted in her breast, and despite the fact she knew her reaction to him and his story were folly, she was hopeless to resist that pull. "What did the duchess do?" she asked between her laughter.

He joined in, their amusement mingling as one, and with him so close, she felt his deeper rumble in her belly. "What do you think she did?"

Her amusement trailed off.

What do you think she did?

It was asked so casually, more as a rhetorical question, and yet, she searched for a sign of a test. For that was surely what this was.

Only, she could not find a hint of his usual cynicism or hardness.

Julia slid her attention away from the marquess, her thoughts upended enough to make her careless. "I believe she left them," Julia murmured. Given his clear devotion, respect, and love for the woman, the duchess had no doubt proven to be a woman deserving of those sentiments because of how she'd treated him as a child. "I believe she indulged you mightily, Lord Ruthven." The fact that he'd escorted her last evening and now stayed with the duchess spoke volumes of the bond between the pair.

"You are… correct," he said softly, almost wistfully as he studied a marble bust of the duchess. His gaze slid away from the sculpture and over to Julia. "I believe given our association with the duchess and our commitment to a new beginning between us, it would be appropriate that we refer to one another by our Christian names. Please, call me Harris."

"Harris," she repeated. It suited him. Strong and yet with a hint of playfulness befitting the charming rogue he undoubtedly was. "And I am Julia."

"Julia," he murmured, collecting her fingers and raising her knuckles to his mouth as though it were the first time they'd met. Her name falling from his lips emerged as though he were testing and tasting it upon his lips. Delicious shivers tingled where he kissed. They raced up her arm and toyed with her heart.

"Why Julia?" he asked, continuing to hold her fingers. With the pad of his thumb, he stroked the inseam where her hand met her wrist, tenderly stroking that powerful digit over the place where her pulse pounded. From a touch so light. And yet so mesmerizing.

"Why what?" she asked, her voice breathless because of that quixotic caress.

He paused briefly. "The name Julia. How did you cease to be Adairia?"

How had she... And then real and pretend got all mixed up in her mind, made a greater muddle by the intoxicating effect he had upon her, and she had to sort herself out to remember who she was.

She'd never been Adairia. She played a game of pretend, on the loss of the only friend and sister she'd known. And Julia went cold inside, his touch suddenly wrong, a gentleness she was undeserving of.

"I was taken in by a family, a mother and a daughter," she said, telling him the story that was, in fact, Adairia's, though one in which the roles were reversed, and Julia became the princess Adairia had always sworn she was. "The mum was a former opera singer who couldn't find employment on the stage. She suffered an illness that left her throat ravaged, and her voice gave out after that. It never returned…and she was forced to quit the stage and turned to selling flowers." How many times had her mother regaled she and Adairia with tales of her greatness…and then her fall? "There was no father," she murmured. Perhaps if there'd been a devoted husband, Julia's mother wouldn't have struggled in quite the same way. "I was lost. Wandering outside Covent Garden when they found me. Crying." Julia's eyes slid shut as the memory of that day slipped forward, the day when her family had become complete. "The girl was near in age to me. But she took my hand and told me everything would be all right. That I could stay with her and her mum."

Only, she now knew that what had completed her family had left another, Adairia's rightful one, with a void that could never be filled. She opened her eyes and brought two separate stories of two different girls converging. "The mother, she liked jewels. She used to talk about the men who vied for her favor and shower her with baubles." Except they hadn't been real gems; rather they'd been paste pieces her mother had clung to in memory of a time when she'd been sought after. Bitterness brought her lips twisting in a painful grimace. "She said jewels were magical and beautiful, and so she called me Julia." Realizing he still held her, Julia slipped her hand from his and let her arm drop, feeling an odd sense of loss.

Harris brushed his knuckles over her chin, angling her face up toward his, and she stiffened, prepared for him to look for the lies that surely dwelled in her eyes. Only, he continued to caress her, stroking his fingers along the curve of her cheek, and she melted, thoroughly bewitched once more by his touch. "Julia... That is... a perfect choice for you."

Actually, it wasn't. She couldn't be any more different than a cherished, valuable gemstone.

Nor, for that matter, had she even been Julia to her mother. She'd been Jewels, because her mother had dreamed of jewels. And there hadn't been a surname, because the man who'd bedded her mother had left when she'd become with child. The sole reason Julia's name had evolved into something decent and respectable was because of the woman whose life Julia even now stole.

In fact, perhaps she was more her mother's daughter, than she'd ever credited.

As he continued to stroke her, she wanted to believe the lie.

Their gazes locked. His fingers ceased moving, and then, ever so slowly, he resumed that back-and-forth glide, his thumb toying with her lower lip. The flesh trembled under his ministrations, and her lips parted.

Her breath hitched, or was that his?

Harris dipped his head, then stopped. He came closer once more. But again resisted.

When any man in the Dials would have simply taken, he showed restraint, and the evidence of his self-control unleashed a flurry of butterflies within.

And then, ever so gently, Harris touched his mouth to hers with a tenderness that threatened to shatter her; it sent a delicious wave of heat and longing through Julia.

She sighed softly.

Harris stilled, and then with a low groan that shook his chest, he deepened that kiss. With every exquisite meeting of their lips, the fire grew and spread, so what began with a gentleness dissolved and a greater intensity and ferocity took over.

Never had she felt like this. Never had she known she could…because this sensation of being in his arms was as heady as touching one's fingertips to a rainbow after the rain. She surrendered herself to him and this moment, and he used that opportunity to slip his tongue inside, touching that flesh against hers.

It ended as quick as it had begun; a delicate dance in passion.

All that glorious sensation came to an agonizing and excruciating stop.

Harris broke the kiss, his chest moving against her also rapidly rising one. He rested the side of his head against hers. His coffee-scented breath fanned her cheek as he brought his breathing under control…and then with an aching tenderness, he dropped a kiss upon her right temple.

She lay against him, the warmth receding, and a new kind of heat taking its place, a mortified, humiliated one spiked by shame. Horror took the place of the wonderful warmth that had come from an embrace unlike any she'd ever known. She scrambled to her feet.

His eyes, hooded by those magnificent tawny lashes, revealed nothing, and she didn't want to see the mockery or disdain that was surely lurking in those cerulean depths, indicating her wanton response to him had outed her as the impostor she was.

She fled.

And coward that she was, Julia was grateful when he let her go.

Chapter 9

The next day, Harris, his presence having been requested by the duchess, found his way to the conservatory, the one place one might always count on finding the duchess.

"I've been begging you to come round for years," she said upon his arrival. "Who knew all it would require to get you to stay and never leave was for me to bring a young lady into my household?" She snorted. "One would think with your reputation that a respectable lady would be the last thing to keep you around, but here you are."

Crossing the length of the conservatory, he joined the duchess at the worktable. "Godmother," he greeted, dropping a kiss upon her smooth cheek. "You summoned."

"I summon people I don't like, Harris. I invite those I love and care about to visit." Pruning shears in hand, she waved off the lady's maid standing in attendance, and the girl curtsied before taking her leave, vacating the wrought-iron bench for Harris.

He slid onto the seat and waited.

She snipped at a leaf.

The green scrap fell, landing on the small heap made by the work she'd already done on the boxwood.

Leaving a person to sit in silence was her way. As a boy,

it had unnerved him. The older he'd grown, however, he'd come to appreciate the time left to sit with his thoughts.

"It is my understanding you took breakfast with the girl yesterday," his godmother remarked.

Not a *girl*. Desire fired in his veins as he recalled the feel of her and the taste of her... He shifted on the bench. "I did."

"It wasn't a question. It was a statement. I know these things."

Because her staff was loyal.

"She doesn't seem to like you," Her Grace said without inflection.

"Why, thank you."

At his droll tone, she glanced up. "Oh, hush now. You're not a stupid boy. You, who charms ladies older than me out of their pantalets, has managed to butt heads with the single young lady I give a damn about."

"Ah, but, dear duchess, I'm wary of the lady for the sole reason that I worry about you." And he didn't trust the motives of a young lady who'd been gone a lifetime only to suddenly materialize out of thin air.

"Come now." His godmother brought her clippers close enough to his chest that he was almost tempted to move away. "Do you really think this lady needs you to go protecting her from a slender, tiny bit of a thing? She's no more than a child."

"There are other kinds of hurt that can be exacted beyond the physical kind," he murmured. Harris raised his hand to cover her own and guided it and the clippers back to the table.

"You're thinking about your bride again," she said bluntly. His godmother was the sole person of his acquaintance who thought absolutely nothing about bringing up that hardest, most humiliating part of his existence.

"I'm thinking that nothing bad can come from being cautious, but that pain is possible if you let yourself believe something that isn't true."

A sound of impatience escaped her, and she resumed cutting, this time with a greater zeal that made him more than a little regretful that he'd not removed the shears from her hands. "Just as not every man is the same as your miserable late father, not every woman is the same as your late wife."

He paused. No, he wasn't so cynical as to believe all women were mercenary and deceitful. But he also knew there were women of that ilk out there, and as such, it was better to be cautious until one could ascertain for certain their motives. He knew the motives of the scandalous sort he kept company with. The young ladies his godmother spoke of? The ones who had only marriage and a respectable life on their minds were to be avoided at all costs.

At his silence, the duchess looked up, a somber set to her graceful features. "Did you hear me?" She spoke with the gentleness she'd reserved for him as a boy who'd just lost his mother and had had for company only an aloof, distant father who couldn't be bothered with him. "Not all women are like that treacherous liar you found yourself married to."

"I know that." Harris grinned. "Because I have a woman of honor and honesty and decency before me even now."

A blush splashed upon the duchess's cheeks. "Go on with

you now," she said gruffly, waving off those compliments—those true compliments—with a wave of her spare hand, "thinking to charm this lady. I was talking about a younger one than myself."

He donned an affronted expression. "You're hardly old. Why, you aren't a day beyond thirty," he said, following that with a wink.

"I'm just forty-five and you know it." She chuckled. "You'd do well to find yourself a bride."

"As you pointed out, I had a bride."

"A *new* one," the duchess clarified. "One who could appreciate that wink."

Which his wife had decidedly not. As the duchess turned her attention back to the tabletop boxwood and snipped away, Harris stared blankly. As a rule, he avoided thinking of his late wife. Not because it hurt with her being gone—he was too hardened for that. Rather, because it was a reminder of how foolish he'd been, and trusting, and the careless mistakes that had seen him... trapped.

The woman he'd ended up with as a bride had been nothing more than a beautiful stranger carrying the babe of a handsome footman who'd never have made her a suitable husband, so she'd trapped an unsuspecting Harris, finding herself an arrangement that would let her carry on with her happy affair, while having Harris stuck in an unhappy union.

Snip, snip, snip.

"I never thought you should marry her, for what that is worth," his godmother remarked, apparently knowing with the intuitiveness of one's mother where Harris' thoughts had landed. "I told your father he was a fool for insisting upon

93

it."

"The Clarendale name and the Ruthven title," he said, unable to quell the bitterness. The late marquess had cared first, foremost, and only about that name and title. Harris had just happened to be the necessary conduit through which that great line would continue.

"But then, there were many ways in which he was a fool." Her Grace paused in her cutting and assessed her meticulous work before resuming her shaping of the bush. "Wedding your dear mother was the only good decision he made. Unfortunately for your mother." She muttered that last part under her breath. Her features suddenly warmed as she glanced up. "But fortunately for you. You were born to that union, and as such, it wasn't all bad."

No, but it had set a foundation early on to prove that many marriages were cold, empty unions. The few memories he carried of his mother were of her being confined to her chambers as she lost babe after babe the marquess had foisted upon her in the bid for a spare to Harris' heir. Ultimately, his mother had lost... herself in that ruthless quest.

His eventual marriage to Lady Clarisse had only added cement to that truth he'd believed as a boy.

The duchess patted his shoulder. "Any man who lived your life would have turned out with the same cynicism, Harris. But there are good people out there, if you just open your eyes to see them."

"People like Lady Adairia, who insists on being referred to as Lady Julia?" He couldn't resist the droll retort.

She smiled. "Precisely." But then her smile slipped, and she turned her famous—and famously fear-inducing—

duchess' frown upon him. "Now, stop scaring my niece."

"You don't know her," he said gently. "All you know, Your Grace, is that she showed up one day with a pendant and professed to be your niece." There were more reasons to be wary than welcoming.

"I will not be able to know her as long as you're scowling around the girl, making her uncomfortable." She rapped his knuckles. "Now. Behave." She clipped out each syllable.

There came the quiet approach of footsteps outside, and Harris was prevented from saying anything else.

For she was there; studiously avoiding his eyes, and iron-ically, Harris, an unapologetic rogue, found himself looking anywhere but at her.

"Come, come, my dear," the duchess called, waving Julia over. From the side of her mouth, she delivered one last whispered warning to Harris. "Open mind, dear boy. Open. Mind."

Julia stood in the doorway, taking in the duchess and her tall, imposing godson. The gentleman who rightly didn't trust her. Who'd also kissed her senseless and no doubt had had all his suspicions and ill opinions of her confirmed with that embrace. She'd acted no different than the whore she said she wasn't. But that kiss—her *first*—had felt like heaven, and it was as though she'd been sparked alive for the first time in the whole of her existence.

Julia remained frozen, unable to move.

Oh, my God. That was why she'd been called. It made

sense now. She'd behaved like a wanton, pressing herself against him and pleading for his kiss, and in so doing, she'd confirmed that she was in no way the innocent and respectable Adairia. Yes, she and Adairia had lived the same life. But Adairia had been born to *this* world, unlike Julia who was the bastard-born daughter of a failed opera singer. These two most powerful members of the peerage could see her ended for the charade she played at.

And he had undoubtedly brought her here to call her out before the duchess, to make Julia answer for her shameful behavior. Her pulse thumped loud and hard in her ears, deafening. For it wouldn't matter to the duchess or her godson the reasons that Julia had set out to deceive them. That if she'd stayed in East London, she'd have met the same fate Adairia had, a gruesome, not-so-quick death. All that they or the world on the whole would care about was that a street rat had invaded their ranks and—

"Julia," the duchess prodded, and Julia jumped. "Come, come, my girl."

The marquess, nay, Harris—it was easier to think of him as different than a powerful noble who could ruin her with a single word—had been too disgusted to look at her moments ago, but he deigned to do so now, and he stared at her from under thick, hooded lashes, his face a perfect mask.

Her mouth went dry.

For a moment, she eyed the path behind her, where two footmen remained stationed.

Oh, God.

Lifting her chin up, she began a slow, long, and painful walk over to the pair staring expectantly back.

When Julia had been a girl and a hanging had been held at the square outside of Newgate, her mother had dragged Julia and eventually Adairia to watch that public spectacle, as people of East London were wont to do.

Unlike the other spectators who'd assembled, gleefully watching as though they'd come to take in one of those Covent Garden productions she hawked flowers outside of, Julia had despised every moment of it. While many in the crowd had cheered and laughed, selling treats for people to snack on as they waited and watched the men, women, and even children meet their maker that day.

Julia had always stared on at those poor souls making their march, her heart hammering and hurting for the fear they'd been no doubt filled with. She'd imagined herself in their stead. After all, the fate of a person born to the streets was as precarious as the London day. Now, she knew precisely how those people had felt. This same terror and horror and… urgency to flee were what that final march had inspired within their chests.

At last, Julia reached the pair.

Silence met her arrival.

Interestingly, even with the elevated rank that found the woman just shy of royalty, Julia found herself preferring to focus on the duchess, as opposed to the marquess, with his penetrating stare that saw too much.

"We have a problem, Julia," the other woman said, thumping her shears once on the table.

Julia drew in a quiet, uneven breath. "D-do we, Your Grace?"

"We do." The duchess jabbed a long finger at Julia's

chest, and she stiffened. "It is those garments."

Those...

Julia followed that point.

And then the significance of that statement and the truth that she hadn't been caught out, left her breathless with relief, giddy. A silly little laugh bubbled past her lips.

The duchess sharpened her focus upon Julia, and she made herself stifle that nervous mirth. "Forgive me, Your Grace, it is simply that I've not worn finer garments. The quality, the color. Why, there can never be anything wrong in any way about them."

The woman instantly softened, and guilt, the more familiar sentiment where this lady was concerned, consumed Julia once more. "Some say they're too garish."

From the corner of her eye, Julia caught the smile pulling at Harris' lips.

"I'd say anyone who says that is just jealous that they cannot pull off such boldness," Julia murmured.

"Yes, yes, well, either way, we shall be having a modiste come in, and she will fit you for a more suitable, appropriate wardrobe that's not tailored down from this lady."

Her heart dropped. "No!" Julia exclaimed, her slightly panicked shout echoing in the rafters of the high glass ceiling.

"No?"

"I should think you'd welcome a trousseau," the marquess remarked.

With his suspicions and ill opinion of her, he would assume that. Because her motives would be driven only by avarice and not by the sheer need of survival that compelled people of her station.

And yet, does the end justify the means? a voice taunted at the back of her mind, where guilt dwelled and shame festered.

She ignored that voice and turned to the duchess. "I am ever so grateful for your generous offer, and yet, I must decline."

"It's not an offer, dear. It was me telling you what I intend to do. Tomorrow, you are to be fitted."

"But... but..." She lifted her arms. "These garments are splendorous." The finest she'd worn. The finest she'd ever wear. For that matter, she couldn't take a single thing more than she already had.

The duchess laughed. "You are very much my niece."

Julia forced a smile that felt tight and painful and harsh on her mouth. *No. I'm not. I'm a liar. I'm street trash with a father who didn't even want me.*

"Isn't she, Harris?"

Harris, who to his credit didn't voice that lie aloud just to please his godmother. He just continued to study her with that cynical gaze that she found herself unable to meet.

"As if anyone could doubt it," the duchess said, and Julia's gaze slid involuntarily over to the greatest of her doubters. "Your new trousseau aside, that is not why I've summoned you. It is because of my godson."

Lord Ruthven.

"Yes, I see he is here." Julia paused. "Still."

He dropped a bow. "Indeed." he murmured, his stare so intense as to rip right through her and her lies. "Is there somewhere else I should be?"

Tension crackled and sizzled, hanging in the air, an electric heat to it that came from the kiss that lingered still on her lips, when she should feel only fear at what his presence meant. Words failed. Julia felt the duchess' eyes on her exchange with Harris, but God forgive her for her red-haired temper her mum had insisted she'd inherited from her da, she couldn't put on the proper show where this gentleman was concerned. Julia made herself glance away first. "No, my lord. It is a great honor to have your presence here again… and again."

The duchess laughed, and releasing her shears, she caught one of Julia's hands in hers and reached for her godson with her other. "You two are of like temperaments."

It was on the tip of Julia's tongue to point out she wasn't like Harris in any way, but she managed to bite back that curt pronouncement.

"It is my hope with Harris now remaining with us for an indefinite time that you two might strike up a friendship."

Julia whipped her gaze up to the marquess', but his expression was veiled, revealing none of the smugness he no doubt felt.

Oh, bloody hell. He'd absolutely no intention of leaving. But then, should she expect anything different? "I… how… wonderful," she brought herself to say. Just as she'd suspected, the truce he'd tried to strike up the other day had been nothing more than an attempt to grease her up.

"Well, it is not wonderful yet. Not with you both fighting as you are. In the hope of you getting to know one another, I thought it would be a good idea if you spent some time together."

As one, Julia and Harris stiffened.

"Your Grace—"

"I don't think—"

She thumped the hilt of her shears. "Silence, the both of you. As we will all be living together, I'll not have you at each other's throats."

"Are you trying to have me thrown out?" Harris demanded.

"I'm merely suggesting that if there is some other place that you might go—and you being a marquess, there undoubtedly is—that you go there."

"The hell I will," he barked.

Her Grace clapped her hands. "Children," she said, breaking across their bickering. "Now, though I do not disagree with Julia that it is altogether ridiculous that you wish to remain here, I also see benefits to the two of you getting to know one another. Now, off you go. A curricle ride in Hyde Park."

As one, Harris and Julia snapped their heads to look at the duchess, and then, once more at one another. A slow-building horror filled him; that emotion mirrored in the young woman's wide eyes.

Well, it seemed they'd agree on one thing, after all.

Bloody hell.

Chapter 10

All number of conveyances, from a casual hackney on to enormous barouches and elegant phaetons, had rattled along the streets of Covent Garden. Julia, however, had always been endlessly fascinated by the curricles.

Whenever they'd gone whipping past, she'd taken a moment away from selling flowers to glance at those quick-moving vehicles and wonder what it was like to ride within them. Because of the way the riders' hair had been wind-tossed, she'd often suspected it felt like flying.

It had been one of the pleasures she'd secretly wondered after and envied those powerful peers the privilege of knowing.

Only to now find herself moving at a brisk clip in one of those very conveyances and dreaming herself anyplace but where she was.

Because she *also* found herself with perhaps the most dangerous person she could—a man who doubted she was who she professed to be, and also one who'd kissed her senseless earlier and whose kiss she'd been unable to shake from her thoughts.

She sat stiffly at his side, hugging the edge of the bench in a bid to put some space between them.

Her efforts, however, proved futile. From the corner of her eye, Julia couldn't keep her gaze from wandering to the leg that brushed her skirt and nearly touched her own. Her mouth went dry.

She felt his stare on her and swiftly averted her attention out at the passing landscape. *Think about the rumble of the carriage wheels. Or the crunch of gravel. Think about anything beyond the fact of just how much Harris, Lord Ruthven unnerves you.*

As he guided the mount down the heavily traveled gravel path, strangers were stealing glances their way.

Her palms moistened.

This was a terrible idea.

Not just the curricle ride with the marquess, but putting herself on display before all the most powerful people in England. All of whom would happily line up at the very gibbet she'd lived in fear of. There was no doubt they'd cheer her on to her death for daring to infiltrate their lofty ranks.

After a thirty-minute, or perhaps forty-minute, journey from the duchess' to Hyde Park, Harris was the first to speak. "You don't much like me, do you?" he remarked casually.

Of anything he might have said, that was decidedly more welcome and easier than being called out for her wanton response to him. Some of the tension left her shoulders. "I daresay I can put the same question to you."

He scoffed. "Come, I was perfectly charming the other morning."

"I'll have you know, if you have to say that you were perfectly charming, you were decidedly not as charming as you believe, my lord."

Instead of indignant outrage, a smile pulled at Harris' lips, not the cynical one he usually wore, but rather, a real one that dimpled his cheeks and wrought havoc upon her heart.

Furthermore, her words for him had been a lie anyway, and perhaps his smile said he knew it. With the exception of his kiss, he had been charming. From the moment she'd entered the breakfast room yesterday, he'd been too charming. He'd not been rude or insulting, but rather, warm. And that had proven more terrifying than his disdain.

"My lord again, am I?"

"When you practiced deceit and offered your name under false pretenses of friendship, then yes. My lord you are, and my lord you will remain." With that, Julia picked up the parasol the duchess had lent her and fiddled with the scrap, struggling.

"Here." Harris handed her the reins of the curricle and took the umbrella from her fingers.

"I have it," she lied. She'd not a clue how to open the blasted frippery.

She tensed at having the pair of chestnut horses under her control, but he'd mastered her umbrella and had the reins back almost quicker than a blink.

"Thank you," she said gruffly, angling the frilly scrap at her shoulder.

Harris guided the curricle down a side path before pulling it off to the side.

She stiffened. "Wh—?"

"I wasn't practicing deceit," he interrupted. "Not in the

way you are thinking. You don't trust me." His wasn't a question. "And if we'd have the truth between us, then yes, I am suspicious of your sudden reappearance." He paused, and his eyes locked with hers. "The duchess mourned the loss of her niece—*you*—for years. It was the saddest I've ever seen her. And after her sadness faded, she committed herself wholeheartedly to hiring the best detectives. Men who scoured the streets of London for a sight or a hint of a little girl lost. There were many false leads, and the people she hired took advantage of her, bringing forward some child or another in hopes of receiving the grandest of prizes. And every time she realized that child was not you? I saw her heart break all over again."

Her chest ached at the image Harris painted of a woman who'd been hurt too many times and who would now be hurt again.

"You don't have to do this. You can leave and spare her more of the hurt…"

"It is because you care about her," she said softly. "Your treatment of me."

"Of course it is," he replied, so automatically there could be no doubting the veracity of his words.

And God help her, there was a softening inside.

But then, honesty had that effect. It was so rare a commodity in the streets as to be rarer than the unicorns Adairia had told tales of.

To give her fingers a purpose, she snapped the parasol shut and set it between them, the tiniest of barriers.

Harris gave her a look. "You find it so very hard to believe that I'm capable of caring about someone?"

"I do." Julia glanced down at her gloves, the ones concealing her callused palms. She clasped her fingers tightly as a memory slipped in of an elegantly clad lady, horror etched in her features as she looked disdainfully upon Julia's floral offering. "Not because I presume to know you," she was quick to add.

She is offensive to me. See that she begs at another corner, or call the constable.

The echo of her footfalls striking the cobblestones as she'd raced from the Drury Lane theater while a certain stop at Newgate echoed loudly in her mind.

Feeling his eyes upon her once more, she looked up and attempted to explain. "The lords and ladies whom I've observed, Harris? They aren't capable of caring about anyone but themselves." They'd let a child starve, with the only regret expressed the fact that they were an eyesore upon the pretty existence they preferred looking upon. "They don't see past their own interests and desires. They like their life pretty and unfettered." Her mouth hardened, and her gaze locked unblinkingly on his shoulder. "They do things like have children carted off so they don't have to be confronted by the sight of them. Or who offer coin in the dead of winter, but only if they can have a feel…"

Even as those words left her lips, she wanted to call them back, but it was too late, and everything curled up—her toes, her fingers, her insides. All tightening with the shame of that admission. There'd been too many times she and Adairia had been so desperate that Julia had sold a touch to save Adairia's virtue, to spare her sister. Shame scraped along her insides, and she sucked in a breath. "And so, yes, the idea that people of your station are capable of caring for anyone? That is... was foreign to me." Her voice emerged as a pained whisper.

Please, stop looking at me.

Please, look away.

Please, just forget absolutely everything I've said.

But then his fingers grazed her chin, and Julia's body tensed as he guided her chin up, forcing her eyes to meet his. "Is that... something you have experience with?" he asked harshly.

She heard the hatred there. The fury.

Shame continued blossoming within her, unfurling like a flower of humiliation, because she already knew what this man thought of her. As such, she wanted to deny it. But she couldn't. Because to hell with him and to hell with those like him. Julia firmed her jaw and jerked her chin up, loosening his hold upon her.

"Aye. That's something I have experience with, Harris."

Harris, because it was easier to call him out that way. Using his Christian name made it easier to feel he was an equal, and not superior to her inferior, the common street trash who on too many occasions had let a man touch her breast through her dress, or grope her buttocks for a pence.

His gaze darkened. The tawny slashes of his brows shot together in an angry line over a pair of frosty cerulean eyes. He growled. "I would happily kill the lot of those lords should your path cross with them again. You need just point them out, and I'll make them regret their treatment of you... and others who surely suffered the same abuses," he said sharply.

It took her a moment to register that the fury coating

that low growl wasn't reserved for her, but rather, for the nameless strangers whom she'd spoken of. People of his station. Lords and ladies who shared his ranks, but... also not his heart. Or his depth of compassion. The kind he'd displayed for the duchess and now a righteous indignation on Julia's behalf. She searched her eyes over his face. "Why?" She managed nothing more than that befuddled whisper that she wasn't even sure she'd spoken aloud. Why wasn't he horrified, as he should be, by what she'd revealed? Horrified not at the people of his station, but at her for selling those touches and for disgusting them with her presence? "Why would you offer to do that?" she repeated with a greater insistence.

It didn't make sense. It didn't fit with who he was or what she believed about him or noblemen, and it left her all muddled in her mind.

"I'm not a monster," he said gruffly. "But you don't know that, do you, Julia?"

It was a rhetorical question, and she was grateful for it, because it allowed her to try to order her thoughts and put to rights the cadence of her racing heart.

"You don't know that," he repeated more gently as he glided the back of his gloved hand along the curve of her jaw, and it trembled under the power of his touch and the words he spoke. "Because you have only known monsters, and I have not... given proper thought to what your experience has been these years."

They locked gazes for a long while, and some quiet, unspoken truce floated to the surface, hanging between them.

He gave a slow, meticulous flick of his wrist, and the carriage rocked into motion once more.

Julia sat with her fists at her sides, grateful when he again spoke that he shifted the topic away from the most shameful parts of her life.

"My godmother has been like a mother, Julia," he said quietly. "I'd not see her hurt, and if that means being cautious and, in so doing, offending you or others, then I am sorry for your hurt feelings, but I will not be sorry for the motives that drive me."

"That, I can understand," she said softly.

It had been easier to hate him when she'd believed he viewed her as an inferior, that his resentment and coldness toward her had stemmed from the place she'd come from. But knowing it was because he cared about his godmother and that, even with his reservations about Julia and her identity, he'd still express the outrage he had on her behalf chiseled away at the icy fortress she'd built around herself. It reversed their roles. It made him a hero and her... well, she'd always been a villain in this.

Julia stared at her lap. "I should not be offended by your unease around me," she murmured. "I am a stranger, and you've no reason to trust me." Desperate to understand more about this man, for reasons she couldn't understand, she sought more of an understanding about his relationship with his godmother; a woman who clearly meant so much to him. "How did you come to know Her Grace?"

"Our mothers made their Come Out the same Season. They were both diamonds of the first water." As he spoke about his family, she glanced over. "And from what I understand, my mother was sought after by every gentleman in the market for a wife." A muscle rippled along his jaw, his mouth tense, and his eyes went hard. "Even those rogues and previously confirmed bachelors, who were not gentlemen."

"Your father was not kind to her," she murmured.

Hatred iced his eyes. "He was not."

She waited for him to say more, but the protracted silence, echoed by the churning of the curricle wheels, indicated he'd no intention of speaking further on the matter of his parents. And by the tense way in which he held himself, he regretted sharing all that he had.

Fiddling with the handle of the parasol, Julia stared out at the passing landscape, at the luxuriant grounds of greenery and flowers she'd never known existed in London. All the while, she considered everything Harris had revealed in just a handful of sentences, ones that had spoken volumes.

She'd simply taken it to be fact that the lords and ladies of such lofty ranks lived to make advantageous marriages. And she realized she'd been holding Harris guilty of the same crime she'd unknowingly committed—passing judgment on people whom she did not know and failing to see them as real souls, with their own hurts and their own struggles.

"The duchess was kind to you, then?" she murmured when he sat still and silent.

He nodded. "After my mother passed, I spent much time in the nurseries, forgotten. Until one day, the duchess stormed the household and took me under her wing. She and Ladies Cowpen and Cavendish." A wistful smile hovered at the corners of his hard lips, and that ghost of a grin, not the artificial one he'd turned on her, proved real and did very real things to her heart's rhythm.

That was when Julia knew with absolute certainty just one thing—she was going to leave. The moment they returned, she'd pen a note, confessing all, and then she'd be gone from this family and this life before she caused any more pain, any more sadness than she already had. Before she earned any more undeserved kindness from the man beside her.

Why did that cause the ache in her chest that it did?

Because you see that he's not a heartless nobleman, but an honorable gentleman who cares so very dearly for an older lady.

And because he expressed outrage on her behalf? *Imagine the outrage were he to discover your complicity, the fact that you not only deterred Adairia from coming to the duchess, but that you came in her stead.*

She was the impostor he believed her to be.

She was—

A flutter of pink out of the corner of Julia's eye brought her head whipping sideways, and she stared, riveted by the sight of the enormous winged creature, fairy-tale-like in its look and graceful movements as it slid along the placid surface of the Serpentine. Then it disappeared under the water so that only a slight rippling remained, and Julia didn't know whether she'd merely imagined the sighting.

Gripping the side of the curricle, Julia angled herself over the edge to squint at the river.

"Julia?" Harris' query came with a concerned question.

There are magical birds there. I tell you, Julia, they're real. Of course, you wouldn't believe it, because they are just so very majestic.

Adairia's adamant singsong voice came as clear and as real as if she were beside Julia even now.

Julia, who'd charted the comments as more of Adairia's effervescent joy and belief in magic.

The bird broke the surface, the distant splash breaking through the memories.

"It is real," she whispered.

"Julia?" Harris repeated.

Her breath caught, and she gripped his arm. "Stop the curricle," she whispered, tugging his sleeve, and then she was scrambling over the side. Julia stumbled, and then caught herself, and took off running.

He was going to lose the lady.

He was going to have to return to the duchess' residence and explain that the fay woman had slipped out from under him and gone racing off.

And the thing of it was, of all the reasons he'd given for the lady to be offended, he came up empty on precisely what had sent her running.

Cursing, Harris steadied the horses, and then, bringing the curricle to a complete stop, he secured the reigns and took off after her.

Her figure proved a speck in the distance, the lady faster than any he'd ever known.

Harris lengthened his strides.

"Julia," he called.

She gave no indication she'd heard him, continuing on,

and then suddenly, she stopped on the edge of the Serpentine.

Planting her hands on her hips, she stared out at the river.

He skidded to a halt as he reached her side. "What is—?"

"Do you see this?" she whispered.

Raising his hand to his brow to shield his eyes from the sun, Harris scanned the horizon, searching for whatever it was that had moved the young woman to shock.

"I don't…"

She shot her arm out, pointing, and he followed that gesture to the placid river.

And God help him, he still had not a goddamned clue as to what—

"They're birds," she whispered, and then she dissolved into an exuberant laugh. "Pink birds, Harris."

They'd been a staple in the park for all the years he could remember, and he couldn't recall the last time he'd noted them. "I… yes, they're pelicans."

"Pink ones," she said, pressing her hands to her mouth and laughing all the more. "Pink pelicans."

He'd never known anyone to find such unadulterated joy in anything so simple. The women he kept company with were ones whose wonder didn't extend beyond the material baubles he provided during his relationship with them.

He found his gaze drawn to Julia, and he took in the bright splashes of color upon her cheeks. He was… entranced. By her joy. By the freedom with which she allowed herself to share those sentiments.

She rocked back on her heels, her features wreathed in an

unabashed joy that held him frozen, captivated by such an effervescent happiness. "I thought they were magical," she said, more to herself, that whimsical smile still dancing upon the corners of her mouth.

And once more he was drawn by that lush mouth. Her slightly fuller, poutier lower lip, captivated him.

"When I was a boy, the duchess and Ladies Cavendish and Cowpen took me to Hyde Park to see the pelicans. They told me the Serpentine was no mere river, but rather…" Harris drifted closer. "A wishing well," he whispered.

She stared blankly at him, giving her head a little shake that conveyed her lack of understanding.

His chest hitched in the oddest way as he was reminded all over again of the harsh portrait she'd painted of the struggles she'd known.

"A wishing well," he repeated. "The Celts believed springs and wells were sacred places. Places of magic, where keepers dwelled below. For a price, they would grant a wish to the wisher. The duchess and her friends would bring me to that spot there." He pointed across the way, and Julia followed that gesture to the adjacent end of the Serpentine. "And they'd take turns giving me coins, and I'd close my eyes each time, think, and then throw those coins out."

Another one of those lilting laughs spilled from her lips. "And *you* believed in that magic?"

"Oh, unabashedly so. I wasn't always cynical," he said, and her smile deepened. Her sharp cheeks contained the faintest trace of dimples within them. "In fact, I was quite a lover of all things magical." Reaching inside his jacket, he withdrew a small purse and fished out a pence. "Here."

She stared at the coin in confusion. "I don't..." Julia shook her head.

"Make a wish," he urged, pressing that coin forward.

Julia blanched and held her palms up as though attempting to ward off an evil spirit. "It is wasteful." Her hands formed an X in a rejection of his offer. "It would be an expensive wish at that."

Expensive.

Had he ever seen a meager pence as something of value?

Once again, he was struck by the realization of just how privileged his life, in fact, was.

"It is a dream." When had been the last time he'd spoken about wishes and dreams? Certainly long before his marriage, and then, following his wife's agonizing death, and the death of her babe, it had been hard to see lightness in anything.

In fact, until this exchange on the shore here with Julia, he'd not believed himself even capable of uttering such words without the cynicism that had come from life's scars.

"Surely a pence is a small price to pay for a dream," he said quietly, and gently, Harris pressed the pence into her bare hand.

Julia's fingers curled over the coin, her grip upon it so tight, the blood left her knuckles. Slowly, she drew her hand in, and as though it were the first time she'd ever looked upon a pence, she studied it wistfully where it lay in her open palm.

"Take it. Make your wish," he urged, keeping his voice a low murmur, half fearing she'd reject that offering. And not entirely sure, for that matter, just *why* it mattered so much that she would toss the coin. Only that it did.

Julia dampened her mouth, closing and opening her hand around that pence several times.

Harris leaned in, lowering his lips beside her ear. A whisper of lavender clung to her skin and filled his senses, dizzying, distracting. "Close your eyes," he whispered. "And let it go, Julia."

Still, she resisted.

Near as they were, he saw every nuanced change in her body. The slight, but discernable, rise and fall of her chest. The glide of the long, graceful column of her throat.

And then she stepped forward, leaving that spring-summer floral scent dancing in the air behind her, Julia tossed the coin.

It hit the water with a noisy, decisive *thunk* and promptly sank beneath the surface.

Drawing her narrow, but regal, shoulders back, Julia dusted her palms together. "There," she said. "Now, if we might—"

Harris shot a hand out, gently but firmly catching her wrist. "Uh-uh."

She frowned. "What?"

"That's hardly the throw of dream-making." He motioned to the place her coin had landed.

She bristled, her adorably freckled nose upturned with her annoyance. "And whyever not? You hardly said anything about one's throw impacting the state of one's dream. Furthermore, I'm not throwing away more of your funds, Harris," she said impatiently, and collecting a slightly too-long hem, she made to step around him.

Harris slid into her path. "You can't let *that* throw be the one to mark your first wish."

Putting her hands on her slender hips, she brought her shoulders up in a belligerent little shrug. "Alas, short of fishing it out, there's no undoing it, Harris."

When she again tried to leave, he stretched an arm out so she was forced to either stop or run square into him. "Fair enough," he said, and in one fluid movement, he fished out another coin and made a show of removing it from behind the shell of her ear. "Fine, then you can't let it be your last. Here."

Julia gasped and touched a finger to that delicate lobe. Her eyes went round with her shock. "How... What... How did you—?"

He grinned at her almost girlish wonder. "Alas, a magician never reveals his secrets." In quick order, he plucked another coin, this time a shilling, from behind her other ear.

She edged her neck back, leaning away and eyeing him as warily as she might the Witch of Endor. "Whatever is that?"

"A shilling."

Julia briefly closed her eyes and drew a little breath in through her mouth, adorable in her thinly veiled attempt to conceal her frustration. Despite himself, he found another smile forming. When she opened her eyes once more, he was quick to wipe away any and all expression.

"I know what a shilling is, Harris," she stated evenly. "I'm asking what exactly you are doing with it."

"Tsk, tsk." He gave his head a regretful shake. "I'm afraid I'm a deucedly bad teacher if, after the whole wish lesson, you still don't gather the way to go about throwing a coin."

She was already shaking her head. "Absolutely not."

"We're not leaving until you make a proper wish."

"I did." She sounded very close to stomping her feet, and he couldn't help it. This time, he did smile. "I'm not simply throwing away three of your coins, Harris."

"Ah." He lifted his thumb and index finger and flipped the coin so that it landed atop the flat of his hand. "But one would never dare claim that a dream was a waste." With that, he lifted the shilling near her chin.

She stared mutinously down at it. "You are determined to have me throw away your coins, my lord?" She was perturbed with him. He knew because of the tightness of her voice and that formal use of his title.

"I am."

"And you are not going to allow us to leave until I play this silly game."

He grinned in answer and waggled both coins.

Muttering to herself, Julia snatched first one and then the other. This time, she didn't bother with closing her eyes, but launched them both in quick order. She stared at them as they fell not even a pace and a half away, nearly side by side, identical as they hit the surface with sad, sorry *plunks*. Until they were gone.

Harris and Julia stared for several moments at the last place those coins had been.

"There," she muttered. "Are you happy?" Not bothering to await his answer, the lady stalked off.

Harris easily overtook her quick, but shorter, strides. "Actually, I am. You, on the other hand, seem anything but, Julia."

She abruptly ground her serviceable boots to a halt. "I'm

not. Do you know why?"

"N—"

"Because I think it is silly," she exclaimed. "I think there are a million and one things you would have been better served doing with those funds, Harris, than giving them to me so that I might play at a children's game." She cast a forlorn glance off to where the coins now lay buried somewhere in the sands of the Serpentine. "Because throwing coins into pretend w-wishing wells isn't going to erase hurts or bring back people we l-loved and lost." Her voice grew to a soft cry, and then she went quickly silent. Touching her fingers to her lips, she recoiled. Her chest rose and fell with the force of her emotion. And then she rushed off.

Harris stared after her. This time, he allowed her the distance and space she so clearly sought, even as he wished to rush after her and learn about those hurts she'd just hinted at.

What Julia had spoken of was a loss where love had factored in, and as such, he could not fathom the depth of suffering that came with that. He started toward her, moving at a slow pace.

As he did, he thought about how that "children's game," as she'd called it, would seem to a woman who'd spent most of her life, until now, going without the comforts and luxuries Harris himself had enjoyed.

He'd been so resentful about the path his life had taken. Until this moment, he'd also failed to properly consider just how self-absorbed he'd been. His pain hadn't been anything compared to what Julia had spoken of.

Julia reached the curricle and wandered over to the horses.

As she lifted her hand to stroke one of the mount's on her withers, Julia's lips moved faintly as though she were speaking to the chestnut creature.

The mare lifted her enormous head, leaning into her caress.

As he made his slower approach, Harris continued to study her in a new way, through a new lens.

It was both eye-opening and humbling to come to the realization as late as he had just how fortunate he was to enjoy the luxuries he did.

"I'm sorry," he said quietly.

She went still. She pulled her shoulders back, but she didn't turn to look at him.

Harris joined her beside the pair of chestnuts, leaving a handful of steps between him and Julia. He patted his hand against his thigh several times, and then, catching himself midway through another distracted slap, he stopped. "I did not consider how that might seem to you. The... wastefulness of it." He slid closer. "Or the loss you may have known."

He left that there, waiting for her to fill the void and answer the unasked question.

A soft spring breeze rolled along the path, the leaves overhead dancing, the branches parting and allowing a slash of light through the trees. The sun's rays played with all the shades of red and blondes and browns that made up her hair. One of those curls slipped loose of her chignon and teased her shoulder.

Reflexively, he caught that tress, and Julia drew in a quiet breath as he slid the curl back behind her ear. "But, Julia," he said softly, "you shouldn't find guilt in allowing yourself simple pleasures. You are deserving of them… and more."

She briefly closed her eyes and faced him. "I'm not." A sad smile played with her lips. "My sister?" Julia sighed, her gaze growing distant. "*She* deserved this world, Harris. She deserved to throw coins and play with pelicans and—" Her voice broke, and she glanced quickly away.

Drawn to her, Harris lightly cupped her cheek, wanting to erase the sadness that had replaced the earlier joy upon her first spotting of the pelicans.

"Harris, ol' chap, is that you?" a booming voice bellowed from behind.

Harris swiftly dropped his arm to his side and cursed the unwanted interruption that had shattered his connection with Julia.

They'd been discovered.

Julia hurriedly stepped away from Harris at the same moment he did her, both moving in opposite directions until there was a safer, more respectable distance between them.

"Rothesby," Harris greeted, the familiarity of the name indicating he knew the gentleman who'd come upon them.

The dark-haired fellow staring back made no attempt to conceal his bald curiosity. With a slight roguish sneer on a face slightly too harsh to ever be beautiful, the gentleman gave Julia a bold once-over. "Introductions perhaps, old friend?" he murmured, never taking his eyes from Julia.

She knew his ilk as well as that all-too-familiar, improper stare he'd trained upon her, the kind that had been directed her way by many a passing gent outside Covent Garden.

Despite herself, Julia found herself drifting closer to Harris, who simultaneously was already sliding nearer her in a display of support and protection that said so very much about who he, in fact, was.

"Uh, yes, of course," Harris said. "Allow me to present my good friend, His Grace, the Duke of Rothesby. Rothesby, the *Duchess* of Arlington's niece, Lady Julia Corbett."

Black eyebrows went flaring up. "Indeed?" The duke eyed Julia with renewed interest. "Perhaps you might join me at White's later this afternoon?"

So they could speak about her. It was there in the possessive way the roguish fellow slid his gaze up and down her person, as though he had a right to look upon her, lingering his attention as long as he wished.

"Given you're staring at me as you speak, my lord," Julia said, "is it safe to assume you're inviting me for drinks at your club?"

There was a beat of silence, Harris' gaze swinging to her, and Julia tensed. A man such as him wouldn't take to having a woman such as her call out a friend, and a gentleman at that.

And yet, another one of those enigmatic smiles graced his lips and dimpled his cheeks.

"What a clever thing you are," the other man said, his approving grin indicating her words had proven anything but a deterrent to him and his attentions. "I look forward to continuing our... acquaintance."

"I am afraid I must join you some other time, Rothesby." Harris spoke in chilled tones. "I am otherwise occupied this day."

Harris might distrust her. But he'd still not allow one of his social equals to insult her, and it spoke volumes about the man beside her.

"That is unfortunate." The other man inclined his head. "We shall meet up one of these days this week." With that, he dropped a bow for Julia. "Lady Julia, an absolute pleasure." The gent managed to turn that last word into a purr, which she knew firsthand was a man's attempt at seduction, and yet, she'd heard enough over the years to be anything but impressed by him.

"Your Grace," she said coolly.

The moment Rothesby had gone, Harris looked at Julia. "I am sorry about that. He is an arse most times, with an eye that's more improper than it should be, but he's also a loyal friend."

"You needn't make apologies for the ill behavior of another, Harris."

"Then allow me to make apologies for my own earlier ill behaviors," he said, and she tensed, reminded all over again that he'd extended the most gracious olive branch, defended her, and now she'd continue to perpetuate a lie.

"You have nothing to apologize for," she murmured.

Several couples converged upon the area that Julia and Harris had made theirs, stealing the all-too-brief, but all-too-welcome, moment of intimacy between them.

He held a hand out. "Shall we?"

She hesitated. Yes, it had been inevitable that their time here would come to an end, and yet, she hated that it must. She wanted to stay here, as they'd been when the copse had been their private oasis, and they'd conversed freely about children's dreams and the magic of wishes. Alas, she had also learned the aching lesson that any and all moments of pure happiness were fleeting. She placed her fingers in his and allowed him to hand her up.

Wordlessly, he caught her gently by the waist, his enormous palms spanning it as he lifted her up onto the curricle bench.

Coming around the curricle, he joined her on the seat.

When he'd guided the chestnuts onward and put the little gathering of others who'd stolen their sanctuary behind them, Julia looked up, studying him as he drove.

There was a seriousness to this man, a cynicism that had a palpable energy, and she wondered at that. What caused one such as Harris to be so very guarded in life? What, when she'd believed the nobility lived lives without struggle or hardship?

As if he felt her eyes upon him, Harris glanced over. "What is it?"

"I had a wonderful time," she said softly, and her answer was not a lie. She had. Today had been the singularly most magical moment of her entire life. "I… thank you."

He inclined his head.

Chapter 11

Since Julia's arrival days earlier, the duchess continued to enlist Harris's efforts where Julia was concerned. He escorted the young woman about London. He dined with her, the duchess, and countesses and afterwards joined them for refreshments and music.

And Harris, who'd always avoided the respectable found himself...*enjoying* his time with Julia.

Why, he'd even enjoyed their latest outing together, this morning. Even when tasked as he'd been earlier today with squiring her and three other women about London, to be seen, his godmother had insisted. He'd found it hadn't been any task, at all.

He'd enjoyed it more than he should and more than could ever be good or safe for him. Especially as with every passing moment he and Julia spent together, the ease in being with her...the bond between them, *deepened*.

It was why after returning Julia, the duchess, and the countesses back to Her Grace's residence that afternoon, Harris headed for his clubs...in search of a drink.

One that he needed desperately.

Stalking through White's, he was headed for his table when his gaze caught on the figure occupying the one adjacent to his.

Rothesby lifted his half-filled brandy snifter in salute, motioning him over.

Bloody hell.

Mayhap the decision to come here had been the wrong one after all.

He briefly considered reversing course. Alas, to do so would yield more questions. Even more. Ones that Harris had little wish to answer.

Even if Rothesby was a friend. Even if they had gotten on since Eton and Oxford, and he'd stood beside him through that tense, ugly ceremony that had been his first—and last—wedding.

"She's quite delicious," his friend said with the usual ease he used when referring to all women.

The man was a rake of the first order. Not at all different from Harris in his appreciation of the fairer sex, and yet, something grated this time. "She is the duchess' niece," he said tightly.

"It's still entirely fair to acknowledge the lady's beauty." Rothesby hailed a servant. "In fact, I'd say the duchess would be offended if I did not remark upon it."

A footman arrived with a snifter for Harris.

He accepted the glass with a word of thanks, and as he poured himself a glass, he considered the other man's words.

Aye, she was beautiful. At their first meeting, he'd been unable to see past his own reservations about her. It hadn't been until he'd run into her in that music room later that night, with the moon's glow bathing her heart-shaped features in the softest light, that he'd appreciated her form and beauty as being different than those he usually appreciated, and all the more… interesting for it.

As they'd made the remainder of the way from Hyde Park to Grosvenor Square, he'd felt an urge to learn even more about the lady, and for reasons that had absolutely nothing to do with his suspicions. Just as the kiss in the marble room hadn't been motivated by anything other than this magnetic draw he neither wanted nor needed. He did not need being pulled toward a possible liar.

And oddly, he'd had a wonderful time, too. What he'd intended as a fact-finding mission, meant to further learn anything he might about this woman whom the duchess had welcomed so readily into her residence, had led to a discovery of a different sort.

"So?" Rothesby asked, pulling Harris from his thoughts.

"So, what?"

The other man gave an exaggerated roll of his eyes. "Come on, man. What is her story?"

"You know her story," Harris said automatically. All of Polite Society knew the tale of the duchess' lost niece.

Rothesby, nearly as cynical as Harris himself, scoffed. "Surely you aren't believing she is, in fact, who she claims to be."

Since the moment he'd learned of her reappearance, he'd been filled only with a cynical intent of protecting the duchess at all costs, the young woman who'd entered Her Grace's household be damned. Only to find himself, after this short time with her, not so very cynical as he'd believed. Not when presented with the honesty she'd shared about her struggle and also in everything she'd revealed about the harshness that had been her life. He had been...captivated.

And hearing Rothesby's jaded words about the lady, it felt wrong to admit what he really thought to this man. Even if their friendship did go back more than fifteen years.

"Why can't she be who she claims to be?" he countered instead.

The duke choked on his drink. "Because you, my friend, know how the world operates." A hand still on his glass, Rothesby stuck his littlest finger in Harris' direction. "More specifically, you know how *women* operate."

"The duchess is happy to have her returned, and as you're well aware, only a fool questions anything that brings Her Grace happiness."

It was undoubtedly the lifetime of friendship between them, and his knowledge of Harris' turbulent life, that allowed him to latch on to that which Harris hadn't said.

"Ah, but you do have reservations?"

He resisted the urge to squirm in his leather seat. "I would be a fool not to have some doubts." A lot. He had a ton.

"Well, worst case is, you've found yourself a pretty piece to replace the countess. How is the countess, anyway?"

At last, they'd moved to safer discourse. "We have parted ways amicably."

"Splendid." The other man smiled widely. "You won't be offended if I extend the lady an offer of my protection."

"Not at all."

"And I do not suppose this timing has anything to do with the sudden arrival of the delectable Lady Julia Corbett...*Julia* Corbett who has an altogether different name than the duchess's *actual* niece."

Harris gnashed his teeth. Bloody hell, the other man had effortlessly and trickily steered Harris back to the topic of the duchess's niece. Leaning across the table, he spoke in a tense, measured whisper. "Have a care with the lady's name," he bit out. "Whether you or I or anyone has doubts, the duchess does not, and she will hardly tolerate the smearing of the lady's name, and for that matter, neither will I. Am I clear?" he snapped.

Lord Rothesby stared back with wide eyes, and surely for the first time in the other man's life, he was absolutely and completely silent. Then a knowing grin curled his lips at the left corner in a mocking, knowing half smile. "You are... abundantly clear."

Let it go.

Say nothing.

"What?" he demanded, and damned if he didn't step through the door and all the way into it.

"Well, it is just that the notoriously roguish Lord Ruthven, with his disavowal of all things innocent, seems a good deal concerned with the lovely young lady and her honor."

Harris's ears went hot. "You are making more of it than it is," he said tersely, taking a drink of brandy.

All the while, he felt the other man's amused, smug eyes on him. "Am I?" Rothesby asked. "*Am I?*" he repeated, placing a greater emphasis upon that same question.

"You are. I am merely assisting the duchess."

Rothesby patted a hand against his heart in an exaggerated way. "My goodness, how very generous and kind you are, Ruthven." The other man put his drink down. "I've two predictions for you."

"I really do not need to h—"

"One, you land yourself in the bed of that lovely beauty, who is decidedly not your godmother's niece, and two, you toss her out on her arse afterwards when you have confirmation that she isn't who she claims to be."

He didn't know why it should matter the other man's opinion. It was, after all, the very one held by Harris himself. Something, however, spoken that way from this man's lips filled him with a potent rage.

"Well, well, well, what is this I hear of carriage rides with young, respectable ladies?"

They both looked up.

A grinning Lord Barrett looked back and forth between Harris and the duke, before claiming a seat.

"This again," Harris muttered, while the other man took a glass from the waiting servant.

Snifter in hand, the other man kicked back on the legs of his chair. "It makes sense you know," Barrett said to no one in particular.

"What?" Harris asked impatiently.

"*Why* you broke it off with the countess."

"You know that?" *Too.* Were there no secrets kept in this damned Society?

"She shared it with my mistress, who shared it with me. Between that and the fact you, the last gent anyone in Society expects, are seen squiring a young miss about, well, eyebrows have been raised. As have been the wagers in the betting books." The viscount motioned to the object in question, where a number of men stood in line waiting to scratch their bets upon the pages. "The world is filled with speculation that you've been tempted by some young lady."

"That is preposterous," he gritted out, his ears going hot, threatening to make a damned liar of him.

"While the others who actually know you also know there is no way in hell you'd go losing your head to any virtuous"—Barrett grinned—"or, for that matter, naughty lady."

Harris swallowed a curse. Well, that had been quick.

Barrett let his chair legs come to rest on all fours and dropped an elbow upon the table. "Rest assured, old chap, that I placed my money firmly in the latter column." The right corner of the viscount's mouth quirked up. "As I know better than anyone that the absolute last thing you'd do is go falling for any woman and that any dealings you have with the lady are surely because of the duchess, whom you've never been able to say no to." Barrett chuckled and proceeded to discuss some of the more outstanding wagers regarding Harris' relationship with Julia.

Barrett's was and had been the safest assumption and wager. Notoriously hard-hearted and disinterested in anything and all things innocent, Harris was the last person in the damned world who'd go losing his head, as Barrett had put it, over a woman. And yet, there was also no denying that Harris was incredibly drawn to Julia.

A woman he'd been wary of, and yet, with every exchange, he appreciated her dry humor and biting wit, and then there'd been the side of her he'd seen today—free and unrestrained—and he'd been captivated.

He stared into the contents of his glass, rolling the snifter back and forth in his palms so the amber drink conjured memories of Julia's luxuriant strands as the sun's light had struck them.

God help him and save his soul, but standing beside the Serpentine with her, he'd wanted to—

"Are you paying attention, man?"

Harris jumped. Liquid droplets spilled over the edge of his glass and splattered the table. A servant was immediately there. With an immaculate white cloth, he wiped away the remnants from the mahogany surface, leaving it immaculate once more.

The moment the young man had gone, Barrett gave him a bemused look. "Good God, man, one would think you are, in fact, woolgathering about the lady."

"Do not be preposterous," he muttered, taking a drink, wanting to talk about absolutely anything other than Julia.

Except, the other man must have heard something in his tone. Leaning forward, Barrett peered at him through narrowed lashes. "Wait... what is *this*?" he said in wondrous tones. The viscount looked over to Rothesby, who, damn him, wore an entirely too-amused expression.

"A *very* good question," the duke drawled.

Oh, bloody hell. Both men were like hounds who had the scent of blood, and knowing them as he did, Harris knew they had absolutely no intent of abandoning this *fun*.

"And here, I was firmly in the column of 'loyalty to the duchess compelled you,' but now I must know more about this Lost Lady."

This Lost Lady...

"There's nothing to say," he said coolly in tones meant to

deter, though they only had the opposite effect.

Barrett grinned. "Which means there is absolutely everything to say. You must describe her."

"I'm not describing the lady, Barrett," he said impatiently. Something about the other man wanting a visual of her grated on his already frayed nerves.

"I can," the duke volunteered. Shooting a hand up, he wagged his fingers. "I had the pleasure of seeing the young lady."

The viscount's all-too-knowing smile widened. "Ah, but it really begs the question as to why Ruthven is so secretive."

Harris's friends promptly shouldered Harris out of their *discussion*.

"Is it secretive?" Rothesby tapped his chin in feigned contemplation. "Or possessive."

Oh, this was really enough. "I am not possessive," Harris snapped.

"Protective, then?" Rothesby supplied.

Reclining in his chair, Barrett gave a dismissive way. "Either way, I don't require any information from Ruthven. The evening papers have indicated she's lovely."

She was... a fay nymph, whose auburn strands he'd desperately love to see tossed about her shoulders. Except...

Harris frowned. "What exactly are the papers writing of her? The lady has hardly been anywhere." She'd not been to a single *ton* event.

Barrett shrugged. "As I said, the evening papers."—By God, the bloody gossip-mongers in this town could ferret out every last secret from every single person if they so wished.—"Servants talk."

"They should be sacked," Harris muttered.

The viscount continued. "The lady's kindness has been remarked upon by them."

He gritted his teeth.

Confusion brought Barrett's brow dipping. "Are they wrong?"

A recollection slipped in of the servants smiling at the breakfast table and her comfortable discourse with them rather than Harris. "No," he said. That had been the first time in his life he'd seen any lord or lady engage so with a servant. "She's... perfectly lovely to them." It didn't matter what the hell the servants were saying, it should be absolutely nothing about the lady.

Ruthven pounced. "Perfectly lovely, is she?"

Bloody hell.

Barrett slapped both hands over his face in an exaggerated manner. "I'm certain to lose my shirt on this wager, then."

Harris kicked the other man hard under the table, earning a raucous laugh from both men. Just then, his skin pricked with the attention turned on them. Men abandoned their seats and rushed to those betting books, no doubt to make more wagers about Harris. "I'm not captivated," he said tightly.

The pair across from him went absolutely still.

Oh, bloody, bloody hell.

Ruthven grinned. "I didn't use the word 'captivated.'" The duke looked to Barrett. "Did you?"

"Not I," the other man shook his head, and grinned.

"Would both of you just quit? I'm not... I don't even

know the lady, and I hardly trust she is, in fact, who she says she is," he said on a furious whisper that managed to penetrate their amusement.

Except, as soon as he'd said the words, Harris wanted to call them back. For they felt like a betrayal of sorts.

Yes, these were his closest friends in the world. One whom he'd known since the age of six, when he'd also been the forgotten son of his miserable father. And also one who'd been betrayed—in a different way—by a woman whom he'd been supposed to marry. Nay, the pair of them weren't the manner to keep secrets from each other, because ultimately each knew the other would keep that confidence until death.

But this? It wasn't about a worry about that information being leaked. It was about revealing something that would call into question Julia's character.

Ruthven's features grew serious. "Indeed?"

Harris considered his words carefully. "You know there have been any number of people who've come forward." Children. Prior to Julia's arrival, it had always been children who'd passed themselves off as the girl.

"Yes," Barrett murmured.

"It is only natural that I've been… skeptical. The duchess, however, firmly believes the lady to be her long-lost niece, and as such, I've made myself available to her and the lady so that I might ascertain this time is, in fact, real."

"Ah, so as many have suspected, you do it for fealty and regard for the duchess," Rothesby put forward.

Harris tried to detect shades of sarcasm or jest in the duke's words, but he was hard-pressed to find them.

"Well, then, we shall toast to hearts that remain free and

clear." Barrett lifted his glass in salute.

Harris was grateful moments later when his friends finally laid to rest the matter of Julia, and worse, Harris' fascination with her, and proceeded to discuss other wagers he'd recently taken out.

And yet, as he sat there, Harris oddly found himself wishing himself away from White's and returning to Julia.

Chapter 12

S ome people were permitted dreams.
   Not most.

Not all.

Just some.

The majority of people—men, women, children of all ages—didn't have the luxury. They barely had an opportunity to rest, let alone dream.

Julia had never been one who could dream. She'd been just another figure among the masses. She'd always known precisely what she was and who she was. Certainly enough to never have entertained the fantasies—or what Julia had believed were fantasies—that Adairia had.

But at the edge of the serene river, with the charming and beguiling, roguish Marquess of Ruthven pretending to pluck coins from her ear and encouraging her to toss those coins and dream, never more did she wish there was such a thing as dreams coming true. Because if there were, and wishes could become realities, then she would have a future with him.

But dreams were not real, and Julia was not deserving of them.

It was why, yesterday, after her outing with Harris, the

moment she'd climbed the steps of the palatial townhouse, Julia had searched out the duchess. So that she might tell Adairia's aunt everything. The duchess however, had been out with the countess's and she'd had a reprieve.

Julia, however, could not let these generous people believe a lie. The duchess had suffered so very greatly, and Julia? She'd no right to any happiness when Adairia was gone. Her heart broke all over again at a loss that would always be fresh. Nay, she'd failed Adairia. Julia wished she could be so selfish as to claim her sister's life.

But God help her, she couldn't.

It was why she made her way to the gardens even now to speak with Her Grace.

For it was time for Julia to return. To squalor and cold and an empty stomach and lecherous touches when there weren't enough flowers to sell. And that was if she was able to sell them. And blast if a sheen didn't fill her eyes and blur her vision.

Julia slowed her steps to a stop. Catching her hand at the wall, she stood there. Squeezing her eyes shut, she took in several slow breaths.

There was still the price to pay for felling Rand Graham's henchman. It wouldn't matter that he'd fallen over his own clumsy feet. The bastard's goal had been to end her, and she'd prevented him from fulfilling that mission.

That was what the sole of her focus should be on. The fact that her life was all but forfeit when she returned to the Rookeries, unless by some miracle, the newest head of East London's streets had found some purpose she might serve to justify keeping her alive. But that had been before a curricle ride, and coins tossed in an imagined well, and a glimpse of how things might have been if she'd not only been born to a different life, but if she'd had a man such as Harris at her side. A gentleman who breathed fire and burned with rage at even the idea that someone had hurt her.

And now, blast her for being a weak fool, after those sweet exchanges, she found herself... bereft at having to leave Harris, and the duchess, and this household. And it wasn't just because of the security afforded her by these walls.

It was mostly the people who lived here. In just a short time, they'd showed her the ties that bound them all together through love and caring. It was a bond she'd shared with Adairia, and one she ached to know with this found-family.

You can stay. A voice whispered that temptation, slithering around like the serpent put there by Satan himself. *You can live the lie, and there is no one to gainsay that you are, in fact, who you say you are.*

Aye, she could live the lie, but it wasn't an existence she would ever be happy living, because ultimately she'd know, and she couldn't steal from Adairia's memory or her family this way.

With that, Julia straightened and, taking the garden gate handle, let herself into a gloriously bright Eden robustly filled with floral bushes and flowering plants—and fitting for Julia, who still grappled with temptation.

"I was wondering how long you were going to wait at that gate," the duchess called over, intently attending the task before her, not so much as looking Julia's way. For which she was grateful. "Join me, girl." It was a command issued by a woman so very clearly accustomed to giving them and not being denied by a single soul.

Taking another deep breath, Julia made herself make the slow, agonizing march over to where the duchess knelt, digging a small hole into the overturned earth.

Her maid hovered at Her Grace's shoulder, her hands filled with small gardening tools that she occasionally supplied to her employer. Alongside the maid stood a strapping footman.

When Julia reached their side, the duchess set her spade down.

The footman immediately came forward to help her to her feet, but Her Grace turned a scowl on him and then climbed to her feet. "I'm quite capable of standing, Owens. I've been doing it since I was all of one," she said dryly. "That'll be all, Gracie," the duchess said. "Have a walk around my gardens while I speak to my niece."

My niece…

Oh, God. She'd known this confession was going to prove agonizing, but this? Standing on the cusp of breaking the duchess' heart was unbearable. Determined to have this telling over with, Julia opened her mouth to speak. "Your Grace, there is something—"

"Those two are quite in love, they are," the duchess said with a sly whisper. She motioned to the dainty maid and the much taller servant at her side.

Julia looked to the pair. Sure enough, the farther away their steps carried them from sight, the more the couple brushed the tops of their hands together, until their fingers touched, and they tangled those digits together.

There was an aching sweetness to the sight of them.

And she froze, unable to do anything but stare.

"Nothing like young love, is there?" the duchess murmured wistfully, calling Julia back to the moment.

She forced her focus away from the lady's maid and footman. "I would not know, Your Grace." There hadn't ever been a sweetheart or a suitor. But that afternoon, on a carriage ride through Hyde Park, she'd had a taste of what it might be like to have one…

The duchess patted the top of Julia's hand. "You will, girl. You will."

No, she wouldn't. But what would it be like to find herself courted by a man such as Harris?

Make a wish.

In that instant when he'd placed those coins between her fingers and she'd tossed it into those waters, she'd done just that. She'd allowed herself a moment to believe in magic and dream of a life she would never know.

But, Julia, you shouldn't find guilt in allowing yourself simple pleasures. You are deserving of them… and more.

Her breath hitched softly, and guilt stabbed like a needle through her heart.

"Your Grace," she tried again.

"Join me, Julia," Her Grace urged, and dropping to a knee, she patted a patch of earth beside her and resumed digging. "I've needed to move these lovelies," she explained when Julia had joined her on the grass. "Are you familiar with them?"

"Lilies of the valley," Julia said instantly.

The duchess fixed an approving smile on her. "Very good."

It was one thing she was well-versed in—flowers. Flowers of all kinds and species. Not because she'd ever received one or even because she in any way liked them. That knowledge had come from sheer necessity. As such, it seemed wrong to take the woman's praise. Drawing her knees close to her chest, Julia rested her chin atop her skirts and stared at those delicate white buds. "I only know because I was"—*am and will once more be*—"a flower seller."

"And it served you well, it did." More of that praise Julia didn't deserve.

"Served me well," she said softly to herself. How had it served her in any way? What skills had it gotten her? What happiness had it brought? "It was merely a means to an end," she said when the duchess stopped and fixed a questioning stare on her.

"Hmph. Any time spent with flowers has its value." Humming to herself, the duchess resumed her planting.

As she worked, Julia stared at the buds Her Grace attended.

Early on in her life, Julia had come to despise flowers. They'd represented toil and struggle. Now, however, she wondered how she might have viewed those blooms differently had her relationship with them been different. Would she have regarded them with the same reverence and love the duchess clearly did?

"Do you know the story of the lilies of the valley?" the duchess asked.

Julia shook her head before recalling the duchess was still focused on her task and made herself answer, "No, Your Grace."

"Legend has it that one day, a lily developed an affection for a nightingale. The bird would perch itself in a tree above her." The duchess paused to gesture to the tree beside them and its canopy of branches, as though it was the player in the story she told. "And every day, it would sing its song. But the lily was shy and remained silent, hidden in the shadows. Until winter fell, and the bird left. The lily was bereft. And she did not bloom again until the spring, when the nightingale returned, and she was happy once more."

"What a lovely telling," she said softly. And also a fantastical way of viewing those flowers that she'd only ever seen for the monetary worth affixed them.

She sat in silence, watching the lady as she worked, loathing herself for being one of those same people Harris had spoken of who'd shattered the duchess' hopes, preying on her. She wished she could leave her to this moment of happiness she found in the gardens with her flowers and the dream she had that Julia was the real woman she wished her to be.

Singing quietly to herself, the duchess collected a lily of the valley and added it to the small hole she'd made in the earth. "There," she said as she made a small circular mound in the soil around the plant. "They prefer partial shade, they do. Of course, it will grow in full sun with water, but there's no good in forcing the poor thing to dwell in a place it does not wish to be. Don't you agree?" She gave Julia a look, and Julia froze.

Those words pinning her to the place she sat.

There's no good in forcing the poor thing to dwell in a place it does not wish to be.

Her Grace may as well have been speaking about Julia herself. And yet…

"I am not who I claimed to be." She blurted out that truth before her selfish desire for more compelled her to silence.

The duchess continued working, not so much as pausing in the work she'd begun, planting another lily. And Julia was caught between a place of wishing Adairia's aunt would say something and also nothing at all. And yet, Julia wanted this exchange over so that she could have closure to this situation, even if it meant a stint in Newgate. Anything to be free of the lie she'd let herself perpetuate against Adairia's family. Taking another breath into her lungs, she spoke again. "I said… I'm not who I claimed to be. I'm not… Adairia."

The duchess stared at her for a moment and then chuckled. "I'm not so old that there's a thing wrong with my hearing," she drawled. "At least not yet." She held Julia's gaze. "And I know," the duchess said simply. A small smile graced the other woman's lips.

Julia had to remind herself to breathe. She glanced about, more than half expecting the big, strapping footman to reappear with reinforcements and a constable. When none did, and it just remained she and the regal duchess, she drew in a shaky breath. "How long—?"

"Since the moment you arrived."

"Oh," Julia said weakly.

Fetching a handkerchief from the front of her apron pocket, she patted at her lightly perspiring brow and then, in a very unduchlesslike move, the duchess joined Julia, sitting beside her on the grass.

"My girl, Adairia had the palest blonde ringlets and the most cream-white of skin." Lightly touching Julia's auburn hair, Her Grace gave her another tender smile, and Julia had the first hope that mayhap the other woman wouldn't turn her over to the law for her transgression.

"She doesn't," she whispered, her eyes on a lone sparrow hopping about the emerald-green grass. Periodically, the creature pecked its beak at the earth before coming up as empty as any person in the Rookeries when it came to finding food. Tears stung her eyes. She'd spoken in the present tense, as though Adairia were still alive. And suddenly the words were falling fast from her lips, all rolling together, and she couldn't stop them from coming. "Sh-she had light skin when we first met. The only people I'd ever known to have skin like lilies was the ladies outside Covent Garden. Before Adairia, I'd never seen a little girl with skin such as hers, but it isn't like that… wasn't like that…" Not anymore. Adairia was gone. "We sold flowers together, and being outdoors from the moment the sun began its ascent to the moment the moon took its place high in the sky, Adairia has… had"—her voice broke—"the same tanned-hued skin as me."

Something wet trickled down her cheek, and she brushed at it, staring at her finger.

A tear.

She was crying.

The duchess dangled a floral-embroidered handkerchief before her nose.

She waited while Julia took the silk scrap and brushed the moisture away from her cheeks.

"You were a friend of hers," the duchess murmured.

Julia let the scrap fall to her lap, clenching and unclenching it in her fist before she realized just how she'd ruined the fabric. She smoothed it out.

The duchess' hadn't been a question, but Julia nodded anyway and added her own clarification. "I was." Only, the word *friend* didn't capture what Adairia had been to her, the bond they'd shared. "She was my sister." And while she could still get words out through the crushing weight of pain that pressed on her chest, she told the duchess everything, beginning with how she and her mother had found Adairia alone, to the ultimate end the young woman had found. When she'd finished, the duchess sat silent.

"I didn't come here to… deceive you." Her lips pulled in a grimace. "Not at first. Rather, I came to see if there was any truth to what she shared with me, and to tell you about Adairia, and to let you know she never forgot her family, and she never stopped b-believing." Even as Julia had pooh-poohed Adairia's dream, Adairia had always known precisely who and what she was. She'd made to rise when the duchess put a hand upon Julia's forearm, keeping her to that spot beside her.

"What will happen if you return?"

If? When. She shook her head.

"What will they do with you now that you know… their role in Adairia's…" The duchess' face crumpled, and she looked away, but not before Julia caught the grief that contorted her features. When she returned her attention to Julia, however, a placid mask was back in place so quick, Julia might as well have imagined that crack in the duchess's composure. "What will they do to you?"

She shivered, her palms coming up to reflexively rub at her chilled arms. Her efforts proved as futile as the sun's rays in warming her.

"I... don't know." She handed the duchess a lie, because she couldn't and wouldn't share the ugly fate that awaited her.

Her Grace leaned in and peered at her face. "You insult me by thinking I believe that answer, my dear."

"Does it matter?" she asked without inflection. "What should happen to me?"

"Yes," the duchess murmured in somber tones. "I rather think it does."

Why was she being like this? Why was she being... understanding? Why, it was actually as though she cared about what happened to Julia.

"I do care about you, girl," the duchess said with an unswerving and unnerving ability to follow Julia's very thoughts.

"You don't know me," she pointed out.

Adairia's aunt collected Julia's coarse palm within her own, earth-stained one and then patted the top of her hand. "No, but I do know that a young woman who showed up here so desperate as to pretend to be someone else certainly has a reason for doing so, and as you were a friend of Adairia's, so you shall remain a friend to me."

Why? Why was she doing this? Julia jumped up. "I cannot stay here." She'd no place continuing to take when Adairia had been robbed of this very experience she'd longed for.

"Answer me this, Julia," the duchess murmured as she sailed gracefully to her feet. "My Adairia? Her being gone… Will your leaving … Will it bring her back?"

She gave her head a tight shake. She'd have done anything. She would have sold her very soul to Rand Graham himself if it would have brought Adairia back.

"I would have you remain here."

It took a moment for those words to register.

Stay.

She wanted Julia to remain. There'd be a roof and a warm household and food in her belly and… "Why?" she whispered, desperately confused and trying to understand.

"Why?" Her Grace repeated. "Look around you." She splayed her arms wide, inviting Julia to assess the space they occupied. "I have a husband whose been traveling for more years than I can remember," the duchess shared, and with that revealing for the first time where the duke had gone. "And what am I left with here while he galivants about the globe?" Sadness wreathed the other woman's delicate features. "How much wealth does a woman need?" she asked that question more to herself. "There are no children of my own. When my husband is gone, almost all of this will go to a priggish, miserable excuse of a man who succeeds him. I'd have the money and properties while I am here be used to give you a place where you can be safe."

Safe…

There it was. Temptation once more.

"Plus," the duchess continued in an exaggerated whisper as she leaned into Julia, "I enjoy having a young lady about to spoil and keep company with."

What the powerful peeress suggested enticed. She made it so very easy to want to say yes and yet… "Your godson… Lord Ruthven, he would never allow it." Nay, he'd send her packing in quick order, and that was only if he didn't have the magistrate called on her.

"Harris? He doesn't have to know."

He didn't have to know.

Which meant… deceive him. Lie to the gentleman who'd taught her of wishing wells, and who'd given her coins to toss away, and who'd insisted she deserved to believe in magic and have wishes for herself. He'd not feel so welcoming when he discovered the truth about her, and for the oddest reason, she wanted to cry all over again and for entirely different reasons. "I cannot," she said around a thick throat. She cleared the swell of emotion there and repeated with a greater insistence, "I cannot allow you to lie to him on my behalf. He cares very deeply for you, Your Grace, and is deserving of the truth."

And once he had it, she'd be gone in an instant.

The duchess looked her over. "Going to force me to take the honest, honorable path, you are." She grunted. "Leave Harris to me. It is my decision to make."

Julia stood there, warring with herself, caught between that which she yearned for and the sense of guilt in positioning herself within the household where Adairia belonged. Not her.

In the end, God help her, selfishness won out.

Chapter 13

Years earlier, when Julia and Adairia had been small girls, some fellow on the streets had attempted to kidnap Adairia. Peddling her flowers, never on the same corner but always close enough that she could be there to help her sister, Julia recalled the panic and terror as that man had maneuvered Adairia's arm in his and begun steering her away.

That had been the first—and only—basket of wares she'd ever abandoned and lost. Dropping them, forgetting them, intent only saving the girl, Julia had run so fast, her lungs threatening to explode, and as he'd bent to pick Adairia up to speed up their journey, only one thing had mattered to Julia—keeping her sister safe.

Julia had found a fragment of a broken cobblestone and tossed it at the man, attempting only to startle him into dropping the girl he was so determined to take. Wanting only to give Adairia and Julia time to flee.

Never anticipating that something so small could fell a grown man. But it had. His eyes had rolled back, and his body crumpled, and as Julia had reached him at last and discovered she'd knocked a man unconscious, she'd known just two things: One, she'd absolutely no regrets, because she'd saved Adairia. And two, when she eventually went to meet her Maker, she was likely bound for hell.

Had there been any doubts as to the afterlife awaiting her, her actions these past few days had confirmed it. Aye, the certainty of it had been cemented this week, not on the ruthless streets of East London, where anything could happen, but in the drawing rooms of a mansion in Grosvenor Square.

Because here was where she'd committed the greatest of thefts, taking comfort and security for herself, while all the girls and young women such as her continued to toil. She broke her fast with chocolate biscuits and raspberries and warm bread and then dined on the finest meats.

Seated beside the duchess, having put her request to her some moments ago, Julia resisted the urge to squirm.

"You want to take the bread and biscuits," the lady said bemusedly as she carved up a small piece of ham.

Let it rest. Going back to those parts of London would be folly, anyway. Yes, it was unlikely given her change of attire and properly cloaked she'd be recognized, but it was still folly…still a risk.

"Julia?" the duchess pressed.

Think of yourself. Think of survival. Julia scrabbled with the inside of her cheek; worrying that flesh with her teeth. Apparently she was a bigger fool than she'd ever credited. "Not all of it," she brought herself to say. "Because of the staff and beggars who come calling. However, I just hoped if there is some excess beyond that…"

"There's always excess."

Yes, Julia had discovered as much in this world. Ironically, it proved the opposite of the state of wanting, where people like Julia always found themselves without.

"I can have one of the servants take the food by." The duchess said something to one of the footmen, giving directives for Cook.

The crimson-clad servant bowed and rushed off, and Julia followed his departure with her gaze.

That was the safest course. It was a way of getting food to people who were in dire need, while also ensuring that no one identified her. But there was absolutely no guarantee that Rand Graham's men wouldn't be waiting for her return and looking more closely than they ought at every woman who entered his streets.

If she stayed behind, however, the servants would decide who was worthy and who was not. Or they'd simply toss the food out, without taking note of which child was the smallest or which woman the lamest. Julia, she knew these things.

"Is there a problem with that?" Her Grace asked, calling Julia's attention her way.

"I would… help, Your Grace," she said when the duchess was raising her teacup.

The regal woman froze with that cup halfway to her lips. "You would help with what?"

"Distributing the food."

The duchess didn't move. "You want to hand food out?"

"I trust it isn't something done," she said.

"It isn't."

Julia felt a splash of color splotch her cheeks. This wasn't her world, and it would never be. As it was, she'd only allowed herself to a temporary arrangement that would soon come to an end. But she was reminded of all the ways in which she was different. "I do not wish to make presumptions about your servants, but they remain unaware of the inner workings of the streets. Certain people have power and collect those handouts only to sell them."

"And you would be able to identify those in need," the astute woman rightly surmised.

Julia hesitated and then nodded once.

The duchess rested a hand atop Julia's. "It isn't done." She patted Julia's hand. "But that doesn't mean it shouldn't be, my girl." Her Grace gave one quick squeeze, and Julia resisted the swell of emotion clogging her throat. "Also, you are to call me Aunt Katherine," she said, patting Julia's fingers once more.

Aunt Katherine.

Adairia would have loved this woman so very much. She wouldn't have known what to do with her most times, but she'd have found her way with the warmth and love the duchess exuded.

A short while later, standing in the foyer, her arms laden with a basket, Julia took in the "small delivery" the duchess had arranged.

There was nothing small about it.

The front door hung open as servants rushed back and forth, filling not one, but two carriages, even the tops of the carriages, with baskets of the morning's baked goods and what Julia would wager were even more items that had been baked after Julia had shared what she had with the duchess.

A servant came forward with a cloak, and Julia accepted it with a word of thanks. Shrugging into it, she reached next for the bonnet.

"Do you think that is enough, girl?" Her Grace asked.

"I think it is most generous." Stretching up on tiptoe, she kissed the duchess on the cheek. "Thank you so much."

A blush filled Her Grace's face, and she waved a hand. "Go on with you." Tears misted the lady's eyes, and leaning close, she spoke in a whisper, her words agonized, her tones hushed so that query belonged only to Julia. "Was Adairia hungry often?"

Too often. Julia had lied to the duchess enough already. "Sometimes," she murmured, opting for a glossed-over version of the truth.

Sucking a breath in through her teeth, Her Grace dashed the moisture from her cheeks. "Well, then, let us hope this shall help others like you and my girl."

A young maid came forward with the last basket, heading for the doorway.

And Julia froze.

Harris stopped at the threshold to let the young lady pass before entering. "What have we here?" he asked as he doffed his hat. The sun's rays streaming through the foyer played with all the many shades of blond and burnished gold in his hair, and despite herself, her heart leaped at the sight of him.

"Julia," he murmured, his gaze locked with hers.

"My lord." It was more a prayer than anything that slipped from her lips on a breathy whisper.

"You came by, dear boy," Her Grace said, and did Julia imagine a reluctance as Harris slid his eyes from hers? "With you missing these past days, I thought you'd finally decided to return to *your* home." The duchess softened that droll statement by turning her face and touching a finger to her cheek.

Harris dropped a kiss upon it. "And leave you, Your Grace? I can't imagine anything would leave me more bereft."

She snorted. "You've arrived just in time. Smelling of brandy, so I can imagine what you've been up to."

"I was at my clubs," he said, and an endearing color suffused the rugged planes of his cheeks.

"No doubt with that Barrett boy and Rothesby. I only tolerate the former because I was friends with his mother, you know."

"I do, Your Grace." As if he and Julia shared a secret, he caught Julia's eye and winked, that seductive flutter of his tawny lashes bringing havoc to her heart.

The duchess removed her gloves and dusted them together. "He might be a scoundrel, but he's a good brother to Calla, and he does serve some purpose."

Warning bells went off. Oh no. Dread settled in her belly.

"I want him present for Julia's entry next week." And there it was.

Julia surged forward. "Entry into what?" she asked, her voice thin to her own ears. Praying she'd heard wrong. Praying the favor being called in even now by a duchess from some duke, and one of Harris' friends at that, had nothing to do with—

The duchess spared her a brief look. "Why, your debut."

Julia could only manage to stare blankly.

"Into Polite Society, girl. Of course, you're being presented to Polite Society." The duchess scoffed. "Why wouldn't you be?" And as Adairia's aunt returned her focus to Harris, panic welled in Julia's breast, and she eyed the door, contemplating making a break for it.

Instead, Julia stood there with an increasing pit of dread growing in her belly. Harris and the duchess' voices moved in and out of focus.

"… already late spring… Almack's is not the best for this… Small, intimate…"

When Julia had confessed all to the duchess, she'd believed that was sufficient. She'd been so relieved to be rid of the lies and forthright about her identity that she'd failed to properly consider the other woman's response. More specifically, her kindness. In Julia, she saw a replacement for Adairia. Something and someone Julia could never and would never be, for the simple reason that there had been only one Adairia. Now, Julia was left playing pretend in a charade with no end in sight.

"… no more than three hundred guests," the duchess was saying.

Julia jolted back to the moment. "*Three hundred* guests?"

"Yes, we'll begin small."

"This is small?" she asked weakly.

"By the duchess' standards." Harris gave Julia a commiserative look that only added a layer of guilt to her quickly compounding regrets.

"By the standards of all Polite Society, Harris," the duchess said, tapping him on the arm. "And I expect you to secure her two sets from Rothesby."

"You know Rothesby—"

"Yes, yes. You hate polite events more than anyone,

except that rascal Rothesby. He's not turned back my invitation. See that he is there for Julia's debut."

She'd be sponsored by a duke and duchess of different titles, and it was ludicrous and madness. The world would know precisely what she was—an impostor. Julia stared blankly at the servants outside loading food into the carriages. She didn't want to be an impostor. She was sick of pretend. She wasn't sick of the security and safety. Nay, a person could never tire of that. But they were unmerited. They didn't belong to her, because she wasn't who the world took her to be.

"Excuse me, my lady."

Julia glanced up at the kindly footman, Stebbins, his arms laden with a basket. Registering belatedly that she blocked the doorway, she quickly stepped aside. "My apologies."

His smile widened. "None necessary, my lady," he said and hurried outside to join the other assembled army of maids and footmen.

"Dare I ask?" Harris asked the duchess.

"You may. Julia is taking food to the hungry."

She felt his gaze swing back to her. "Indeed?" Harris asked, and Julia tried to make sense of that quiet murmuring.

"Yes, she is. And you should be a dear boy and accompany her."

And in an instant, Julia found herself and focused on more pressing matters than her entry into Polite Society. She turned quickly to the duchess. "Lord Ruthven does not want to do that, I'm sure." There was, no doubt, anything else he'd like to do, not to mention that every moment more she spent with him only wrought further havoc upon her senses.

"Are you in the habit of speaking for a person?" the duchess asked with her usual bluntness.

"I... on occasion?"

The duchess froze and then tossed her head back and laughed. "Harris will go with you."

"But—"

"He is happy to do it."

The gentleman inclined his head. "Happy to," he said softly, and Julia hesitated a moment more before she placed her fingertips upon his sleeve.

Yes, this was a mistake for so many reasons. Everything about the intimate moments she stole with him could only prove problematic, making it that much harder to disentangle herself from this life, and yet, as he escorted her to the carriage, she couldn't resist the lightness in her breast at the very real sincerity that had threaded his words.

Since the moment Julia had showed up at the duchess's, Harris had been skeptical of her and her motives. He'd cynically judged her at every turn.

He'd worried about the duchess being fleeced, and yet, in the end, what Julia had taken from the duchess hadn't been jewels or silver. It hadn't been fine baubles or expensive pieces. Rather, she'd amassed food—and with the permission of Her Grace—all to distribute that food to other people. Hungry ones.

Not for the first time since Julia's arrival, Harris had found himself completely humbled and more than a little bit… ashamed.

There'd been a level of self-absorption to him. Not for the first time since Julia's arrival, he was struck by the depth of his own obliviousness to the struggles known by others.

Real struggles that were of both the emotional sort, as he'd known, but also a far greater strife that came in the uncertainty of the safety and security he had taken for granted.

Seated across the bench from Julia, he studied her.

She sat with her chin propped on her fist, staring out at the passing scenery.

And it occurred to him how little he knew her, about her life and how she'd lived, and scarily, he realized how very much he wished to. For what did it say about her and her existence that she sought to return to those streets she'd spoken so harshly of? That the moment she'd put that existence behind her, she hadn't forgotten those who lived there who shared a like suffering. And it was nigh impossible to question the motives of one who asked for nothing more than bread to distribute. Just as it was hard to not look at oneself and one's own narrow, self-absorbed focus before her arrival.

In the crystal windowpane, their gazes caught. Unlike the ladies he chose to keep company with who would have played coy, Julia immediately released the fabric of the curtain. As the gold velvet fluttered back into place, she faced him on the bench. "What is it?" she asked, and it was one of the first moments he'd ever detected a slightly rougher hint of East London on her speech, the sound of it so faint as to be borrowed from a long-ago dialect that had been more familiar to her.

"I don't know what to make of you," he murmured, speaking plainly and truthfully with her. Removing his gloves, he beat the articles together.

"I don't..."

"You declined a modiste when almost anyone would relish having an entire new trousseau. You'd rather be handing food out to those in need than indulging in your own comforts."

Her long auburn lashes swept low. "And you find me odd for that."

"On the contrary, Julia." He leaned forward. "I find you fascinating for it," he said quietly, and there absolutely should be the usual, healthy dose of fear where that realization reared itself once more.

Her expression grew shuttered. "I'm hardly fascinating, Harris. I've lived the life of a commoner."

From anyone else, those words would have been a flirty appeal for compliments. But not from this woman, who spoke to him, as she did to the duchess and the servants, with a staggering honesty that was so very refreshing. "On the contrary, Julia. There is everything intriguing about you."

Her fingers trembled, and she immediately curled her hands into little fists upon her lap. Drawn, as he'd been from the first day, Harris lowered a hand atop one of hers and then collected those digits in his to steady their quake. Gently pulling free her gloves, one at a time, he freed them from the fabric and then folded his palm around hers.

Her breath caught.

It wasn't an unfamiliar sound where he and women were concerned, but this little intake of air was different than those inhalations from the more experienced women he'd always preferred to keep company with. With Julia, that little gasp was a cross of soft pleasure and surprise, as though his was the first and only touch she'd ever known, and there was an intriguing appeal to that. One that recalled their embrace and also recalled all the things he'd dreamed of doing with her since then.

He lightly caressed the pad of his thumb along the inside of her wrist, and he felt the slight increase in her pulse. Her fingers went soft in his hand, unfurling as she opened herself to his touch.

The carriage rattled along at a slow clip, and as he stroked a finger along her palm, he was grateful for the clogged afternoon traffic that granted this moment and this exploration.

"Beautiful," he murmured.

"They're callused and raw," she said gruffly and made to pull away, but he tightened his hold.

"They're real," he said simply.

"That doesn't make them beautiful, Harris," she returned, her voice strained. "It makes them ugly and harsh."

Like me.

The undertones of those unspoken words hovered in the carriage and ripped at his chest. That was truly how she saw herself? She didn't see the generosity of her spirit, the courage she'd shown at every turn, refusing to be cowed by him from the start. Harris carefully considered his words. "Yes, they are imperfect hands, Julia," he began, and her slender form tensed. He made himself continue. "They speak of hardship." And the struggles she'd known. An image of her peddling flowers slipped in. Of Julia, reliant upon the generosity of self-indulgent lords and ladies, people like him, to stay alive. It sent a sharp stabbing pain through his chest. He stared at her profile. "But they also speak to your survival, Julia," he murmured. A feat he, by the very nature of his birthright and comfortable upbringing, knew not a thing of. "And I can only admire you for that strength."

"It wasn't strength," she said with a bitterness better suited to a woman many years her senior. "It was luck."

"Perhaps both, but never just the latter," he said. She really had no idea how strong she was. "There's a beauty in these hands for what you've managed."

"What I've managed," she repeated to herself.

Harris trailed the half-moon curve at the top of her palm. Back and forth, he continued to caress her.

And then it was as though she released her guard. Another sigh slipped out, this one the sound of surrender as she relaxed her grip once more. Raising her palm to his lips, he placed a kiss upon the inseam where her hand met her arm, and then he proceeded to move a slow trail of kisses a touch higher. All the while, he studied her from under hooded lashes, riveted by her slightly parted lips. Encouraged, emboldened, he turned her hand in his and kissed the top, worshiping the other side of those long and beautifully real fingers.

Her chest rose and fell, the little rasps of her sighs as she breathed in and out. The headiest sounds of her desire raised his by degrees.

She bit her lower lip, her slightly crooked teeth sinking into that plump flesh, and he fought the groan that rumbled in his chest.

"I want to kiss you," he said hoarsely, torn between wishing she were the voice of reason and desperately wanting her to want that embrace, too.

"And I want you, too, Harris." Her response came throaty and sultry, and with a groan, he drew her atop his lap.

His mouth was on hers in a moment, her kiss as raw and unbridled as she was with her truths, and he devoured her mouth, wanting to consume her. She angled her head, and he deepened his kiss.

As he adjusted her so that she straddled his legs, the muslin skirts of her cloak and dress shifted in a hedonistic rustle, and he sank his fingers into the expanse of flesh he exposed. "I have wanted to do this since I kissed you in the Marble Room," he rasped against her mouth.

She moaned, and he took advantage of that whimpering capitulation and slid his tongue inside to toy with hers.

Julia lashed her tongue against his. All the while, her hips rocked in time to the sway of the carriage, her body moving against his in perfect rhythm. Harris reached a hand between them and found those honeyed curls between her legs.

She instantly stiffened.

"Let me in," he coaxed, nipping lightly at the corner of her lip. "Let me feel how much you want this, too."

Julia hesitated a moment, and then with a sigh, she eased

her legs and opened herself fully to his search. "This is wrong," she panted, her breath coming in noisy rasps as she moved in time to his stroking. "I-I should s-stop."

"Ah, but do you want to?" He slipped a finger inside her wet channel, and she whimpered. "If you tell me, Julia, I will."

"Please…" His entire body screamed in protest. He made to withdraw, but she covered his hand with hers. "Don't." That last word emerged as a desperate plea.

Emboldened, Harris added a second, stroking her. There grew a restlessness to Julia's thrusts, a frantic, frenzied rhythm. Whimpering, she buried her face in the crook of his shoulder, and he teased her with his touch.

"Come for me, love," he urged, breathless, wanting to feel her surrender. Wanting to give her this pleasure. He increased the cadence of his fingers inside her. "You are so beautiful," he whispered, pressing a kiss against her temple.

Julia gripped the front of his jacket, her fingers forming little claws in the wool as she clenched and unclenched the material. She cried out, but anticipating her surrender, Harris was already taking her mouth in a kiss that devoured and silenced. She ground herself into him, thrusting wildly, pushing herself into Harris and his touch in a moment that went on forever, one that he wanted to go on forever.

She tensed and collapsed against him, breathing but a single word. "Harris." And he was certain there wasn't a more magnificent sound than those two syllables, his name falling from her lips.

Harris held her close. Folding his arms around her quaking frame, he rubbed his hand in a slow, smooth circle over her back.

The carriage rolled to a stop, rocking slowly forward and then back before coming to a complete halt.

Julia jerked upright, the top of her head catching his chin, and he grunted.

"Bloody hell," she whispered, scrambling off his lap and back onto her bench. She'd just managed to shove her skirts back into their proper place when the servant drew the door open.

The footman, Stebbins, who'd proven himself unabashedly smitten since she'd joined Harris for breakfast earlier in the week, held a hand up.

"Where are you going?" Harris asked.

"When I said I intended to help, Harris, surely you didn't think I intended to remain comfortably inside this carriage while you and Her Grace's servants saw to handing out the goods?" she asked with a wry little twist of her lips. With a murmured word of her gratitude, Julia allowed herself to be helped down.

Harris hurried after her, jumping down.

She'd already taken full command of the execution, and he found himself besotted for reasons that had nothing to do with his body's physical awareness of her and absolutely everything to do with the control she took.

He found himself falling back and letting her take that control she sought and exercised so magnificently. Accepting a basket from Davies, a footman, Julia handed out the items to children who assembled around her. She had the look of a lady dropping breadcrumbs while little birds gathered around her.

He frowned.

Only, they weren't little birds, but rather, the smallest, saddest-looking children. Their garments hung open in a sorry state of disrepair, hems having long since lost the threading that held the closures together.

Julia worked quickly, doling out her offerings and offering smiles and kind words as she did. How very different she was from the last woman with whom he'd kept company, a woman who'd gotten so very offended that he'd dare hand out flowers to peddlers who'd use those scraps to resell.

There came a light, little tug on his jacket.

He looked down.

A little girl with the widest, biggest brown eyes stared up at him, her little face gaunt and smudged. "Ye got stuff, too?" she asked hopefully.

Did he?

She turned a hand up, displaying a reddened, coarse, callused one that matched Julia's in all but size.

And his heart wrenched, painfully.

"Well?" the little girl prodded impatiently.

"I do." And taking his cue from a woman who'd proven herself entirely more honorable than he, Harris fell to a knee. Reaching inside his jacket, he removed a purse, and withdrawing several sovereign from the little sack, he placed them into her little palm.

The beggar child's eyes went enormous. "Blimey," she whispered and then quickly folded her hand around the coins and darted off.

One by one, other little girls rushed over for an offering, and Harris divided up the monies he carried.

"Are ye a prince?" one of the girls asked, her voice rich with wonderment.

"Oh, hardly." Reaching behind her ear, he made a show of removing a coin and presenting it before her. "More like a magician."

She giggled and swiped that coin from him before darting off.

Over the top of the curly head of one of the children, his gaze locked with Julia's.

Her eyes were soft in ways he'd never before seen them. The smile on her full mouth was romantic, and he, who'd never understood—nay, never believed—a man could truly be besotted by any woman beyond anything that was sexual, at last understood the plight of those fools.

Another little tug on his jacket jerked him back to the moment, and he resumed passing out every remaining coin he had. When none remained, and too many disappointed children wandered off, their dirt-stained features stamped with disappointment, it was like Harris took a fist to the gut.

A little girl hovered there, staring hopefully up. "Ye sure ye don't got any more?"

His heart ached for the desperation there in the little girl's face. And in her, he saw...Julia. Julia as she'd surely been when she'd been the same age as the child before him.

Harris felt the front of his jacket, and then lifted a finger up. "I have it." He fished his timepiece out; gold and etched with his initials.

As one, Julia and the little girl gasped.

"Here you are," he murmured, over their joint shock, and he pressed the timepiece into her tiny palm.

The moment the gold touched the girl's fingers, she took off running.

Harris looked to Julia. "Shall we—?"

She stared back with horror-filled eyes.

"What is it?" he asked.

"Why would you do that?" she demanded.

He furrowed his brow, and cast confused glance about. "Do what?"

"You gave her your timepiece," Julia said flatly.

He looked at her, and he'd wager he looked as confused as he felt. "And?"

"And?" Julia echoed, and then releasing a sound of exasperation, she tossed her arms up. "Because you don't do it, Harris," she whispered. "You'll get the girl killed." With that, she marched off.

"That doesn't make any sense," he said, rushing after her.

Heading for the carriage, Julia didn't even break stride, not so much as pausing to glance back. "It wouldn't to you."

"Then explain it to me," he pressed when he finally managed to reach her side.

A servant drew the door open. "Because you put her in harm's way," she said bluntly.

With that, Julia took Stebbin's hand and allowed the young man to help her inside the carriage.

Frowning, Harris scrambled in behind her.

The servant shut the door with a hard, decisive click.

"I put her in harm's way by giving her a timepiece."

"You made her a mark." Julia spoke to him the way she might have delivered a lesson to any one of those children who'd gathered about her a short while ago. "A target."

And in a way, he was as lost as them, shockingly and embarrassingly so. Mayhap even more. "I'm afraid I don't understand how giving them an item of value is any different than providing them with funds."

"Coins can be easily hidden and are invariably quickly spent. They'll fill a belly with food that will be quickly consumed and then gone. They can purchase boots, which are personalized, and that narrows the number of people who might attempt to filch them from a person." Her dark irises grew haunted, her sightless gaze sluicing through him. "But items of such wealth, a timepiece, a cloak, they stand out when the last thing people in East London can afford is to stand out. People..." Her voice fell to a haunted whisper. "Terrible ones, they will kill to take those items."

Her words painted a dark image of a ruthless world, a dog-eat-dog one lived in by only the most vulnerable, fighting for basic survival. His entire body... hurt. Her revelations, so matter-of-factly stated, left him gutted inside. "Is this what it was like for you?" he asked, his voice hoarse. Had someone inadvertently, through their attempt at generosity, put her in harm's way? Oh, God. Once again, shame weighed on him as he was presented once more with the extent of his own self-absorption that he'd failed to understand what her life had been like and what the lives of so many were like.

"This is what it is like for everyone here, Harris," she said simply.

It didn't escape his notice that she'd failed to answer him, and in so doing, she'd only confirmed that nauseating fear in the pit of his stomach. He recalled their first meeting, finding her in the duchess' parlor. She'd been attired in a garment that had revealed its wear and age, but had also revealed an item of value. "The cloak." Those two words came past a thickened throat.

Julia gave him a questioning look.

"You were gifted that cloak."

"She meant well, the young lady who handed it over," Julia murmured, confirming his worst worrying. "But yes, it set us apart. It made whichever of us wore it a target." Her eyes slid shut, and her face tensed. "It is why I allowed her to keep the article, but only to wear it in our apartments."

"Who?"

The lady blinked slowly. "Beg pardon?"

"Who did you allow to keep it?" he asked, that question compelled not by the earlier suspicion that had driven him where Julia was concerned, but rather, by this ever-increasing need to know about her.

She blanched. All the color slipped from her cheeks as she visibly recoiled. For a moment, he thought she'd prevaricate. "My sister," she said, her voice catching. "She loved it so damned much, and it was so very bad for her, but I could not deny her anything." Julia sucked in a noisy breath. "Even if it was in her best interest."

For a second time that day, the carriage rolled to a stop, and coward that he was, Harris found himself grateful for that interruption, one that allowed him to try to steady his disjointed thoughts and turbulent emotions.

Julia looked out the window. "What is this?"

"I thought you would enjoy a visit to Gunther's."

"Gunther's," she echoed dumbly.

"Ices."

"No... I know. I've seen..." Her voice trailed off as she looked through the crystal pane once more. "I've never been," she murmured.

Nay, she'd opened his eyes to how little she'd seen and known in life. That was, when it came to pleasure. And energized by the possibility of offering her some of the joy that she'd been so long without, he pushed the door open and jumped out.

"Come," he urged. Waving off a besotted Stebbins, Harris caught Julia by the waist and lifted her down.

Only, the moment her feet touched the pavement, he remained frozen, his fingers still upon her. Uncaring about the gawking passersby. Captivated by the feel and heat of her.

She drifted closer. Or did he do that? Perhaps they both did, their bodies angling nearer.

God, she was magnificent in so many ways, a siren who tempted. A mermaid for whom he'd happily bash himself against jagged rocks.

Bang.

He and Julia both jolted as Stebbins brought the carriage door firmly shut, shattering the moment and clearing Harris' head.

He held his elbow out. "Shall we?"

With the crowded London streets watching on, Harris led Julia inside.

Chapter 14

H e'd taken her… to Gunther's.

She, a guttersnipe born to the streets, was seated at a private table on the fringe of that famous, gleaming shop window. One Julia had passed enough times in the course of her life that she'd lost count. As a girl, she'd always stolen covetous looks at the lords and ladies seated within the shop. The children with their nursemaids or mothers.

Eventually, she'd stopped looking. It hadn't been about envy. No, not that. Though there had certainly been some of those sentiments. She'd stopped looking because of the hunger that had come in seeing a treat and imagining what it would taste like.

Now, she found herself seated in front of that very window overlooking the London streets. She watched Harris speaking with the young man behind the counter.

And yet, as magical as this moment was, as wholly entranced as she was by the fact that a man such as him, would take a woman such as her, to a place such as this, it was not that which had stolen her heart this day. Or at least not this alone.

It was the fact that he'd knelt on the dirty cobblestones outside Covent Garden and spoken to those waifs, of which she'd recently been one, treating them as though they were equals. Then giving out enough money to have seen Julia secured for the whole of her life.

But then, that had been the man he'd proven to be when he'd been just a stranger rescuing a street waif—to his lover's annoyance.

In this moment, with this stolen life, she could almost believe this was real. That someone like her could have a future with someone like him. Which was preposterous.

And yet, neither did it stop her from wanting him as she did, from wanting that future.

Her heart skittered several beats as he finished speaking to the shopkeeper and started for their table. With every step that brought him closer, a fresh wave of butterflies were released in her belly, and they fluttered and danced. She, cynical Julia Corbett, who hadn't believed in love or thought herself capable of weakening for a man, found just how very wrong she'd been.

He reached the table and settled into the chair opposite her. "I have questions," he said without preamble.

She stiffened, and just like that, her foolish musings burst like a fragile soap bubble.

"Do you prefer chocolate or muscadine?"

Of anything he could have said, this was it? "That is your question?" she blurted.

He gave her a skeptical look. "Yes. Was there something else…" Understanding lit his eyes. "You thought I intended to put questions to you about your identity."

Her identity. Which was decidedly not Adairia. An impostor. She managed nothing more than a weak nod.

"No," he said. "I'm not challenging you. Not anymore."

Oh, God. Not anymore. And this, when he should.

This was too much. Guilt was a flavor that would surely spoil whatever treat he'd purchased for her.

As if on cue, a young woman appeared and set two etched crystal bowls before them.

She'd been wrong. Surely there was nothing more luxuriant, more resplendent a food than this. Her eyes slid closed as she let her tongue absorb all the taste and texture.

She opened her eyes to find Harris watching her, his gaze dark, though the darkness was different. It wasn't the suspicious, cynical glint he'd worn during their earliest exchanges. But rather, it was the same heated one that had glinted in his eyes as he'd given her so much pleasure. And if she were the blushing debutante whom he'd undoubtedly one day wed, she'd have felt a proper shame for the yearnings that now consumed her, God forgive her as a wanton. However, in this moment, she could not hold any regrets. Not a one.

"You did so much for so many today." And now he'd treat her to ices at Gunther's.

He scoffed. "Do not make more of my actions today than there is. If it hadn't been for you, I'd have not been there. If it hadn't taken you challenging me to open my eyes, I would have remained blind to my own self-absorption."

She made a sound of protest, but he waved it off.

"There's no excusing it. I've been bitter, and for what? Because my father had no use for me or the mother who bore me, whom he treated as a broodmare? And then marrying at eighteen, I was entirely focused on myself and my feelings."

He'd been... married? Her mind stalled. What if he was still married? She'd just assumed... But she didn't really know him or his circumstances, no more than he knew hers. Her stomach turned over. Dipping the tip of her spoon into her chocolate ice, she tried for a nonchalance she did not feel. When she spoke, she tried to make her voice as casual as possible. "You... have a wife, then?"

Lowering an elbow, he angled his body in a way that prevented any audience from observing his mouth as it moved. "Do you think I'm the manner of man who wouldn't honor my vows?" he asked, his voice faintly teasing and yet...she registered belatedly how she could have, with her question, inadvertently offended him.

"No," she said swiftly. "I just... forgive me."

And on the wave of guilt for that assumption she'd made came this glorious wave of relief, the manner of which filled her chest with the greatest lightness and left her giddy. Except, if he was no longer married... Her heart froze. "You're a widower," she whispered, shame, an all-too-familiar emotion around this man, taking up the place of her earlier happiness.

He stared at her for a long while. "I... the duchess did not tell you?"

"She did not."

"I expected she would." Harris attended his ice, scraping chocolate around the edge of the fluted bowl, and for a moment, she thought he'd say nothing else about his wife. Undoubtedly, an exquisite-in-every-way lady, so very different from a street waif like Julia. And Julia was torn between wanting to know absolutely every detail about the woman who'd been his marchioness and wanting to know nothing at all. Because somehow, along the way, she'd come to care about the man seated opposite her, more than she should. And that, however, was why she desperately longed for him to keep speaking.

"Did you love her?" she ventured. The handle of her spoon bit sharply into her palm, and she reminded herself to relax her grip.

"I didn't even know her," he said, still studying his chocolate ice. "She was an actual stranger to me." A smile more sad than cynical formed on his beautiful, hard lips, and she wanted to brush away that melancholy grin. "Not even in the sense of the cold unions the nobility makes. It was at a formal ball. I heard a scream and went running. She was there in the garden, her dress torn, and it was just... me and her." He chuckled and, with a wry shake of his head, sat back in his seat. "And then, of course, every other member of Polite Society was there. Her family's appearance had been orchestrated."

She gasped as his meaning became clear. "She trapped you."

"Indeed."

"What happened to her?"

"She did it to pass off the babe she carried as mine and to give the child a name. In the end, she died bearing that babe, and... that is all."

That was all...

How very casually he spoke, and yet there was nothing simple about his words.

"So if I've been... cynical, unfairly judgmental, and

suspicious of your motives, it is entirely because of my own insecurities."

That was when she knew, unequivocally and with an absolute certainty, that she could not perpetuate this ruse. Yes, she'd told the duchess all, and for a brief time, Julia had even managed to convince herself that was enough. If the duchess didn't expect her to share the truth with Harris or anyone else, then surely that was enough? But she'd been lying to herself as much as she'd been lying to Harris.

She stared out the shop window at the lords and ladies passing by in their brightly clad, rich garments and at the street waifs peppered into that larger crowd, their hands tilted hopefully up.

Those were her people. That was where she belonged.

Because regardless of whether the duchess knew and accepted Julia, the truth remained: Julia was not and never would be Adairia. And presenting herself before the world, letting people, letting Harris, believe that lie? It was craven and wrong.

Just then, her gaze landed on a girl with the brightest blonde curls that were a shade of golden that Julia had seen only once. The spoon slipped from her fingers and clattered to the table, and then her heart fell.

Not Adairia.

Of course, not Adairia.

Rather, another struggling, begging street peddler. Just then, a lady on the arm of a gentleman stepped in the line of sight of Julia and that beggar girl. The woman knocked into the child, upending the girl's basket of flowers. Rage flitted across Julia's vision. How many times had she been that young woman? Poor. Pathetic. So treated by Polite Society.

"Julia?" Concern laced Harris' tones.

Julia was already out of her seat and flying across the shop. Squeezing past the couple just entering, she pushed through and raced outside. "You there," she shouted, and uncaring of the crowd that had paused at her cry, Julia collected her hem and rushed toward the lord and lady. "What is the meaning of this?" she demanded, and the pair turned to face her.

Through her rage on the young peddler's behalf came a dawning recognition. There was a familiarity to the exquisite creature, a beauty that could not be forgotten, and Julia briefly faltered as she found herself transported to another street where this woman had been annoyed by a different peddler—Julia. And the beauty had been on the arm of a different gentleman.

Every word she'd planned to utter flew out of her head.

"I beg your pardon?" The woman winged up a perfectly formed black eyebrow. "Are you speaking to me?"

Regal as a queen, resplendent in the finest gold silk, the woman before her no doubt was a lady unaccustomed to fielding questions from anyone. Of course, there wasn't a hint of recognition on the part of the lady. People like Julia—as she'd been, like this peddler girl gawking openly at their exchange—were invisible to her.

"You knocked this young woman's items from her arms." In fact, there'd been a deliberateness to her actions.

"And what exactly is it you are expecting?" the woman rejoined, peering down a small, pert nose at Julia.

Julia drew back. "An apology at the very least."

"To her?"

"Yes, to her." Sweeping over, she put her face closer to the lady's. "You may be her social superior, but that does not mean she deserves to be treated so unkindly."

The woman's mouth moved, opening and closing several times before she managed to give voice to her indignation. "Who do you think you are?"

She should have expected that the lady wouldn't recognize her. Attired as she was, in silks and jewels, Julia bore little resemblance to a street waif. A woman as pitiable as she'd been hadn't merited so much as a second look, and she'd felt more than a little annoyance that Julia's struggles had stalled her pleasures. "I daresay I might say the same of you," Julia shot back.

The dark-haired beauty cast a stunned glance to the handsome gentleman at her side.

He lifted his broad shoulders in a shrug.

Then the lady's gaze lit on a figure behind her, and a mix of surprise and shock brought those dark slashes of her eyebrows shooting up. "*Ruthven?*"

Julia whipped her gaze over. At some point, Harris had taken up a place near her shoulder.

It didn't escape her notice the breathless quality of the lady's already sultry tones, or the way her features softened all too briefly before she looked once more to Julia. And then back to Harris. And those ice-blue eyes narrowed, all warmth that had come when she'd spied Harris instantly gone.

"Is everything all right?" he asked in cool tones, and it occurred to Julia he was offended on her behalf, and she went warm all over, from the inside and out. His features were drawn and tense, his eyes hard, as they'd been upon their first formal meeting in the duchess' parlor.

"A friend of yours?" the other gentleman drawled, and she glanced behind her.

He also knew the handsome gentleman, then.

"Indeed." Harris inclined his head. "Allow me to present Her Grace, the Duchess of Arlington's niece, Lady Julia. Lady Julia, Lady Sarah Windermere, and of course, His Grace, the Duke of Rothesby, whom you met at Hyde Park."

Julia immediately found herself the subject of intense scrutiny from that pair.

Her stomach and heart all fell as one. "Your Grace," she said weakly and remembered to curtsy.

This was the same gentleman who the duchess had been hopeful—and insistent—would take part in Julia's debut.

"A pleasure to see you again," he drawled. "We have heard"—the hard gaze he pinned upon her was pointed— "much about you over the years."

He assessed her with the same cynical suspicion as Harris had, and yet, it was not this most powerful of peers who stirred the greater sense of dread.

Rather, it was the woman at his side, who leveled a shrewd glance on Julia, peering so closely at her that she'd the sudden urge to hide. Of course, it hadn't been her intervention that had merited such a study, but rather, Julia's presence here with Harris and his show of support.

Ice traipsed along Julia's spine.

She'd not find friends in these two. Just the opposite.

"Come along, Rothesby," Lady Sarah said, and lifting her

chin, she swept off.

The duke dropped a bow for Julia. "Ruthven."

Harris lifted his chin in acknowledgment.

The moment they'd gone, Julia dropped to a knee and proceeded to help the young woman gather up her things.

"Thank you, miss," the girl said in a rough Cockney.

Julia waved off the child's gratitude and made to speak when Harris joined them.

Both Julia and the flower peddler stopped as he oversaw that task.

"He a prince, my lady?" the girl whispered.

Yes, Julia rather suspected he was.

Before she could answer, however, Harris glanced up. "Hardly. I've no crown. I'm just an ordinary man." With a little wink, he resumed cleaning up the mess made by Lady Sarah.

Just an ordinary man? Nay, there was nothing ordinary about Harris, the Marquess of Ruthven. He was the gentleman who, when she'd been a mere stranger in the street, had not only come to Julia's aid, but had also offered up a crate of flowers to peddle, along with a purse. Now, he'd help this young girl, who reminded her so very much of herself and Adairia when they'd been nine or ten or so.

And God help her, she fell in love with Harris, the Marquess of Ruthven. In this moment, his head bent and the sun toying with his tawny strands while he helped a common woman, she lost her heart so very completely to him.

"There you are," he said as he finished up, and she gave thanks for his focus being directed on the task at hand as she tried to get herself back down to earth. "What is your name?" he asked with such gentleness that Julia only further continued her fall for him.

The girl directed her gaze at her tattered boots. "Rose," she whispered.

"Rose. If you go to 1400 Grosvenor Square, hand the head butler this." Fishing an item from his jacket, he removed a card and handed it over to the girl. "Let him know Lord Ruthven sent you and asked that he find you employment. The driver…. will take you there after I see this lady home."

As the girl headed over to the carriage and Stebbins helped her up onto the bench with the driver, the little girl pressed that card close to her chest and stared adoringly back at Harris with all the awe that fueled Julia's heart's very beat.

Oh, God, there would be absolutely no recovering from this.

Julia was lost.

Chapter 15

J ulia was going to make her debut.

And there could be no doubting that because of her beauty, and spirit, and the dowry the duchess had fixed on her, Julia would find herself quickly wed.

But along the way, so much had been confused.

For *Harris*.

He'd become confused.

Each moment he'd spent with her, his reservations had faded, and he'd forgotten he was supposed to be worrying about her intentions for the duchess and had known only that he... enjoyed being with her. He enjoyed her bluntness. He appreciated her realness, either when she was telling Harris where he could go or in those more unguarded moments when she was so unfiltered in her exuberance and joy at pleasures that, because of their simplicity, had gone previously unappreciated by him.

Now, he found himself relishing the time he spent with her and refusing to let himself think about the inevitable outcome of her entry into Polite Society.

As Harris made his way to the duchess' ballroom, he heard annoyed, nasally tones spill out into the corridor. "No. No. No. It is one, two, three, crisp and even. From the top…"

Harris had made himself stay away after what had happened at Gunther's and her brave display on the streets in challenging one of Society's most powerful peeresses and a duke. She'd not only abandoned her own pleasures that day, but she'd given up those comforts to go to the rescue of someone most people failed to see. There'd been a raw honesty to her joy and surprise that day, none of which could be feigned and all of which had proven contagious.

And he'd run like hell.

Only to be drawn back, not because of the suspicions he'd carried, but because, strangely, he'd found himself missing her.

Only to arrive four days later to the duchess' ballroom and discover she'd gone.

For a breathtaking siren stood in her place. Frozen in the doorway, Harris drank in the sight of the woman at the opposite end of the ballroom, her auburn tresses drawn and twisted like a coronet about her head. The sun's rays toyed with those tresses, highlighting hundreds of shades of browns and reds and blondes, more colors than he'd ever known a shade of hair could be. He moved his gaze over her lean, lithe frame. He'd always admired a voluptuous, gently rounded form, only to find out what a damned fool he'd been, only to discover just how wrong his eye had been. A wave of desire jolted through him. The pale yellow satin gown she wore accentuated a nipped waist and delicate bustline. She'd the look of a Spartan warrioress accustomed to time in the sun.

"Harris has arrived!"

Midwaltz, the lady missed a step, and the audience across

the way all turned, effectively breaking that trance she'd held over him.

Finding himself the focus of the suddenly silent, small crowd of people in the ballroom, he felt his neck go hot.

"Are you going to just stand there?" The duchess waved Harris over. "Do join us, my boy."

Ironically, for the first time in almost two decades, dumbstruck as he'd been at the sight of Julia, he felt like the boy his godmother had called him out as. A green one at that. Donning a grin, he headed across the ballroom. "I cannot imagine anything I'd enjoy more," he said when he reached the small gathering. Harris sketched a bow. All the while, it took a forcible effort to not gawk at the lady beside him, who'd gone from duck to swan.

"Ahem," the bespectacled governess hired by the duchess said, and Julia promptly sank into a curtsy.

"My lord," she murmured. Her tones, husky and sultry, wrapped around him, and this time he didn't fight it—he couldn't fight it—he moved his gaze over Julia, drinking in the sight of—

Lady Cowpen shoved an elbow into his side. "She's been practicing." She gave him a sly look. "Coming along rather nicely."

Of its own will, Harris' gaze slid over to Julia once more, and he resisted the urge to swallow. God, the distance had been needed.

"Indeed," he murmured, and a delicate blush filled Julia's cheeks. Realizing his blunder, Harris coughed into his hand. "That is… indeed?"

Julia flashed a wry grin. "Lady Cowpen is being generous. I'm just a"—she brought the pads of her forefinger and thumb together so they nearly kissed—"*smidge* away from 'dismal failure.'"

"I rather doubt that," Harris said.

The duchess patted his hand affectionately. "Charming as ever, this one is."

Aye, Harris was known amongst Society for being a charming rogue, and yet, the words he'd spoken just then had been the truth.

"Perhaps we could enlist your assistance with Julia's waltzing lessons," his godmother suggested. "Lord knows this one here has been dismal"—she motioned to the tiny fellow staring impatiently at their tableau—"and hardly as pleasant of character."

Color filled the dance instructor's cheeks.

Julia was immediately shaking her head. "Oh, no. I'm certain his lordship has any number of more important matters to attend than… than… getting his toes trampled by me."

"Of course he doesn't." Lady Cavendish chuckled. "You're probably keeping the boy from his clubs and wagers."

He frowned. She'd paint him in such a…

Correct light? a jeering voice taunted at the back of his mind. For the older countess was not wrong. He'd not appreciated just how empty and shallow his existence had been, only to be presented with it so very bluntly.

Slowly lifting a resigned gaze to his, Julia brought her fingertips to rest upon his coat sleeve, allowing him to escort her onto the dance floor. She moved with all the speed of a person who made the march to the gallows, and despite himself, Harris felt a wry grin forming on his lips. "With all your *enthusiasm*, you're hardly good for my self-esteem, Julia."

She snorted. "I hardly think a gentleman such as you would require any sense of validation from one such as me," she said as they continued the walk to the middle of the room.

From one such as her...

"Do you think I'd treat you somehow different because of what your experience has been?" he asked when they stopped their walk. Was her opinion of him so low? And yet, what grounds had he given her to think anything different when he'd challenged her at every turn?

She stared at his cravat, her lashes unmoving, her gaze locked upon those folds. "No," she said softly, her voice faraway. Then, as if she remembered herself, she blinked. "I don't believe that, but neither am I so naïve as to believe that you could possibly wish to," she said matter-of-factly.

The lady couldn't be any more wrong. Ever since the carriage ride, he'd been able to think of nothing but her; yearning for her. Harris reached for her hand once more to guide her fingers upon his sleeve, but she drew them quickly back.

She remained with her long limbs at her sides. "You don't need to do this, Harris." Her voice was faintly entreating. "I'm sure there's any number of things you'd rather be doing than... than... this."

"Actually, there isn't." The moment he'd arrived and found her there, the only thing he'd wanted to do was take her in his arms. He held her gaze. "I want to dance with you, Julia," he murmured, softly near her ear.

She grimaced. "I'll have you know what I'm doing here is not dancing." She gave a discreet gesture to the little fellow, who was tapping his timepiece and watching them. "Mr. Dour has informed me."

He strangled on his laugh. "Mr. Dour?" he asked, drawing an answering laugh.

"I am not being rude. It is his name."

"And a suitable one at that. I can't imagine a more pinch-faced fellow than that one."

They shared a laugh, and some of the tension left Julia's narrow shoulders.

"What's going on out there?" Lady Cowpen's loud whisper to her friends reached across the ballroom.

"In fairness to Mr. Dour, I'm really quite dreadful."

His lips twitched. "Are you always this honest?" Harris didn't allow her a chance to answer. "Now, do not give Mr. Dour more credit than he's due." He held his hands aloft. "If you're unable to dance, it merely means you've not had the right partner, Julia," he murmured, and waited.

She dampened her mouth. That delicate slip of pink flesh darted out and traced a path along the seam of her lips.

She gave the slightest nod, and with that surrender, he settled his hand at her waist. His fingers curled reflexively upon her, the heat of her singeing his palm, and he drew her closer.

They'd been getting on so well. There'd not been any of the usual animosity or needling. Nay, just the opposite. It had been comfortable and wonderful. So much so that it had been so very easy—too easy—to forget that she was of an entirely different world and life than Harris'.

Until he'd gone and asked that question.

Are you always this honest?

That one single query, so innocuously directed at her, reminded her that Harris had been right about her from the start. She was an impostor. Granted, now with the permission of Her Grace, but an impostor nonetheless.

And oh, how very desperately she wished for it all to be real.

Julia's entire heart and soul hurt. How ironic he should pose such a question to her when he'd been the one who'd been mistrustful from the start.

For it didn't matter that she'd told the duchess all. It didn't matter that Julia remained here, with the woman in full possession of the truth of her existence. It mattered what she didn't say. To this man.

It shouldn't matter. What he thought of her.

"Julia?" he asked with such a tender concern that it only made the hurt all the greater.

She forced herself to don a smile. "Should I have told you I'm a splendid dancer and have you discover my lie for yourself?"

"You could have made all your displeasure with me known by stomping all over my toes," he pointed out, drawing a laugh from Julia, and the tension eased from her frame.

"See?" he murmured, confirming he'd teased to set her at ease and, in so doing, had proven he'd been correct after all at being more skilled in some ways than the man the duchess had hired to school Julia.

"I do," she said softly. The haunting strains of the violin filled the ballroom, and she and Harris remained frozen, rooted to their spots on the dance floor, and as his gaze moved over her face, she followed the path his eyes took, matching the search he did of her. How had she believed him cold and unfeeling?

How, when he'd proven caring of the kindly ladies across the room and of the street waif she'd been when he'd come to her rescue? And the children of the Rookeries whom he'd helped…and Rose, the girl he'd offered employment to.

"Well, get on with it, boy," one of the countesses shouted, and Julia and Harris jumped.

A half grin quirked his lips up at the corner, doing wild things to her heart's rhythm. "Lest I find myself earning any more of their displeasure, we should begin."

With that, he guided her through the motions of the dance.

Concentrating her attentions on each one-two-three step, she fixed her focus on the snowy folds of his cravat.

Off to the side, Mr. Dour punctuated the song count. "One, two, three. One, two, three."

Julia missed a step and trampled on Harris' boot. She winced. Perhaps success didn't hinge upon one's dance partner or instructor after all.

"One, two, three," she mouthed and tripped again.

God, she was dreadful at this. It didn't matter who instructed her. She was out of her league in every way. Her absolute absence of grace was a product of who she was.

"It is a one-two-three count, my lady," the dance instructor called in his nasally whine.

"Did I ever tell you about my math tutor when I was a boy?"

One, two—

It took a moment for Harris' words to penetrate her counting. Julia lifted her gaze from his jacket front. "My lord?" She immediately stomped on him once more. "My apologies," she muttered. This was futile.

"My math tutor. Mr. Digits."

She snorted out a laugh, to the audible displeasure of her instructor. "That is nearly as unlikely to believe as Mr. Dour for my mean-spirited dancing master."

"Oh, yes, well, mine I named myself. I was a boy who despised math, and he was someone who quite loved it, and so I said he should have a name that better suited him. He indulged me." He flashed another wry grin. "Which, in retrospect, had a good deal more to do with the fact that I was a marquess' son."

Julia tripped over Harris' toes, but this time, he righted her before she could falter and whisked her in a dizzying twirl that wrought havoc upon her senses.

If Harris had been even a hint as remotely charming a boy as this grown man before her, then servants and instructors and peerage alike would have been hard-pressed to deny him anything.

Nay, that is more the effect he has upon you.

He was a man who muddled a woman's senses.

"Well, Mr. Digits insisted math was fun."

"And you disagreed?"

He waggled his eyebrows, those tawny slashes giving him a devilish look that pulled a laugh from her. "Oh, quite strenuously. Until he lined up peppermints and biscuits and rock candies, and my ability to earn those treats was tied to my ability to use those numbers to properly count them and multiply them and divide them." He lowered his head closer, his breath tickling her cheek. "And do you know what I learned, Julia?"

She managed to shake her head, and this time as she missed her footing, it had nothing to do with her miserable attempts at dancing and everything to do with the dazed state induced by Harris Clarendale, the Marquess of Ruthven.

"That, when made enjoyable, math wasn't the struggle I took it for, and it more than had its uses. Now, close your eyes."

She made a sound of protest. "Harris, I'm going to tread over your feet all the more."

"It's not seeing the steps. It's not counting them. It's feeling them." He adjusted his hold on her waist, angling her body closer to him, and she curved reflexively in his embrace, like those strings being strummed so expertly by the violinist, her heart quickening. "Do not think of it as counting one, two, three," he murmured, his lips close to her ear. "Think of it as feeling that count."

Her lashes fluttered shut, and she turned herself over to the magic of being in his arms.

Harris swung her about in another dizzying twirl.

"One, two, three. One, two, three." His husky baritone counting the rhythm of the waltz took the clinical aspect of Mr. Dour's earlier instruction and infused a seductive quality that pulled her deeper under his spell as she became lost to the steps of the dance and the feel of his arms.

Once, when she'd been a girl, she had indulged Adairia's fantasy, escorting her back to those streets of Mayfair. They'd snuck off after selling their flowers and taken up a place outside of a sprawling residence. Together, they'd pressed their noses against the windowpane and taken in the crowded ballroom, watching the fine lords and ladies dancing as Julia now did. In that moment, and in so many moments to follow, she'd dreamed of being held as Harris now held her. She'd closed her eyes briefly and imagined it, wished for it, and her mind was all muddled as to whether that yearning had, in fact, materialized into this, a moment that was nothing more than a dream. For none of her longing could have properly prepared her for what it was to be in Harris' arms, completing the intricate steps of a waltz while he guided her, applying the slightest pressure to direct her as needed.

All magic, however, invariably ended.

Harris brought them to a stop, and she forced her gaze open as reality intruded.

"Not a single misstep, Julia," he said softly. Raising her knuckles to his mouth, he placed a lingering kiss upon them. And with that touch of his lips upon her heated flesh, Julia discovered just how powerful and quixotic nothing more than the brush of a modest kiss upon a hand, in fact, was.

Her fingers trembled in his hand, and he applied a slight

pressure with his palm, briefly enfolding hers, and she didn't want him to release her. She didn't want him to stop touching her or—

"Bravo, my boy!" The duchess' pleased cry slashed across the moment, recalling Julia to the present and the reality of the audience across the room surveying her—their—every action.

Hurriedly disentangling her fingers from Harris', Julia stepped aside.

"Now, you curtsy," the countess called, all matter-of-fact business that reminded Julia for all the ways Harris had wrought havoc upon her senses with his dance, this hadn't been anything more than a lesson. "Curtsy, my lady. Curtsy."

Belatedly offering one of those deferential dips, Julia couldn't help the swell of regret at the end of that all-too-fleeting dream and wonderment.

"Quite the quick study, isn't she?" Her Grace called over. "Just required the right instructor."

"Indeed, Your Grace." Catching Julia's eye, Harris winked, a teasing, yet still-seductive fluttering of those long tawny lashes that put them as players in a game.

"You've handily taught the girl the waltz," the duchess said.

"Might I advise Her Grace, the lady would be best served to learn the quadrille," Mr. Dour intoned.

While the duchess and her friends went back and forth with the bold-in-his-opinion Mr. Dour, Harris leaned down and whispered, "Though hardly as enjoyable as the waltz, there's a different pleasure that comes from the quadrille."

Her heart thumping, she looked up. "A… different pleasure." Whatever pleasure found could certainly never match what she'd known while waltzing with him.

"The quick parting and coming together with one's partner, the fleeting touch of taking a hand and then losing that connection, and the thrill of waiting for the next time you might lock fingers when you are reunited each time," he said. The husky timbre of his baritone sent a million little shivers racing along her back. Harris' gaze slipped to her mouth, his attention hovering upon it, and for a moment, she thought he intended to kiss her publicly. For an even greater moment, she wanted him to.

But then his lips formed a wry half grin.

"Harris?" The duchess' impatient query brought his attention thankfully away from a hopelessly besotted Julia, sparing her from the humiliating fascination she had with him.

Cupping his hands around his mouth, he called over to the duchess, "I was explaining the quadrille to the lady, Your Grace."

"Well, we are trying to determine which the girl needs to master now, so do attend us, Harris." Lady Cowpen thumped that cane Julia had come to find the elegant peeress used as a stylish accessory.

Harris touched a hand to his chest and bowed his head in a show of exaggerated penitence that earned a bevy of laughter from the ladies at the side of the ballroom.

And there was a keen sense of… disappointment. That was all he'd been. He'd stepped in as a de facto dancing teacher, and she'd merely been the beneficiary of his talents.

He, a man who moved with such grace and with a command of his every step, had undoubtedly charmed every woman who'd stepped into his arms. Every one of those ladies—just like Julia—had certainly been lured by his pull and mastery, and she hated that realization, for it served to remind her that she was not somehow different or special to him. A man who charmed as he did—that dark-haired beauty in the streets, the three women before them, Julia… There was no doubting the reasons he'd earned the reputation of rogue that his godmother had spoken of. And she hated herself for the sting of jealousy and the heavy regret those truths brought.

"Which one do you think it should be, Harris?" the duchess shouted over.

"You know my opinions on most sets outside the waltz and in some part the quadrille."

Her Grace snorted. "The less touching, the better."

"Ah." He lifted a finger and waved it at the trio. "The more fun, the better."

The duchess froze and then laughed. "Do not even think of it. Enough of your roguish nonsense—" Her commands were in vain, as Harris had already released Julia and headed at a quick clip for the trio of ladies.

The countesses chortled as he came, his arms up as he went.

"Harris, cease that this instant," the duchess said. "I'm entirely too old for these games."

Except, it did not escape Julia's notice the small smile that teased the woman's lips the moment her godson reached her side, or the way she slid her hand onto Harris' sleeve.

With that, he proceeded to shuffle the pair of them at a quick clip along the dance floor.

Julia hurriedly vacated the place she had at the center of the room, allowing that unlikely pair full command of the floor.

The woman and her godson moved at a brisk, sideways gait.

It was the most tender, heartwarming dance she'd ever witnessed between a man and a woman who was very clearly like a mother to him. Julia had never known that tenderness in any way with even her own mother, who'd been so bent on surviving, there hadn't been time for much affection.

In that very instant, watching Harris and the duchess laughing, Julia lost her heart to him all over again.

There'd be room enough for terror later, when the thousand fears and horrors learned in her lifetime of struggle and strife won out and reminded her that those who played with fire were invariably consumed and destroyed by it. But in this moment, she saw only Harris, a dashing rogue, a strikingly handsome gentleman not off drinking and wagering, as the duchess had accused him of, but rather, here, waltzing with Adairia's godmother.

"He is quite a dear boy, isn't he?"

She started. Having been so absorbed in her greatest of falls, Julia had failed to note Lady Cowpen's approach.

"The dearest," she said, her voice heavy with emotion.

The other countess took up a place at Julia's opposite side. "He's got a reputation of being a rogue, and he presents a cynical side to the world, but he's still the lovable, good-hearted boy he always was."

Lovable.

Good-hearted.

Yes, there could be no doubting, in the short time she'd come to know him and witness him and his kindness, that he cared deeply for the women before him. And Harris was the manner of man who, when he cared, he would defend and protect until the end.

As she watched him and the duchess, sadness filled her.

For that love and loyalty and devotion were how she knew that when he ultimately discovered her truths—or lies? it was all mixed up now—he'd never forgive her. He'd never see her as part of this household or family. For the simple reason she wasn't. And she never would be. This had never been her place. Rather, it had been Adairia's, and it had been dangerous to let herself believe that anything more could possibly come of her being here. Or wanting anything more with Harris.

Nay, she could not stay here. Not much longer. Soon, it would be time to put an end to make-believe and go…somewhere. She couldn't go back to live in Covent Garden; not without eventually being recognized. The duchess would surely help Julia start anew…somewhere else, in some other way.

And she couldn't stop the swell of sadness at the realization, one that had nothing to do with the lavish lifestyle she'd stepped into and everything to do with the people here whom she'd be forced to leave.

Chapter 16

L ater that night, Harris found himself reentering the more familiar world than the proper, respectable one he'd been playing at these past weeks.

Not, however, for his usual reasons.

Cutting a path across the crowded gaming hell floor of Forbidden Pleasures, he sought out the friend he could always anticipate finding here.

Sure enough, seated at his usual tables, a vibrant beauty on his lap and a dark-haired exotic creature at his side, he angled his head, studying his cards. All the while with his spare hand, he fondled a generous globe of the latter woman.

The moment Harris stopped at his table, the Duke of Rothesby looked up, a spark of surprise in his gaze. After Rothesby whispered something in each woman's ear, they got up and sauntered off.

"Well, well, well, the scoundrel returns to his proper place after all," his friend drawled, motioning to one of the vacant chairs. "Join Barrett and me for a round?"

With a word of thanks, Harris took the seat pulled out by a servant and accepted the brandy held out by another.

"Deal in?" Rothesby was already gesturing to the young viscount.

"I must say I'm more than a little glad to see you here," the ginger-haired gentleman drawled. "I had a sizable wager."

More of this?

Harris' ears went hot as both men went back and forth, congratulating each other for not believing the improbable tale that he'd been reformed and going on to estimate the extent of their earnings.

And they weren't wrong. The idea that Harris was capable of such a change *was* improbable. He couldn't and wouldn't be reformed. After he'd been humiliated and betrayed in the most public way, and then found himself the widower of the woman responsible for that treachery, his judgment had been called into question. It was easier to live a carefree existence, carousing and living for his own empty pursuits than risking feeling anything that was too deep. He didn't want to be one of those rogues who was reformed. Or he hadn't? Did he?

He stared absently down into his drink. It was all… confused. All turned upside down by a young woman who offered her pastries to footmen standing at attention to serve her. And who, according to Harris' godmother, had requested only food that the lady herself would hand out to those in need. And whom he'd taken in his arms today for a waltz that hadn't been like any other he'd danced with any other woman before. A memory slipped in of their carriage ride and his blood heated as he recalled—

"Ruthven?"

He jerked his attention upward to find both men staring quizzically back.

Conducting a swift study of the cards laid down, he

examined his own hand before tossing down a three.

"The duchess asked that I speak to you."

The young duke was already shaking his head.

"It could be worse," Harris pointed out. "It's not Almack's."

"Same respectable crowd, just a different ballroom."

"And what of me?" Barrett asked in feigned outrage.

Harris spared him a quick look. "The duchess isn't quite so desperate that she'd rush to assemble a bounder like you there," he said dryly.

The viscount slapped a hand to his chest and made a show of falling back in his seat, earning a laugh from Rothesby.

"I'm highly insulted," the other man said, his words having zero teeth. Barrett was one who well knew Polite Society's opinion—or rather, lack thereof—of him and had made it clear through his actions and increasingly outrageous wickedness that he didn't give a damn. "Either way, I've become well accustomed to Rothesby being embraced with open arms for that illustrious title he carries. Who would deny a young duke anything? Particularly when there are marriageable misses about? Debutantes and virgins." Barrett shuddered. "No, thank you. I shall leave that pleasure entirely to Rothesby."

Rothesby stuck a finger up in a crude gesture, earning another laugh from the viscount.

"Pleasure," the duke muttered. His recently deceased mother was also one of the duchess' dearest childhood friends, and as such, he was invariably called forward whenever the duchess or one of the countesses required a duke's influence with their daughters or, in this case, a niece. "And what does she require? That I place my ducal stamp of approval upon her?"

Ducal stamp of approval.

It was a gratingly arrogant comment about Julia from a man who was hardly a match in terms of character, or in any way. "The last thing she should require is yours or anyone's approval. And yet, it would also ease her way before Polite Society."

Both men went quiet.

Suddenly, Barrett sat up. "Now, now, now. What is this?" he murmured. "Are you... offended on the lady's behalf?"

"He did come to the lady's rescue outside Gunther's just four days ago," the duke drawled.

"Oh, the lady didn't require my rescuing that day," Harris snapped. "If anything, it was you and the countess who did."

Harris resisted the urge to yank at his cravat. "She is the duchess' niece." Harris tried—and failed—to make his voice as casual as possible. The damage had already been done. "Of course I feel some sense of responsibility where the lady is concerned."

Barrett let an open palm fall to the table. "Bloody fabulous, I'm going to lose my damned shirt." With his spare hand, Barrett swiped his half-drunk brandy and downed the remainder of his glass. And then, muttering to himself, Barrett grabbed the bottle near Harris' hand and poured himself another.

"You're making more of it than there is," Harris said,

looking back and forth between his friends. *But are they?* a voice needled at the back of his head. How much of his earlier annoyance at the other men's discussion stemmed from loyalty to his godmother, and how much had come down to his appreciation for Julia? Pushing aside those uncomfortable musings, he settled his gaze on an incredulous Barrett. "Furthermore, you are not going to lose your shirt," he assured. "You aren't," he said more insistently when his friends gave him matching dubious looks.

Then, angling themselves in a way that cut Harris out and made theirs a conversation of just two, Barrett said, "First, he gave up the most-sought-after widow in London, though Rothesby should thank you for that."

"Unrelated," Harris said, but he might as well not have even spoken.

"Then a trip to Gunther's." As he enumerated his list, the viscount lifted a finger, counting while he went.

The duke lifted his glass toward Barrett. "And do not forget passing out bread to strangers in the street."

Both men shifted their focus Harris' way, and he resisted the urge to squirm. "You heard about that?"

"That you were staring at her, besotted, as she did, and then you proceeded to distribute items together?" Lord Rothesby rejoined. "I hear *everything.*"

"God, you are worse than any old woman with your possession of gossip," Harris said between clenched teeth, earning another laugh from an entirely too amused Barrett. Suddenly regretting the decision to come here and the favor he'd put to the other man, he rushed to end this discussion. "Either way, you have my assurance that my feelings for the lady are entirely respectable." Aside from this yearning he had for her; a hungering that had existed almost from the start. "I'm merely here to enlist your support as she makes her debut."

"And this from a man who questions all women's motives and didn't believe for a moment the lady was, in fact, who she claimed," the duke murmured.

As Rothesby's wasn't a question, Harris sat there stiffly without a response.

Finally, the duke lowered the snifter in his hand to the tabletop and leaned forward. "Of course I'll throw my support behind the lady, if the duchess and you wish it." He lifted his spare hand. "However, I'd advise you to be warned, man. You've been hurt and betrayed before by one deceiver, and I'd not see it happen again because of some waif on the streets passing herself off as someone she's not."

Harris didn't know why those words spoken by the other man, his best friend, should make him want to punch him hard in the face, and yet, they did. Because, in a short while, he'd come to know and appreciate Julia and believe in her. He believed her, too. "You needn't worry about me. I'm not a child."

"No, you're something worse. You are a besotted man," Barrett said, his tone ringing with all the bitterness he'd exuded since his heart had been broken by a treacherous woman with whom he'd considered himself in love. But she'd been using him only to get to the man she really wished to have, Barrett's brother-in-law.

"I'm not besotted," Harris insisted. And yet, that denial felt weak to his own ears.

"Are you sure of that?" the duke asked, leveling his gaze with Harris'.

Harris opted to take that question as a rhetorical. For the truth of it was, anyone would be hard-pressed not to be taken in, even in some small way, by Julia. She wasn't the self-absorbed type, like Harris and almost all the people he kept company with.

Harris put in the requisite amount of time necessary to not raise further questions, playing several more hands of whist before quitting his gaming hell for the night. Taking the reins of his mount, he headed to the duchess'. Unlike before when Julia had first arrived and Harris had set himself up at the duchess' out of concern for his godmother and worries that Julia's intentions were nefarious, now his return to that household was different. It had taken just a short amount of time to see that not only did she care about the duchess, but that she wasn't capable of hurting another.

A short while later, Harris was handing the reins off to a servant and making his way through a household now doused in darkness. He headed down into the kitchens and found himself at a different table than those of his usual haunts. How was it that he'd not realized along the way that it had all grown tiresome? Tedious. The wagering and the string of mistresses. There'd been an emptiness to his existence he'd not known was there... until his life had been filled in a different way.

A tray of pastries had been set out, as it so often was. Since as long as Harris could remember of his boyhood, the duchess' cook had always had treats assembled and left waiting.

Collecting the tray, he started back through the household, carrying the assortment of treats in a new way. How many times had he snuck down to find them? How many times had they, in fact, been left out for him? That, however, had been more than a simple luxury, one that he'd taken for granted. Those confectionary treats had always been there, and as such, he'd never had a proper appreciation for being so fortunate as to have them and the love that came with them.

As he walked through the household, he peered into room after room, searching out just one.

And then he found her.

Much the same way of the night of her arrival, she was seated at the pianoforte, her back slumped, her shoulders stooped. Attired in a modest night wrapper belted at her waist, she remained seated, giving no indication that she heard his approach.

"Unable to sleep?" he called over.

The lady swiveled on the bench, a reluctance to her movements as she did. Nay, even with the span of space between them, he caught the wariness etched in her heart-shaped features.

"May I join you?" he said, when she remained silent.

Julia immediately hopped up. "Of course."

Both her hesitancy and formality were at odds with the eagerness that had filled his chest the moment he'd spied her there.

As he came forward with his confectionary offering, he considered her and her reaction. What accounted for her hesitancy around him still? And more, what accounted for his absolute loathing of her hesitancy? He was so very comfortable in her presence, while she should still be unnerved around him. And he hated it.

He reached her side.

She was quiet, as he'd never before seen her, her gaze worried.

"I come bearings gifts," he said in a bid to break the awkward impasse.

Blinking slowly, she moved her gaze from him to the tray in his hands and then back to him. "I... thank you."

Still, she made no attempt to take them, and Harris set the pastries on the pianoforte. Distractedly, she took the tip of her finger to the silver circular platter, setting it into a slight spin, the strawberry and blueberry and apricot preserves forming a kaleidoscope of colors.

At the same time, she gave no indication of any pleasure at his presence this moment. It was a humbling way to find himself. He, a man who'd rarely found himself without interest or attention of some sort.

"Reservations about your debut?" he murmured.

At his mention of the ball scheduled for tomorrow, her gaze grew veiled, her expression shuttered, and those tangible signs of her guard going up were like another punch to the gut. A reminder of her mistrust of him, and worse, the reasons she had for it. He had been a pompous, priggish arse in so many ways. Blind to the world around him. Self-absorbed.

In an absent way, Julia touched her index finger to the spinning tray, stopping it. She sighed, and in an endearing, girl-like way, she plopped herself onto the bench. Dropping her elbows onto the keys, she set off a discordant jangle. "I didn't anticipate… this," she said gruffly, her gaze nearly perfectly aligned with the pastries.

He found a space on the far corner of the bench. "What part of it?"

"Any of it," she exploded and then drew in a steadying breath. "Any of it," she repeated, this time more calmly. "The fine gowns. The luxuries I couldn't even have dreamed of for the simple reason I didn't know that ones such as they existed." The timbre of her voice grew slightly pitched. "And now a London Season, Harris?"

He reached over and covered her palm with his, conferring support, and under his touch, the heat of her fingers transferred to his, and the tension in those digits eased.

The long column of her throat moved. Her voice fell to a whisper that, even with the midnight quiet, he strained to hear. "I didn't want it, you know."

"I know," he said quietly. He knew that now. At every turn, she'd rebuffed whatever gifts the duchess had attempted to give her. Instead, she'd sought to take more meager offerings and give them over to the less fortunate instead. "It will be all right."

She needed to tell him in her own words. She'd resolved to do so. Having come to know the duchess as she had, Julia knew the duchess would insist Harris accept Julia in Adairia's place. No doubt Her Grace had taken care to omit some of the hardest parts Julia had shared with her.

Because of that, she'd spent the better part of the night crafting and scrapping and recrafting any number of explanations and words to explain why she'd come here and who she was, and yet, she had found none that suited. That was, none that would result in anything more than his assured loathing and disgust, and coward that she was, she didn't want this to end.

But then he went and offered gentle murmurings of support that muddled her intentions and stalled what she knew she needed to do.

Julia bit her lower lip hard.

Why must he be so… kind?

And warmhearted.

And tender.

It made all of this impossible.

It will be all right.

And yet, how could it be? How, when he discovered the truth, it would change everything between them? And it certainly would not be all right when she finally put an end to this charade she'd carried out, with the duchess' permission.

Julia exploded to her feet. "No, I need you to hear me. I don't want this, Harris." She gestured to the ballroom. "I don't want any of it. I didn't think to come here and have a wardrobe made for me." She began go pace. "I needed to escape. To be free of…" Rand Graham's influence and his intent to destroy. "All of it. But then there was Her Grace and the countesses." Julia stopped abruptly, her back to Harris, unable to face him. "And you," she said, her voice cracking. She jammed her fingertips against her temples and fought the panicky little giggle threatening to strangle her. Good God, who would have imagined that she, Julia Corbett, of the Dials would go and lose her senses and reason and fall so hopelessly for a gentleman?

Gentle hands came to rest upon her shoulders, and her body immediately stiffened, but then Harris lightly massaged her shoulders, forcing the tension from her person, and she leaned reflexively back into him and the warmth and support he offered.

"It is going to be all right, though, Julia," he whispered against her ear. "I will be with you."

When he uttered those words, there was nothing else she longed for more.

She remained that way, continuing to selfishly take of his kindness, a kindness he'd certainly not feel were he to know he held an impostor in his arms.

Drawing in a deep breath, she turned in his arms. "Harris—"

"Do you know, Julia, I've been staring at this tray for nearly twenty minutes."

This time, her plans to tell him were brought to a halt for a different reason—confusion. She cocked her head. "My lord?"

He caught her plait and teased the ends of those strands knotted with a bow. "Do you know, I quite despise that formal title on your lips. There is a wrongness to it. It is Harris," he corrected.

He couldn't be any more wrong. Between the stations and lies that divided them, there was no other way in which she should address him—if even at all.

Still, she stole his name for herself one more time. "Harris," she allowed.

"The pastries," he resumed, motioning to the items in question. "I headed to the kitchens and knew Her Grace's cook would have them waiting. I collected them, and I've been staring at them since, and thinking about what I said to you earlier. I told you I counted pastries."

At the look he gave her, a look she struggled to make sense of, she shook her head. "I don't understand what you're saying, Harris."

"I realized how I'd taken luxuries for granted. That since I was a mere boy, I'd not appreciation for the plights of others. And I didn't even really have one, until now. And that is humbling, and shameful, and wrong."

"You didn't live in my world, Harris—"

"That doesn't mean I shouldn't have been aware of it," he cut her off. "The point I'm making, Julia, is… the duchess? She wants to shower you with every luxury you went without. And you have more reason than absolutely anyone to take whatever gift you are given."

Her eyes slid shut. The Lord was punishing her. There was nothing else for it.

But then, the devil had always lived stronger in her, and it was why she opened her eyes, leaned up, and kissed Harris, delaying the inevitable and taking this last moment from him.

Harris stilled, and then his hands were immediately on her. His fingers sank into her hips, and he kneaded that flesh, working his hands over her person, scooping her under her buttocks and drawing her close.

"You deserve more than a stolen moment in a carriage or on a piano bench," he rasped between kisses.

Drawing back, Julia took his hands firmly in hers. She angled slightly away from him, her chest moving with the same desperate force as his. "I deserve to decide who I want to have this moment with," she said, breathless. She'd managed to hold on to her virtue, a nearly impossible feat in the Dials, and reveled in the power that came in giving herself to the man *she* chose. She wanted this. She wanted this one moment with him to take with her when she went. Taking his palms in hers, she brought them to her breasts.

His eyes darkened, and he instantly curled his palms over those swells. Then, ever so slowly, he glided the pads of his thumbs over the pebbled peak of each, teasing her nipples.

She bit her lip to keep in a moan.

He continued to tease that flesh, and then, lowering his head, he kissed her through that fabric, the thin cotton a flimsy barrier to the heat of his mouth. Nay, instead, it only lent a heady eroticism, a kiss that promised everything, with only the thinnest of divides between his lips and her breast.

Harris sank onto the bench and drew her closer so that she stood between his legs. With a restraint that proved he left this moment fully in her hands, he slowly loosened the belt at her waist.

Julia moved his hands away, and then, holding his eyes with hers, she made quick work of untying it. Shrugging out of her wrapper, she let it fall to the floor behind her, and then, tugging her nightdress up, she tossed it aside so that she stood naked before him.

He sat motionless, and then, the same way he'd touched

her before, he palmed her breasts, filling his hands, and she'd been wrong. This was the headiest, most erotic of acts. Leaning forward, he flicked his tongue along the tip of her right breast. Back and forth, he continued that erotic love play.

She moaned, her legs going weak beneath her, but he filled his hands with her buttocks, keeping her upright and continuing his worship. And then he drew a sensitive tip deep, suckling of her.

"Harris," she pleaded, tangling her fingers in his hair and urging him on.

He continued laving her breast, his mouth making wet, noisy, suckling sounds that only raised her desire to a fever pitch. Of their own volition, her hips moved as she arched them in time to his ministrations.

Harris shifted his focus to the previously neglected pebbled tip, bestowing the same attention to it. A hot, heavy wetness formed between her legs, and she couldn't bring herself to feel a proper shame.

Moaning, Julia let her legs fall open.

"Do you want this?" he asked harshly, cupping her between her legs.

"I should say I do not," she panted. She lifted her hips in a bid to get closer to his touch. "It's certainly shameful, but I want it, Harris. So badly," she keened.

Passion darkened his eyes, and he reversed positions. He perched her on the pianoforte, all the while continuing to stroke his fingers within her, teasing her nub. The keys tinkled a discordant medley of passion and yearning as she moved under his masterful touch.

Every arch of her hips brought more of that uneven music filling the Music Room and her ears, blending with the rasp of their ragged breaths, all mixed together.

Of their own volition, her legs splayed wider, and he palmed her there, cupping her in that place where she needed him most. Giving her what she craved.

Julia bit her lower lip hard to suppress the wanton little moan filtering past her lips.

"Do not hide your pleasure from me, Julia," he whispered, his husked baritone surely the one that Satan himself used when tempting the weak to sin. "Let me hear it."

And God help her for being weak, she let the next keening whimper fall, making no attempt to stifle that wicked sound.

"I love your breathy little moans," he praised, sinking onto the pianoforte bench.

"Wh-what are you…?" Her words trailed off into an airy whisper of nothingness as stroked his long fingers along her naked calf, and then higher.

The chill of the room caressed her skin, hot melding with cold.

And then, slowly, he lowered his head, and she held her breath, scarcely daring to breathe as he dropped a kiss on the inside of her thigh.

She shivered. The sough of his breath tickled in the most delicious way.

"I want to make you scream, Julia," he enticed between the kisses he left upon her inner leg. "You'd like that, too, wouldn't you?"

He hovered with his mouth near the apex of her thighs,

and her breath caught loudly.

Harris threaded his fingers through her damp curls, and she bit her lip, arching, pleading with her body's movements. "Do you know what I want more than to hear your pleasure?"

All words failed her.

"I want to feel you." With that, Harris slid a finger inside her sodden channel.

Whimpering, she nodded her head jerkily.

Harris lowered his lips to her ear, suckling at her lobe. "Tell me with your words, love."

Resisting the shamefulness of that, she managed to shake her head.

He continued to stroke her, a delicious rhythm that brought her hips in a rise-and-fall motion that was beyond her control.

And then, suddenly, he stopped.

She whimpered.

"Uh-uh, love," he teased. "Tell me how much you want it."

He removed his fingers, and her entire body buckled at the loss.

"So badly," she panted, and he slipped another long, masterful digit inside, rewarding her for her surrender.

Grateful for that gift, she slid her eyes closed and sank onto the keyboard. Then he began to work her, moving his fingers in and out of her. Over and over.

Moaning, Julia clenched her legs about his hand, thrusting her hips in a bid to assuage that throbbing ache. It wasn't enough. She needed more of him.

Then something hot and wet touched her there, in that most private of places, and her eyes went flying open, and a gasp escaped her as she registered it was his mouth, giving her the most intimate of kisses.

Her hips shot up, and she immediately arched her hips back.

"Do you like this, Julia?" he whispered between each glide of his tongue.

Panting, she let her head fall back and surrendered fully to this moment. He alternately lapped and suckled of her. She shouldn't like it. This was shameful and wrong, and her hungering for this wickedness was surely a product of her birthright—

He tasted her once more, and she slammed her hands behind her, pressing the keys hard. "Mmm." She lifted her hips frantically into his questing mouth, grinding herself against him in a bid to get closer... to him, closer to that glorious peak of desire he'd brought her just yesterday.

"You taste so good," he panted against her thatch, his breath hot against her moist curls. "But I want all of you, Julia."

I want all of you.

He paused, lifting his gaze, his meaning clear, his request clearer. Forcing her heavy lashes up, she held his stare. "I want that, too."

She wanted this memory, all of these glorious ones, before she left and faced the ugly that was awaiting her.

Shoving back the threatening images that danced at the corners of her mind, refusing to let them enter and steal these last moments of joy, she cupped Harris' cheek with a hand that shook.

Passion darkened his gaze, and then he was moving away.

She silently cried out at the loss of him.

But he was only draping his jacket on the floor and then returning to lower her on top it. Raising herself onto her elbows, Julia watched unabashedly as Harris tugged his shirt off, and she drank in the sight of him, the chiseled planes of his flat belly, the light matting of hair upon his chiseled chest.

Harris tossed that lawn article aside. His boots and breeches followed, and then he stood before her, gloriously naked. She lowered her gaze to that enormous shaft jutting proudly out between his legs. He was enormous, hard all over, and that part of him was no different. Desire flooded her core. Julia lifted her arms up, reaching for him.

And then he was coming down, covering her body with his and lowering his mouth to her breasts once more. Bringing those mounds together, he flicked his tongue back and forth teasingly, laving both tips together until Julia was incoherent with need. Until her thoughts dissolved, her speech along with them.

He drew slightly back, and her eyes flew open.

Julia turned a questioning look upon him, silently pleading that he'd not developed some ridiculous sense of honor, praying he'd not stop.

"Are you certain you want this?" he asked, his voice gravelly and rough from desire and the restraint he exercised.

She held his eyes. "This is the only thing I'm certain of any longer, Harris," she whispered, and not wanting any more questions or breaks in this magic, Julia leaned up and kissed him.

It was as though the touch of her lips freed him.

She faintly registered his knee nudging her legs apart, and Julia let them fall wider.

Harris lay between them, bracing himself on his elbows so that he framed her body, and then he moved slowly. He stopped at that barrier she'd so protected through the years. Julia's chest rose and fell fast and hard.

He touched his lips to her temple; placing a tender kiss there that brought her eyes fluttering shut. She forced her lashes open; wanting to see him; to memorize each angular plain of his face, committing it and him and this moment to her memories, forever.

Dropping his brow to hers, he held her gaze. "Forgive me," he whispered, and then thrust.

She gasped; her body convulsing at the unexpectedness of that intrusion.

Harris instantly stilled; allowing her body time to adjust to his enormous length inside her. "I'm so sorry," he murmured, taking her lips under his once more, and she melted under that kiss, and then, he withdrew.

She tensed; fearing he'd stop, wanting this moment to go on forever.

But he only slid inside her, again.

Her sodden channel slicked the way for him, and even as the fit was tight, he glided smoothly within her.

Julia let her head fall back, and her eyes fell shut as she took all of him within her. Her heart raced, pounding hard against her rib cage in time to their matched ragged breathing.

Harris buried his head against her neck, his breathing harsh, as though the restraint he showed took a physical effort.

Julia wrapped her arms around him, and gliding her fingers up and down his back, she lifted her hips and urged him to move.

And he did.

Slowly at first, gentle in a way she'd never known sex could be, in a way that she'd never observed in the rough, quick takings she'd seen more times than she could remember over the course of her life. As he thrust and retreated, he teased her with his fingers until Julia was aware only of a pleasure so acute, it hovered on the precipice of pain.

"Please," she begged him. "Harris."

His face tense, his jaw clenched, he thrust deeper. Harder. Faster. Giving her exactly what she hungered for.

He gripped her hips sharply, his fingers digging into her flesh in a primitively possessive way, as though he wished to lay claim to her, and that was all she wanted and would ever want, to be possessed by him. Every thrust pulled her higher and higher to that climax she'd experienced in his arms, and she wanted to taste that explosion once more.

The pressure grew between her legs, so very sharp, and Julia bit down on her lower lip, and then she reached that glorious pinnacle. Crying out his name, she lifted into Harris' thrusting and came. Her toes curled until the soles of her feet arched at the exquisiteness of her climax.

Harris' hips took on a slightly jerky, erratic rhythm as he rammed himself into her deeper, and then, with a low, pained-sounding groan, he withdrew and spent himself in a shimmery arc onto the floor beside them.

He released a final raspy breath and then collapsed onto his side, drawing her beside him.

And as Julia lay there, curled against his side, folded in his embrace, she realized how wrong she'd been.

Having this one glorious moment in his arms would never, ever be enough.

Chapter 17

He was going to marry her.

He'd bedded her, and that was, of course, the right and honorable thing to do.

Nay, this went beyond mere honor. This was a visceral need to be with her. To see his world anew through her eyes, and to see the greater world through her eyes too. He just needed to collect his mother's ring.

Whistling a jaunty tune, he headed through the entrance of his foyer and tossed his cloak to the waiting butler.

"My lord, you have a visitor."

The somber thread in his butler's voice managed to penetrate his joy and halted Harris in his tracks.

"Mr. Steele," Manfred murmured. "I took the liberty of showing him to your office."

"Steele," he echoed. Of course. He'd hired the man on behalf of his godmother. And yet, somewhere along the way, he'd brushed aside the fact that while Harris had been with Julia, the detective had been investigating her.

Manfred cleared his throat. "Should I not have done that, my lord?" he ventured. "I can tell him you are unavailable."

Harris started and gave his head a shake. "No. No. Of

course. Not at all. I'll… see him."

With that, he shifted course and headed for his offices. As he went, he was unable to escape the unease.

Stop it.

There was no reason for it.

The man had been due to report back on anything he discovered—or didn't discover—about the duchess' lost niece. Just because Steele had come to see him didn't mean he'd found out anything concerning about Julia.

Except, the minute Harris opened the door and found the grave-looking gentleman waiting, all those assurances he'd given to himself slipped away as that feeling of dread reared its head. The emotion slithered like a snake and spread its serpent's poison as it went.

"Steele," he said. Closing the door, he crossed over to his desk.

Steele immediately came to his feet. "Lord Ruthven," the other man greeted, availing himself to the seat as Harris motioned to it. "I've come with a report on the person you asked me to investigate."

Guilt.

"It wasn't necessary," he said gruffly, knowing Julia as he did. "Her Grace is confident in the veracity of the lady's claims, as am I now." There'd never been a need to involve the famed detective, and guilt soured in his gut at the fact that he'd gone against the duchess' wishes and enlisted the man's assistance. "Therefore"—he pulled out his center desk drawer—"your services will no longer be required."

"Your intuition was correct, my lord," Steele said quietly, and Harris froze, his fingers hovering over the banknotes he'd been about to write.

"Correct?" he repeated dumbly, not following the other man's words.

Or is it that you don't want *to follow them? Because you don't really wish to know what he's actually saying.*

Grabbing a folder from the chair beside him, Steele opened the file, and as he spoke, he handed over a series of pages. "I can report definitively that the lady is not, in fact, the duchess' missing niece, Lady Adairia. There have been a number of people who've identified the woman now residing with your godmother as Julia Smith."

With every word uttered by the investigator, Harris' heart beat faster and harder in his chest, his pulse hammering away in his ears, threatening to drown out the remainder of words that Harris didn't want to hear. And yet, he had to.

"The young woman is not who she claims to be," Steele explained. "She is, indeed, an impostor. I am still uncovering details of her origins, but she was a flower peddler born to a failed opera singer in the Dials. Her identity has been confirmed by a number of individuals."

An odd humming filled Harris' ears, and he fought to follow the detective's revelation.

Her name was real.

That, at least, was true.

That had to mean something.

"Surely... these people cannot know that?" Even as the question left him, Harris knew he was merely grasping at straws, desperate to believe anything other than this. Still, hope couldn't stop the queries from coming. "After all, how can they?"

"Because she is well known. There is confirmation from those old enough to remember when the young woman's mother was carrying the child. They recall her birth and early years." Steele reached for another paper. "This, however, is where the story becomes interesting."

Harris briefly closed his eyes. *It's not a damned story,* he silently raged. What they now discussed wasn't a tale in a book with twists and turns, but details about Julia, a woman whom he'd come to care about... and believe. Harris made himself lean forward, stretch a hand across the desk, and take the latest page. How was his hand not quaking? How, when every part of him shook inside?

A vise squeezed at his chest, threatening his ability to get air in through his lungs.

"I trust it is difficult learning the duchess has been deceived once more," the investigator said, with more a calm pragmatism than with any actual tone that conveyed regret or sadness.

The duchess has been deceived once more. This *was* a path they'd wandered down so many times before this, and yet, not like this. This time, it was different. Or Harris had believed.

Harris had let his guard down with Julia. He'd come to care and... His mind shied away from the possibility of what else. And all along, she'd been a pretender. The greatest of them all. She'd made him believe in her innocence, and he'd become enrapt with her awe of the simplest pleasures and captivated by her willingness to help those in need. Had it all been pretend? A grand facade she'd expertly played? Or had her actions been motivated by guilt for the comfortable life she'd taken for her own, all the while remembering how people in those streets still lived? He steeled his jaw... and his heart. Once again, he'd been duped. Deceived.

"The news is not all bad," Steele said, pulling Harris back from his raging thoughts.

"Really?" Harris asked, unable to keep the bitterness from coating his query. "The woman whom my godmother accepted into her household and who managed to convince"—*me*—"her and everyone around her that she is, in fact, another, and there's somehow... good?"

Please, let there be more. Let there be something that proved Julia was more than a duplicitous creature who'd managed to invade a heart he'd believed incapable of feeling everything it had for her.

"The young woman and her mother, when she was alive, had a second child with them." Steele held his gaze. "The girl went by the name Adairia."

Harris stilled, his own misery and regrets suspended by that revelation.

Steele nodded, confirming the question Harris hadn't asked.

"I am still gathering what I can about both Miss Smith, along with her supposed sister. Unlike those who could account for Miss Smith's mother's pregnancy, there are no such confirmations in the case of the other young woman, who has recently gone missing."

"Gone missing, you say?"

Steele nodded.

A dark, niggling thought took shape at the back of Harris' mind. One that he balked at, one that his entire soul arched away from, because he couldn't give it life. He couldn't give any credence to the possibility that the woman he'd come to care about and for was somehow capable of an even greater treachery than the one she'd perpetuated here. Still, he made himself ask anyway. "Was she... Was Miss Smith," he clarified, making himself say her name, "somehow involved in..." Oh, God, he couldn't even finish the thought.

"There is no indication of that," Steele said matter-of-factly. He paused. "As of yet."

As of yet.

Meaning there was no definitive answer at this point.

Meaning it was entirely possible.

Sweat popped up on his skin, moisture slicking his palms, and he dragged a hand through his hair and then made himself rest those shaking palms on the damning file. He'd let down his guard, and he hated himself for it. And he hated her just as much for having made him weak for even that instant. "Thank you for this information," he said.

How was it possible his voice was so even? How, when he was shaking inside?

"Given the information yielded by my investigation, I took the liberty of stationing men outside Her Grace's residence in the event that the young woman flees, and we lose any potential connection she might have to the duchess' missing niece." Steele stood. "I would also like to schedule an interview with Miss Smith for later this afternoon at the duchess's residence." He handed over a card with a time marked on it.

"Of course." Harris had to tell his legs to move and shot

to his feet. He took that damnable card and stretched his free palm out. "Thank you," he said, shaking the other man's hand. "I appreciate the work you've done."

Work that had made Julia into a liar, and that knocked Harris' world off-balance.

After Steele left, Harris remained rooted to the floor, not certain how long he remained there. Time had ceased to have any and all meaning. Minutes, moments, or hours—whatever they were, they all crawled by.

None of what had been revealed here should come as any surprise. After his marriage, he'd been cynical by nature. What Steele had revealed was consistent with what life had shown him about the ruthlessness of the human spirit and the natural ease with which a person was capable of deceit.

And yet, even with all of that cynicism bestowed by life, Harris had believed in her. He'd believed her.

Squeezing his eyes shut tight, he sucked in a painful breath.

What was worse, he'd fallen in love with her...

And now he was left with the agonizing task of telling the duchess and the countesses that they'd been duped, and in the worst possible way.

A short while later, seated across from his three mothers, it became apparent the moment he uttered his discovery aloud: "You knew," he said dumbly, staring at the trio of women.

"Of course we knew," the duchess scoffed. "Though I do find it in bad taste for that Steele fellow to not inform me of his findings."

"Gentlemen," the twins muttered together in annoyance.

"Always presuming we aren't deserving of information that is directly about us," Lady Cowpen said.

The ladies gave commiserative nods before going back to their notes and discussion… about Julia's debut.

That was it?

That was who and what they'd take umbrage with? Not Julia? Not any aspect of Julia's treachery, but rather, the fact Steele had come to Harris first?

Pressing his fingertips into his temple, he rubbed at the increasingly aching megrim he was developing.

He tried again. "And what of the missing young woman?" he asked carefully.

Tears formed in the duchess' eyes, and for a moment, he regretted the question that had brought his godmother more pain. Her loyal friends each took one of her palms in theirs and held them, conferring support in a touching display of friendship.

"Adairia died," the duchess said, her voice surprisingly strong. "But Julia is here."

Ah, so this accounted for the duchess' graciousness and forgiveness. She'd found in Julia a link, a replacement for the niece she'd lost.

"She lied to you," he said with a bluntness he hoped would penetrate.

"Only at first," his godmother said, and with that, she gave all her focus to the page in front of her and began taking notes once more.

Lies.

My God, the world has gone insane.

Surging to his feet, Harris paced a path over the floral

carpet.

And seethed.

As he'd suspected, it had been nothing more than lies. All of it.

Every fear he'd had. Every doubt had proven correct.

Of course, one would never know it by the serene smiles worn by the three elderly ladies who'd delivered the announcement. The same ladies who'd since moved on in conversation, sipping tea and munching on chocolate while planning Julia's entry into Polite Society.

"Come, come, Harris, join us," Lady Cavendish urged. "We had the maid prepare you coffee."

"We also have some of your favorite biscuits," her sister piped in, her mouth full even now with a powdery treat.

He stopped abruptly and stared over at them. "Biscuits?" he said incredulously. "Biscuits?" Because, well, it really required clarifying.

Her mouth powdered with sugar, Lady Cowpen held her plate aloft. "Biffcits," she said, and then swallowed the remainder of her bite.

The world had gone insane. There was nothing else for it.

"Sit down, Harris," the duchess said impatiently. "I am getting dizzy watching you pace so, and I do not like it."

He promptly joined his godmother, taking up a place on the King Louis XIV chair opposite the trio. "I'm sorry, are you—?"

"No need to apologize, dear boy," Lady Cowpen called over.

"I'm not apologizing," he gritted out.

"Well, that is just rude," Lady Cavendish said, and his neck went hot as she turned to her twin for sisterly support. "Have you ever known Harris to be rude?"

He opened his mouth to get a word in.

"Never," the other countess responded, shaking her head. "It is not like him at all."

Her sister leaned close, whispering loud enough for the next household on Grosvenor Square to hear her. "This is what Polite Society says he's like. I just never thought I'd see that rudeness turned my way."

"I've not done anything wrong," he exploded. "I'm not being rude. I'm being perfectly calm and rational!"

"That certainly remains to be seen," Lady Cavendish mumbled. "All that back-and-forth running you're doing around the room."

He felt the rush of color flooding his cheeks and briefly closed his eyes to rein in his temper. It didn't help to diffuse his outrage and annoyance. "I'm not the one you should be turning your ire on." He jabbed a hand toward the closed door. "The deceitful woman resting comfortably somewhere in the duchess' household, however? She is another matter. She is the one deserving of your displeasure." And most decidedly not him.

If looks could kill, he'd have been smote by the furious stares trained on him by the three most terrifying matrons of Polite Society.

He'd never seen it before this instant. He'd always been the favored one, the son born to their dearest friend. That was, until now. Now, he had a taste of how the rest of the *ton* felt around such a terrifying presence.

"Are you quite done throwing your tantrum, Harris?" the duchess asked in her perfectly crisp, duchess tones, those she reserved for the ones who'd displeased her.

His tantrum?

Of course, the safer answer would be a decided and prompt yes.

Even when thoroughly insulted, as he'd just been by Lady Hawthorne.

Only, the duchess—and Ladies Cowpen and Cavendish—however, had been like mothers to him. And as such, he'd face their displeasure and confront it head on before he conceded this. Even so, when he spoke next, he did so with more measured tones, attempting to break through whatever madness gripped the three ladies. "She is... an impostor," he said quietly. "She lied to you." *To me. To all of us.* "And you want to welcome her into your household to stay on as a guest for... for...?"

"As long as she wishes to remain," his godmother said coolly. "I've already initiated talks with my solicitor. If she'll agree, I'm adopting her."

How was he the villain in this? "Indefinitely, then."

She raised her dainty floral porcelain teacup and took a small sip.

"You aren't thinking logically—"

"Have a care, Harris. I may be your godmother, and I may love you dearly, but I am not a woman who will take to having my logic insulted and my decisions questioned."

He remained motionless, and then, with a silent curse, he surged to his feet and began to pace again.

She is a dupe.

A liar.

Just as he'd suspected.

His strides grew increasingly frantic.

He thought of her at the park, at the edge of that damned Serpentine, looking oh-so-very-bereft, filling his head with lies about her inability to believe in magic and wishes. All the while, she'd been deceiving the duchess… and him. And now, in just a couple of days' time, she'd turned Harris into a villain before these women he loved.

"He's at it again," Lady Cowpen lamented.

"Will you sit?" the lady's twin asked on an exaggerated sigh.

The hell he would.

The hell he could.

Harris continued to frantically pace. "I'll not," he seethed.

Lady Cowpen brought her cane down across the next place he would have stepped, a lily embroidered upon the Aubusson carpet. "Sit."

"This isn't your decision, Harris." The Countess of Cavendish, who'd always been the easiest to charm, proved as recalcitrant as the other ladies in the room. "We want her to stay."

"You want her to stay," he repeated incredulously.

The three friends nodded in perfect unison.

"The hell she will." Growling, he attempted to make his way around Lady Cowpen's cane, only to find his feet dueling with that carved cane, dancing sideways and back again.

"Well, good thing for your godmother that this is not

your household to make that decision," Lady Crowley snapped.

"Enough." The duchess commanded greater with that quiet utterance than most military generals did an entire army behind them. Looking to the seat he'd vacated, she conveyed without words her expectations.

He stiffened and reclaimed the seat, throwing himself down into the folds. Resting his hands upon the arms of the chair, he drummed his fingertips.

"Now," she continued, "I understand you do not trust women, since you were trapped by your late wife—"

"This has nothing to do with Clarisse." The denial exploded from him.

She fixed a gaze on him, and he slouched back in his seat.

"You think all women are liars."

"And Julia is."

"But sometimes people lie out of necessity, Harris. And ultimately? Julia confessed. She told us."

That knocked him back in his seat. "She did?"

His godmother nodded. "She did. We've already said as much. *Do* keep up, Harris. Stop repeating everything I say."

That gave him pause, and he sat in silence with that revelation. Why had she revealed herself to the duchess? Why, when the duchess had given every indication that she believed Julia was her long-lost niece?

Liars lied, and yet, Julia had shared the truth with his godmother. What were her reasons for doing so? Had she felt... guilt for the decision she'd made to deceive them? And if so, what had driven her to the point that she'd felt the need to dec—

He caught himself. What in hell was he doing? What in hell was he thinking? He was going to find himself as weak as the trio before him.

Stop finding defenses the woman does not deserve.

Harris set his jaw. "She undoubtedly did it because she identified that you'd respond just how you have."

"Well, that is the silliest argument I've ever heard," Lady Cowpen mumbled around another mouthful of pastry.

"It's all so very disappointing, you know." Her twin dabbed at the corner of her right eye. "He's usually such a clever boy."

"I'm unclever? This from a group who has not considered that you now have a stranger, who we know not at all, in this household. You're all but inviting her to fleece the duchess."

"Are you suggesting Madeira is unclever?" Lady Cowpen demanded.

A hot flush suffused his cheeks once more. "I would never." Rather, he'd been suggesting the three of them collectively had suffered some kind of blow to their ability to reason. "That was not my intention—"

"Because I'll not have you insulting my twin. Only I am permitted to do that, Harris."

His godmother set her teacup and saucer on the rose-inlaid table between them. "That is enough. The matter is settled. Julia will stay. She will continue with the same training she's already begun and she will have her Season—"

Harris choked.

"—and be welcomed here."

"You still intend to do this?" he asked flatly. "Present her as your niece?"

"I will not lie. I will just not make an effort to correct wrongly drawn conclusions."

He bit his tongue to keep from pointing out that a lie of omission was still a lie.

"Now, I don't need you here bickering. Rather I intend to explain how it is to be, and if you are displeased with my decision…" She looked to the door, and he followed that pointed stare, more than half expecting to find the interloper there. But instead, he found the panel firmly shut.

Harris furrowed his brow and then froze as her meaning slammed into him. "Are you suggesting you'll show me the damned d-door?" he sputtered.

"Have a care with your language, Harris." She made a tsking sound and leaned over to pat his knee the way she'd done when he was a boy. "Of *course* not." She paused. "I'm *telling* you. If you aren't happy about my decision, and the lady's presence offends you so much that you can't treat her with the same decency and respect you treat all your wanton widows, then you are welcome to leave."

His wanton widows? Really? That was what she'd somehow turn this into? A condemnation of him and how he lived his life?

"Harris?" she pressed.

"I will be all things polite," he gritted out. Polite when he showed Julia the damned door.

She smiled. "There. That was not so hard, was it? You are dismissed."

Shoving to his feet, he dropped a stiff bow and let himself out.

The moment the footman stationed beside the parlor door drew that panel shut, Harris cursed. His steps grew furious as he strode the length of the hall.

They'd been lied to.

What was worse, his godmother had taken the liar under her wing, and as someone who knew firsthand that woman's loyalty, he knew there was no shaking her of her decision. Nay, unless she herself arrived at a conclusion, no one—not Harris, not her best friends the countesses, not even God Himself—could sway her.

Nay, the only way to see that the duchess was no longer being taken advantage of was by going to the woman herself and showing her the damned door himself.

"Where is Julia?" he demanded of a passing maid.

The girl started. "Th-the gardens, my lord." Bobbing a hasty curtsy, the girl bolted off.

Splendid. Now he was scaring damned maids.

With that, he went in search of Julia.

Chapter 18

J ulia had always hated flowers.

And yet, studying the bright pink, fully unfurled peony, she found it hard not to appreciate the wonder of that bloom. Perhaps flowers weren't so very bad, after all. Mayhap, blinded by her struggles as she'd been, she'd just failed to see and appreciate their beauty.

She'd never before seen those flowers when they'd still been growing from the lush earth, unfurled, fresh, and lush.

A tiny black ant crawled around, making those whispery petals its playground.

At the quiet crunch of gravel, her head came shooting up.

A lightness suffused her breast, as it always did at the mere sight of him. "You!" she exclaimed, flying to her feet.

He reached her side. "Me." His lips curled at the corners, and Julia faltered.

He wasn't smiling. Julia worked her gaze quickly over his beloved face, the harsh lines even harder, the muscles tensed, his mouth unyielding. And his eyes were frosty, distant. Removed. He was very much the cold stranger who'd greeted her upon her arrival. Julia's heart slipped in her breast.

And she knew.

She knew it with the same intuition she'd known Adairia was dead when she'd discovered her gone. Or the day her mum had died.

Awfulness had a way of carrying a lifelike presence and force.

Her stomach knotted viciously and painfully. "What is it?" she asked softly. "Why are you looking at me like this?" What accounted for this sudden coldness?

"Tell me, how should I look at you?" he countered frostily, his voice cold enough that, even with the sun's warm rays beating down upon the earth, it managed to bring the gooseflesh up on her arms. "How should I look at a woman who is both a liar and impostor?"

She went motionless. A liar and an imposter? "What?" her voice barely registered to her own ears over the sound of her pulse hammering away in her ears.

His nostrils flared. "An investigator confirmed all that a short while ago. And my godmother confirmed as much not long ago."

Her stomach lurched. He hadn't known...? No. That wasn't possible. "I believed the duchess had told you and that is why you had stopped with all the questions," she whispered. "You knew before we made love. I asked you if you talked to the duchess," her voice grew slightly panicky.

"We spoke about your Come Out," he snapped. "She asked for me to watch over you."

"Oh," her voice emerged breathy and weak to her own ears.

Harris *hadn't* known the truth about Julia. Instead, he'd learned it from an investigator whom he'd hired to look into her. Of course there would have been. She'd been naïve and foolish to expect there hadn't been. Just as she'd been naïve and foolish to think she could freely take these moments with Harris without there being an absolute loss of his affection once he found out about her. "I thought you knew," she said into the void of miserable silence.

A harsh laugh ripped from his chest, and she winced at the acerbic quality of that mirthless sound. "When exactly when would I have found out, Miss Smith? When were you going to tell me that your being here is a lie and that you aren't, in fact, who you claim to be? Before or after I fell in love with you?"

She opened her mouth when his words registered.

Julia rocked back. "You... love me?"

"Was that part of your plan?" he asked bluntly.

There was no hint of warmth or wonder, just an absolute disgust that added another tear to an organ that would never, could never, be repaired.

"Of course not," she pleaded, turning her palms up in supplication. "I didn't think someone like you could—"

"Because I'm a cold, cynical nobleman?" he snapped, cutting her off.

"No," she stammered. "That isn't what I was saying." God, she was making a mess of this. Julia sucked in a jagged breath and raised her eyes to his. "I didn't think someone like you could love someone like me."

In the end, he didn't. In the end, in this moment, he looked upon her with the same antipathy and disdain the whole world always turned her way.

Julia caught the flesh of her inside cheek between her

teeth.

In fairness, she'd not been truthful with him. She might have told the duchess the truth, but Harris had deserved to hear it from Julia. She knew that now. She'd known it then, too. She'd simply taken the coward's way and allowed the duchess to take the lead, and there was no forgiving that. Even so, selfish as she was, she didn't want what they'd shared to end, not like this. Not at all.

Julia made another attempt to explain away something that could never be accepted. "I tried to tell you last night in the Music Room. I wanted to talk to you and then…" Her cheeks warmed.

He continued to stare hard at her, his gaze unrelenting in its coldness. He'd not make this any easier for her. But then, why should he?

Julia took a slow breath. "Then… last night… happened, and I was lost in what we shared, Harris. I didn't want that to end."

"What we shared?" he repeated with such acrimony, her chest ached. "What exactly did you share?" he asked in such flat, emotionless tones her heart clenched viciously. "We made love and you?" He scraped a derisive stare over her. "You gave me lies."

Julia flinched. Lies? "I didn't lie to you," she whispered; her voice trembling, she lifted her palms up.

He took a furious step toward her. "While I told you about my wife, and my marriage, and—"

"I shared parts of myself with you, too, Harris," she implored. "And I didn't lie. I told the duchess the truth." Julia had just erroneously assumed his godmother would share that revelation with him. Panic built inside. *Was it that you erroneously assumed what you did? Or did you let yourself believe what you wished so you didn't have to have this very discussion you now are with Harris...?* Julia took in a deep, shaky breath, and tried to make him see. "I'm not Adairia, but Adairia was my sister."

He surged forward. "She was *not* your sister," he barked, and Julia recoiled from that vitriolic rage. "She was the duchess' rightful niece." He jabbed a finger at the air, punctuating that truth. "And you, madam, are nothing more than a charlatan. A pretender. Just like my dead wife"

Her heart splintered slowly, the break infinite and never ending, the rending continuing with every disgust-coated word that left his lips.

He was correct once more. Julia, however, didn't know what caused her very soul to ache more, though—the fact that she couldn't reach Harris in any way, or the fact that he was right.

The fight seemed to go out of Harris. Falling back on his heels, he dusted a hand tiredly over his face.

I've done this. I've hurt him. I was the one responsible for breaking his trust and... his heart.

"I trust you do not like me much, my lord," she began softly.

"I shall not tell you what I'm really thinking about you or my feelings on your being here," he said coolly. "Because if I do, then I'm the one who'll find myself thrown out on my arse, while you"—he flicked a derisive glance over her person—"will be free to remain."

He might as well have kicked her in the stomach, so

strong was the urge to double over and give in to the pain of his dismissiveness and coldness.

"I have no intention of tattling on you," she said quietly.

Harris stared at her for a long while. His features a glacial mask as they were, she couldn't make heads or tails out of what he was thinking, and perhaps that was for the best. Because she didn't really want to have any more of his contempt turned so fully upon her.

Then he whistled slowly through his teeth. "My God, you are good. What were you before this? A Covent Garden actress?" He peered at her. "I thought from the onset that there was something familiar about you."

"I told you I'm a flower peddler," she said, searching for a hint of remembrance of that day when they'd met briefly in the street, and he'd saved her life.

"You also told us that you were Lady Adairia, and"—he swiped a hand in her general direction—"look how true that proved to be."

It had been inevitable.

He'd never trusted her. He certainly wouldn't now knowing Julia was nothing more than a common street rat.

If she'd understood those sentiments had been inevitable, why did it stab so at her heart?

Leave him to his unfavorable opinion. He was deserving of it. "I am... sorry," she said, her voice catching. Locking her fingers together, she stared down at the joined digits. "It was not my intention to... lie to you or Her Grace." She grimaced. "Not at first. It... just... happened."

"It just happened, *Julia*?" he echoed, and then he gave his head a disgusted shake.

"What do you want? How can I make this right?" she pleaded. Even as she already knew...

"There isn't anything," he said with a coldness that froze every hope.

Nay, it was futile. She'd known Harris just a short while, but she knew him to be a proud man. He would not so easily forgive once deceived.

They stared at each other, at an impasse. He locked in his hatred of her, and she, her abiding love for him.

In the end, both were spared from speaking next.

Stebbins appeared, and they both looked over, having failed to hear the kindly footman's approach. He cleared his throat. "Her Grace has requested Lady Julia's company in the library. She has a caller."

Neither said anything for a long while, and Stebbins shifted back and forth on his feet.

"Thank you, Stebbins," Julia finally said. "That will be all."

He lingered there, offering her a supportive look before bowing deeply and taking his leave.

Would he be kind still if he knew the truth? Which was inevitable.

Julia looked to a stone-faced Harris. "I am so very sorry," she repeated. "Sorrier than you can ever know. I was scared. I didn't know where to go, or what to do, and so I came here." She lifted her chin. "Now, if you'll excuse me, my lord?"

"Oh, you know, I don't think I will, Miss Julia Smith. Is that even your name?"

"It is." She managed to keep her voice even. "My mother was a mere 'Smith'. She was an opera singer and chose

Mackenzie as the surname she used." A performer who'd been a master of pretend and make-believe, Julia's mother had made up a more interesting surname. "She felt it had a grander sound." *Stop rambling.*

His eyes narrowed. With scorn? Pity? She wanted neither sentiment from this man... or anyone.

"I don't trust you."

"You never have," she said sadly.

It was as though the fight went out of him, and his features slipped from that previously unyielding mask. "But that isn't really true." Such pain crept into his gaze, she wanted to hold him and ease the pain that she had wrought. "I came to trust you and confide in you, and..." He stopped talking, and giving his head a shake, he looked away. When he looked back, all that harsh frostiness had firmed up his features. "And despite my initial reservations, and against all my better judgment, I was proven correct."

And with that, she tired of his berating. Yes, he had a right to his feelings, but what else would he have her say? What else would he have her do? She might have lied to him, but even if she'd been truthful with her identity and presence there, he'd never have liked her or trusted her because of where she'd come from. Julia tilted up her chin. "My, how very proud you must be to have ascertained the truth. Do you want a prize?"

His eyes went black, and for a moment, she thought she'd stepped too far with her jeering. She took a hasty, reflexive step away from him.

"Do you think I'm going to hit you?" he snapped.

It wouldn't have been the first time she'd found herself

with an errant cuff or slap from a lord to whom she'd stepped too close. "Of course not," Julia said. She knew, however, Harris wasn't the manner of man who'd put his hands upon a woman. Odd that the pain of his rejection proved far greater than any blow she'd been dealt. She hugged her arms around her middle, attempting to ease the agony of this loss, one that had always been inevitable. Needing to put some distance between herself and his palpable hatred, and to keep from crying in front of him, she let her arms drop. "If you'll excuse me? The duchess is waiting." She turned to leave.

"Julia?"

Hope brought her whipping around.

"Mr. Steele has requested to meet with you. I expect he is your caller waiting in Her Grace's library."

Her mouth dried up as fear seeped in. "I... see." The whole of her life, she'd attempted to stay on the right side of the law. A person in St. Giles was presented with enough danger in those streets that earning the notice of a constable and facing Newgate, or worse, had been a risk she and her mum and Adairia had never undertaken. For the whole of her life, she'd lived as honorably as she'd been able, never committing a single crime. Only to find now that she'd ultimately landed herself in that great place of peril after all. "Are you going to turn me over to a constable?" She made herself ask the question she most feared an answer to. "Are criminal charges to be brought against me?" she continued, her voice shockingly steady.

He winged a tawny brow up. "That would depend. Have you done anything that would merit a place in prison?" He gave her a probing look. "That is, other than adopt a false identity and pass yourself off as someone you're not?"

It didn't escape her notice that he'd failed to provide Julia with any assurances as to her fate, that he'd not ruled out Newgate. And her heart somehow found a way to break apart all over again. For this was really what he thought about her. His opinion was so very low. It was how she knew that absolutely nothing she could say was anything he'd either understand or forgive. "I'll speak with this investigator," she said, and turning on her heel, she made her way out.

Harris joined her in a walk that felt never ending through the duchess' sprawling residence. He was stiff and silent at her side, and she mourned the loss of what they'd shared. She missed his teasing and their banter. She missed everything good and wonderful they'd shared. Her fractured relationship with Harris was the absolute last thing that should consume her in this moment. About to face a detective and have her fate and future decided, she should be thinking about what questions he had for her and what would happen to her after she answered them. How ironic to discover that she, who'd never been a dreamer, or hoped for love or anything more in life, should find herself so totally bewitched and consumed by Harris Clarendale, the Marquess of Ruthven.

At last, she and Harris arrived.

Julia lingered there, her gaze drifting to the tall, commanding gentleman who stood at the center of the room and then back over to Harris. His features remained shuttered.

"I know it was wrong that I withheld that information

from you," she said quietly, her fingers clenching and unclenching in the fabric of her skirts before she caught that distracted action. "But everything else I told you... was truth. My name is Julia. My mother chose my name for the reasons I gave you. I never knew my da, and Adairia... she was my best friend. She was my sister, mayhap not by blood but in every way that did and does matter." Her voice grew earnest as she spoke. "But then Adairia was"—killed—"lost." She could still not bring herself to say it, to think about the fate her friend had met. "And I was scared, Harris. I knew... know what they are capable of." She fixed her eyes briefly on the detective waiting for her. "And I panicked. All I thought of was hiding."

His penetrating gaze bore through her, and there was a spark of emotion within his eyes, a softening?

But then he looked away. "Steele is waiting," he said gruffly.

At that dismissal, absolutely all hope was lost.

Drawing in a breath, Julia nodded and entered.

Even with his renewed disdain, she proved weak, for as she moved deeper into the room to join Mr. Steele, she found comfort in Harris' presence.

They reached the investigator.

"If I may ask you to wait outside while I speak alone with Miss Smith?"

Her stomach muscles knotted.

Harris frowned. "I will stay quiet through your questioning, but I will remain."

"I believe it better if I speak with the lady alone."

Harris opened his mouth to further challenge the investigator.

"It is fine," she said quickly. "I have no concerns speaking alone with Mr. Steele." It was a lie. She was terrified out of her damned mind at the prospect of being alone with him.

Harris held her gaze for a long moment.

"It is fine," she repeated, lying for his benefit.

The moment he'd gone, Harris closed the door quietly behind him, and she was alone with Mr. Steele. His features were strong, but there was still an unconventional handsomeness to Mr. Connor Steele, whose name wasn't unfamiliar in the streets of East London.

"Miss Smith. Please." As though he were the owner of this very room, he motioned to the leather button sofas.

The moment she was seated, he availed himself of the chair next to her. He was broad and powerful, and the chair squeaked and groaned under his weight. "There is something I'd like to speak with you about," he said without preamble, dispensing with niceties and getting to the heart of business.

Removing a sheet from within the folder he held in his fingers, he handed it across the table.

Julia stared at the parchment. "What is this?" she asked carefully.

"Are you unable to read—"

"I can read," she said tightly. And yet, for some reason, she couldn't make herself collect the page from his hand. She didn't want to bring herself to read whatever secrets were contained upon that page.

He returned the sheet to the table. "There was a woman," he spoke in gentling tones, the ones Adairia had always used with their skittish mouser and ones Julia would wager had led countless others before her to spill every last secret and shame to the man before her. "The young woman was a struggling peddler of flowers in the streets…"

"That is a bit of an oxymoron, Mr. Steele," she said, her nervousness resulting in inadvertent levity.

"The woman was something of a loner. A former ballet dancer," Nay. She'd been an accomplished actress and opera singer. "she fell on hard times. Well-mannered. Well-spoken. She was very refined for the Rookeries. She possessed the most striking crimson curls that people always spoke about. They defined her quite distinctly."

"I know all of this. My mother insisted I learn proper English and manners. Toffs give more coin to the well-spoken." Restless, Julia glanced down at the page on the table, and her gaze collided with a name on the middle of the sheet. She swiftly jerked her head up, her heart hammering.

"Do you recognize that name?"

She nodded once, suspecting that query about a simple identification was an attempt at gathering how truthful she intended to be with him.

Steele continued, "The young woman fell in love with a man with a notorious reputation, a man known well by everyone in the Dials and St. Giles." He paused. "His name was Mac Diggory."

A memory slipped in…of her mother telling the story of how she'd arrived at her name for the stage.

Mackenzie was your father's name.

She inhaled deep and shook her head. "No. That's not possible. You're mistaken. I never met him. I only saw him from a distance. My mother"—Julia lifted her palms and brought them slashing down toward the floor—"had no dealings with him."

"No," Steele said in his increasingly infuriating, overly kind way. "She did have dealings with him… prior to her falling pregnant. After she was heavy with child, Diggory was no longer interested." With more of that grating gentleness, he pushed another sheet of paper across the table.

Julia gave her head a shake and pushed the page back at him.

"That doesn't change what's written there," he said gently.

She hesitated and then made herself grab the page. She skimmed the words written there, making quick work of them.

… relationship with Diggory lasted two years…

… the relationship also bore a daughter… by the name of Jewels…

… sold flowers with her mother from the age of four or five, until her recent disappearance…

Julia slammed the page down. "You're wrong." Her heart raced. He had to be.

"I'm not, and I trust you know that."

"I don't know that," she said sharply.

And yet…

Your father was a sailor. Big and brawny and powerful.

Julia frantically searched her mind for everything she remembered about the man named Diggory. Tall. Powerful. Sweat popped up on her skin.

A Scottish fellow named Mackenzie. Everyone feared him, but he was ever so gentle with me.

Mackenzie…

Everyone feared him.

A little moan escaped her, and she bit her lip to keep the remainder of that misery in.

Squeezing her eyes shut, she fought to breathe, but her airflow was nonexistent because of the cinch about her lungs. If what was written there was truth, then that would mean Julia shared the blood of London's most evil, ruthless villain. A monster among men whose reach had been so great, it extended beyond the grave and lived on in a crew still loyal to upholding his memory and the power he'd amassed.

Her entire being arched and twisted away from that truth.

"Diggory had an obsession with the peerage."

"I know that," she said tightly. Between his clubs and the tales of the children he'd kidnapped, the whole world had known of that sick fascination.

Steele leaned in. "After she fell heavy with child, your mother ceased to have any contact with Diggory, but it did not stop her from believing she could reestablish her connection. There are some who've confirmed her efforts. Your mother, Delilah…she found a child with noble roots."

It took a moment to register what he was saying, what he was suggesting. And when she did, Julia went first hot and then cold and then hot again all over. She was already shaking her head.

"It is my belief that she did so in an attempt to make herself appealing once more to Diggory. At that point, however, he'd no interest in daughters born of the peerage."

She jerked, feeling like she'd been run through. "I

don't..." *Believe this or understand.*

Except...that day she had first spied Adairia slipped forward.

"Look at that little girl, Julia. She is lost. Go fetch her."

It had been her mother who had pointed out the sobbing child. It had been Julia's mother who'd urged her to collect her.

And Julia had. God help her, she had done precisely what her mother wished that day, never knowing...never suspecting that anything other than altruism had guided her.

I am going to throw up.

"That girl your mother found and didn't return was Adairia," he finally said, jerking Julia from her tortured thoughts.

Her mother had found Adairia, but she'd never made any effort to locate the girl's family, and in that failure, what she'd done was no different than had she kidnapped the child. And no matter how unwitting, Julia had been just as responsible.

She dug her fingertips against her temples.

Steele dragged his chair closer, sitting so near their knees almost touched. "If you knew, Julia," he said quietly, "there is no crime—"

She let her shaky hands fall to her lap. "I didn't," she cut in on a whisper. "I'm not..." Nay, she wasn't the things this man claimed. She wasn't evil.

Oh, God. Her entire body recoiled from what he'd shared. Lies. Untruths.

"Perhaps you felt you had no choice. You were a child yourself," he said with a gentleness she'd wager he used with all the criminals whose sins he sought to pull from lying lips. "I knew Diggory. No one would fault you for doing that which you had to… in the name of living."

No.

Had she known?

Closing her eyes, she dug her fingertips against her temples. *Think. Think.*

What if she'd known?

Pretty as a princess, she is. A real ladylike sort, isn't she?

"Your mother fell out of his favor. He'd no need for"— Julia—"children who didn't fit with his plans," Steele said. "She saw her. She took her."

Julia gave her head a shake and pushed the page back at him. "No," she repeated. Steele, however, refused to take that sheet.

"She saw Adairia as a way to curry favor with the one man who held all the power over St. Giles."

A moan escaped her, and her fingers curled into balls, wrinkling the paper. "You're wrong." Only, now it made sense as to why Rand Graham's men had attempted to silence Julia. Graham and the ones involved assumed she knew something.

"I'm not," he said quietly, and the sadness in his eyes was real. The pity.

And that was when she knew the truth he handed over, the one she'd known deep inside.

"Why are you telling me this?"

"I'm telling you this because I've reason to believe Adairia is alive, and if she is, and you have some connection with Rand Graham and his gang, you might be able to lead me to her."

Her entire body jolted as through the horror that had gripped her came a slashing bright light of hope. Julia scrambled to the edge of her seat. "What?" she whispered, afraid to dare hope he spoke the truth. Afraid to believe this one piece she desperately wanted to be real.

Except, if what he said was true, then that would mean… Julia had left Adairia to her own devices.

Her hope died a swifter death than a flickering candle in a gust of wind. "They would have killed her already."

"An ethereal woman with whitish-blonde curls was seen with Graham…"

Oh, God.

Julia choked on her horror. Death… it would have been preferable… to this. She pressed her palms against her face, wanting to blot out the implications of what this meant. Graham had made Adairia his plaything. Julia, who'd kept Adairia safe from the advances and assaults, had now failed Adairia so spectacularly.

"Miss Smith," Steele said with a gentle firmness.

Julia let her arms fall, and she stared blankly at the man seated across from her.

He rested a hand on her shoulder, jolting her from the torturous thoughts spiraling too fast out of control. "Who sired you doesn't define you. Nor do the actions you were forced to take as a child."

I didn't take them, she silently screamed. Except, she might as well have. If what he spoke was true, she was as complicit as her mother and every other man or woman who'd committed crimes on the streets of London. Her pulse pounded hard in her ears.

"I was a pickpocket. My wife... sired by Diggory."

She raised a vacant gaze to his. What was he saying? His wife...

Julia jerked her stare from his. It was another detective's trick. "What do you intend to do?" she asked.

"What I have to. Inform the Duchess of Arlington the information I'm now in possession of."

He had to tell them. The duchess employed him. And Julia was a stranger. She was nothing more than a stranger.

But I can make this right. He'd all but given her the names of those in the Dials who'd have a hand on Adairia. If she got to them... If she could find Adairia... "May I tell them... first? About my mother, that is," she pleaded, searching for more time for herself. "I promise, I will..."

"Miss Smith," he said kindly.

Julia bit down hard on the inside of her cheek. "No. No. I understand." She glanced down at the page in her hands.

"That one is for you."

A panicky laugh built in her chest. Like a little gift. A damning, shameful gift he'd proffered. There was another for the duchess... and Harris.

And there could be no doubting that Harris, with the past heartbreak he'd known at his late wife's hands, would never trust that Julia's motives had ever been anything pure. Unless she righted past wrongs. She scraped a hand through her hair, knocking loose combs that clattered with little pings upon the hardwood floor.

"If there is anything you can tell me... if your mother made mention of any of his hideouts, places that I and others might not be aware of."

He truly believed she was in bed with Diggory's accomplices. "I don't know these things," she whispered. "My mother told me nothing about him. Everything I know is because I lived in East London the same as anyone else. He didn't…" *Hide.*

A memory slipped in.

Your father wasn't a man who hid. He was as swashbuckling as a pirate. Bold as you pleased.

"Miss Smith?"

She blinked slowly.

"Is there anything else you think you might provide that could prove helpful in locating Adairia?"

The one who'd stepped in to fill the void left by Diggory also would not hide. Nor would he allow an investigator to slip through his doors and freely take something, or someone, out from under him.

She shook her head. "I… don't know."

Steele stood, and she had to remind herself to move. She shot to her feet. "That will be all, then." With that, he collected his belongings. "I intend to share all of this with Her Grace and Lord Ruthven."

As he should. He'd been hired by them. Julia had another urge to vomit, and she swallowed reflexively again the bile burning her throat. "Of course."

If what he'd said was true, then Adairia had not been lost that day outside the Covent Garden theater. She'd been all but kidnapped by Julia's mother as an offering to Mac Diggory. Julia's entire life proved a lie. Her mother's motives, once seeming good and pure, were soaked in the evilness of what had truly driven her.

There could be no doubting that every ill opinion held by Harris would only be confirmed when he learned about Julia's mother's actions. Nay, neither he nor the duchess, nor anyone, for that matter, could or should forgive Julia. Not given what, according to Steele, her mother had done.

And it turned out she'd lied to him after all. She did have a surname, and it belonged not to a kind Scottish sailor who'd failed to return, but rather, to the most ruthless, hated man in all of East London.

She steeled her jaw. There was just one thing left to do, one thing that could make up, in some small way, for her mother's sins. She would find Adairia and bring her back to the home she'd always wished to be.

With that, Julia did what she should have done that first moment that lie to the duchess and Harris had left her lips, she fled.

Chapter 19

T he duchess' niece was alive.

It was a familiar tale they'd been told countless times before.

This time, however, those suspicions had been brought by one of London's most successful and famed detectives.

When Steele finished his telling, the room remained silent. The older women, who were never without a word between the three of them, were absolutely quiet.

From where he stood in the corner of the room, Harris took in the duchess' reaction.

"Adairia is… alive," the duchess whispered.

"I have every reason to believe she is," Steele affirmed. "I have spoken to the young woman to ascertain just how much she knows of Miss Adairia's fate. I cannot say for certain as to whether Miss Smith had a hand in the lady's disappearance."

Harris' body tensed, his chest tightening as he silently screamed a declination. She couldn't have. Even as she'd proved a deceiver in other ways, he could not believe she would be capable of… that evil.

The duchess frowned. "Of course she did not have a hand in her disappearance," the duchess snapped. "As thickheaded as you men are, it is an absolute sin and crime that you are allowed to rule the world as you do."

The detective hesitated a moment, and Harris straightened. A familiar sense of unease tripped up his spine. "What is it?" he asked.

"Are you familiar with a man by the name of Mac Diggory? He—"

"We know who he is," Lady Cowpen snapped. "A thief of children."

All of London had been fascinated by the stories of the rightful heirs and lords he'd kidnapped as young children. Those stories had only fueled the duchess' hopes. Harris, however, hadn't put much stock in the possibility that Adairia had been taken as those other male children had been.

"Julia Smith was a daughter of Mac Diggory."

Harris' gut churned all the more.

"I questioned the lady as to whether or not she'd assisted in the kidnapping of Lady Adairia."

"Of course it could not have been her. She is near in age to Adairia. When the girl went missing, Julia wouldn't have been older than five or six herself. And you'd think she had a hand in that?" She made a sound of disgust.

Harris stilled. No, the timing of it all didn't make sense.

"I would direct you to worrying less about Julia's supposed guilt and more about my missing niece. You come into this household and make these charges against her. You should know I am going to adopt the girl. She has a safe home here." The duchess gave him a pointed look. "Safe from all."

Steele's cheeks flushed. "It is my responsibility to put

those hard questions to her."

The duchess blanched. "You made these allegations to her?" She didn't wait for him to answer, but swung her focus back to Harris. "Never tell me you allowed this meeting to take place?"

Harris' gut spasmed. With his own initial hurt and resentment no longer fresh, he saw the logic in Her Grace's words. Yes, there'd been the lie, but Julia had been truthful with the duchess. And not only that, while she'd lived here, she'd thought only of helping others. "I expected that, given she'd lied about her identity," he began weakly, "there was the possibility—"

"That she lied about everything?" she barked. "The reason Julia came here was because the same people who harmed my niece came for her. Her life was in danger, and she'd nowhere else to go. She offered to return, knowing what awaited her."

The muscles in his body tightened, and a sharp sensation gripped his chest. For everything Julia had shared, she'd not told him about the peril she faced.

"There is the possibility—" Steele began.

"Not another word from you, Steele." With that, the duchess came to her feet. "I need to make sure Julia knows she always has a home here. If you scared her witless, there will be hell to pay, Mr. Steele." A sound of disgust escaped her, and she swept across the room, marching over to the nearest bell-pull, where she rang for a servant.

Stebbins immediately appeared.

"Fetch Lady Julia this instant."

The young man bowed, and closing the door behind

him, he dashed off.

The duchess, however, wasn't through with her wrath, this time turning her ire on Harris. "You can be as mistrustful and as angry as you want about what happened to you, about being deceived by Clarisse. But that woman? She trapped you. Julia was a friend to my Adairia. She was and is deserving of our support and our security."

Yes, she was.

A young woman who'd fought him on taking a pence to throw into the river, because she'd seen it as wasteful, wasn't the manner of schemer who'd been out to fleece. He saw that now. Shame soured his mouth, sitting on his tongue like vinegar.

The door burst open and the duchess's butler stumbled in, with a caller close behind.

"A Mr. C-Colins," Her Grace's butler, gasping and out of breath announced the latest addition to the room.

"Who in God's name is *Mr. Colins*?" the duchess cried before anyone else could speak.

"Colins is one of my men," Steele said swiftly, stepping forward. "What is it?"

"The lady is gone."

Gone.

Harris' stomach dropped. She'd fled. It was damning, and yet, it also spoke to her fear.

"Gone?" the duchess echoed dumbly. She looked between the two detectives. "You *allowed* this?"

The subordinate looked to his superior, and having been dressed down by the powerful woman before them, Harris had a strong sense of relief that Steele was the one being made to answer.

Steele, however, spoke with all the blunt directness and confidence of a man in full possession of the decisions he'd made. "I expected she'd run. And I expected she'd take us where we needed to go to find your niece. My other man will be tracking her."

"Yes, you did, Steele." Her Grace hissed his name. "By risking Julia's life."

Oh, God. Harris went cold as the implications set in—they'd used her as bait. They'd sent her after the very ruthless people the duchess had insisted she'd been hiding from. Julia had directly placed herself in harm's way with men who'd think nothing of putting their hands upon a woman.

His thoughts came to a staggering, abrupt stop. Beads of sweat popped up on his forehead as a memory trickled in.

The young woman being assaulted in the street, facedown on the pavement with a brute atop her, pinning her to the ground, and another standing in wait.

And then the memories kept coming.

To the evening he'd raced back to the duchess' to find Julia waiting.

"You," Julia blurted.

"She recognizes Harris."

The sick sensation in his gut grew.

"Thank you, sir."

"I recognized you."

"Forgive me. Oi didn't mean—"

Harris' eyes slid shut.

No, it couldn't be.

He covered his face with his hands.

It had been her that day. That had also been the peril that had sent her fleeing. How desperate she must have been to come here and allow him and the duchess to believe she was someone else.

For there could be no doubting that the danger she'd faced had sent her here. She'd been fleeing whatever retribution those men had sought. And he'd been so self-absorbed that he'd not even recognized her as the woman whom he'd helped on the street.

I'm going to throw up.

How could he have not known? How could he have failed to recognize her? What kind of bastard was he that he couldn't, at the very least, have heard her out? Nay, because he'd been blind, and worse, cynical. And that cynicism had clouded his judgment and made it so Julia felt she couldn't trust him.

I don't trust you. I don't believe you. I think you are here to take advantage of a desperate woman's hope.

His heart beat at a panicky rhythm. Nay, why *would* she have trusted him?

"Harris, what is it?" his godmother asked, worry underscoring her query and drawing him from his tortured thoughts.

Stalking over to Colins, he gripped the man by his jacket front and dragged him close. "Where is she?" he demanded, rage and fear warring for supremacy within him. "Where did she go?"

The other man remained silent, casting a glance over at his superior.

Harris gave Colins a slight shake. "Answer me, goddammit," he said, his voice sharp.

"The lady summoned a hack. Ordered him to drive her to Brewery Street."

Harris released him quickly. She was there because of him. He'd given her no reason to trust him, and she'd willingly raced into danger, putting her life at risk... because he'd failed her.

"Take me to her. Now."

She was going to be all right. Because she was strong and spirited and capable and because he wanted to spend his life with her... if she would have him. He'd spend the rest of his life making her happy and atoning for the ugly way he'd treated her.

As he followed after Steele and Colins, he couldn't let himself think about the possibility that they might not get to her in time.

Chapter 20

Julia had always despised the likes of Mac Diggory and now Rand Graham. Evil and violent and eminently unkind. She knew Satan reigned superior over the Lord, because there was no accounting for how such men should be the people in power on Earth.

For all her fear and disdain of Diggory and Graham, she'd also always been in awe of them. They were people so powerful as to not have to hide and shirk and sneak. Rather, they lived as bold as they pleased in a world that existed for the likes of they and Julia.

She'd also had sense enough to steer clear of those places they frequented and inhabited, because once one stepped into their sights, one was invariably trapped.

Now, she made her way through those same streets she'd gone out of her way to avoid, to meet with the very people she'd also sought to avoid.

Because of Adairia.

To save Adairia, she'd have stepped in front of a runaway carriage.

But you didn't, a voice taunted.

You assumed her life and lived on comfortably, all the while she'd been struggling.

Julia tried the door of Rand Graham's residence. All who dwelled in these parts knew where the king of them, dwelled. Unsurprisingly, the rusted panel did not budge. Rather, it jingled and served as a damning announcement of her presence.

Suddenly, the panel was jerked open, and for all her determination to come here and find Adairia, terror reared its head.

A tall, broad man, scarred across the face and as menacing as Satan himself, stared back.

Her feet twitched with the reflexive urge to turn and flee.

Graham's man looked her up and down. His eyes were dead, which was oddly more terror-inducing than had they been filled with the gleeful threat of violence she'd met in the eyes of Graham's other men.

"State your business," he demanded in crisp, surprisingly high-quality English tones. Graveled and rough, though, they countered the lie of gentility within them.

She'd left Adairia once before this, and that was a weakness she never intended to let herself fall prey to again. "I'm here to speak with Mr. Graham," she said, angling her chin up. "My name is Julia Smith, and I am a daughter of Mac Diggory." Because, God help her, if that blood connection to the now-dead gang leader conferred protection, then at least something good had come of her association with him.

The guard displayed no outward response to her pronouncement. After a pregnant pause, he drew the panel open a fraction more, and Julia hurriedly stepped in.

Of all of the horrors she'd expected to face, this was decidedly not among them.

Seated at a smooth mahogany table, Rand Graham, with his dark devil's curls, tossed a card down. The young woman across from him, wholly absorbed in whatever game of cards they played, fanned hers out in the center of the table.

Adairia?

For a moment, Julia did a quick glance about, thinking she'd stepped into another household and had come upon a different young woman with those unique whitish-blonde curls.

Over the top of Adairia's head, Rand Graham shifted his eyes a fraction, that harsh stare landing square on Julia, and she came back to herself.

Julia rushed into the room. "Adairia!" she said sharply, and the young woman whipped around. Relief and joy all swelled in her breast. It was her.

"Julia!" Adairia cried as cheerfully as if they'd met across one of Her Grace's crowded ballrooms. Her friend sprang to her feet.

For a moment, Julia lost her bearings and jerked to a stop. Perhaps they did meet across the duchess' marble floor after all, because dressed in the yellow silk she was, with Adairia elegantly clad in a pale pink satin, neither of them bore a resemblance to pathetic peddlers in tattered garments.

Her friend rushed over, closing the distance between them. "You're here!" she said happily.

"What is going on?"

"This is… Rand…" A pink blush fell over Adairia's cheeks. "Mr. Graham."

Rand. "*Mr. Graham?*" she echoed in disbelief. Her gaze slid over to him.

CHRISTI CALDWELL

"Yes, we were just playing a game of faro."

"Faro?" she said, knowing she sounded like one of those parrots with which the old sailor Captain Marlow had limped around their end of London, but there was no helping it.

Adairia beamed and nodded. "I'm quite good." She looked to London's most ruthless gang leader. "Isn't that right, Mr. Graham?"

Julia's gaze swung to the well-clad figure with whom her friend spoke so easily and comfortably.

His dark lashes fell like blankets on his cheeks, making his eyes narrow pinpricks that revealed absolutely nothing, but not before she'd detected the absolute deadness in eyes so dark blue they were nearly obsidian.

Julia shivered, drawing her cloak closer. "If you'll excuse us for a moment, Mr. Graham," she said tightly.

He pushed back his chair and slowly unfurled to a towering six feet, five inches and stalked over.

She tensed as he paused beside her, giving her a once-over. And then, shockingly, he continued on for the doorway. The moment he'd gone, he closed the door behind himself, and some of the tension slid from her shoulders. His footfalls, however, never moved far beyond the hall, and she'd wager both her and Adairia's lives that, at that moment, he lingered at the door to listen in.

Finding herself, Julia stalked over to Adairia and immediately drew her into her arms. The relief at finding her alive outweighed her shock and annoyance at the seeming friendship she'd struck up with the very man who'd been attempting to kill the both of them.

"I thought you were dead," she rasped. Closing her eyes, she buried her head against Adairia's shoulder.

"No. I'm quite alive and well."

Julia made herself release her friend, but kept her hands upon her shoulders, afraid if she ceased touching her that she'd disappear from Julia's life once more, and this time forever.

"I am ever so happy to see you," Adairia said casually with a smile.

A smile? She would smile about this? As though there was any humor to be found in the fact that she'd been taken and Julia and the world had believed Adairia dead? "Why do you look so happy?" she asked, desperately trying to understand. "He's a vile, deplorable man," she reminded Adairia, keeping her words quiet.

But then, aside from the day she'd been sobbing for her mother outside that theater, Adairia had always worn a smile. In the hardest, coldest winters, when they'd had to snuggle close under a threadbare blanket to steal whatever warmth they could, to the times they'd had no food and only the tempting scents wafting from the bakeries they'd passed on the way to their work.

And Julia was proven wrong as, for this time, a frown brought the younger woman's lips down at the corners. Adairia stepped out of Julia's arms, putting several steps between them. "He's really quite friendly and kind... and misunderstood."

Friendly?

Kind?

Misunderstood?

Julia briefly closed her eyes. Only Adairia could and would see potential good in a place where absolutely none existed.

"He's been trying to kill you," she spoke bluntly. And because that apparently meant nothing at all to the other woman, she added, "He's been trying to kill me."

"Actually, he wasn't." Adairia returned to the velvet-covered gaming table and proceeded to gather up the cards, stacking them and adjusting the deck so it was neatly ordered. "He was attempting to bring us each in to meet with him so we could talk. There are others within Mr. Diggory's previous faction who are attempting to silence the Lost Lords and Ladies. But Rand is decidedly not one of them."

"Rand?" Julia couldn't keep from asking. Her friend was on a first-name basis with the ruthless gang leader.

Dread deepened in her belly at the pale pink blush that marred Adairia's cheeks. "Yes, Rand."

Oh, God. This was even worse than she'd feared. Her impressionable, romantic sister from the streets had gone and fallen for him. "Surely you don't believe that," Julia implored anyway, refusing to believe that Adairia could ever come to care in any way for such a man.

Adairia paused in her tidying and looked across the table to Julia. "I do believe that," Adairia said with the strength of conviction. There was a maturity to her tone, and her command of this exchange didn't fit with the gentle, innocent soul after whom Julia had looked these years. And what was worse was the hardness in Adairia's pretty blue eyes.

"Rand has been perfectly kind and polite."

But the naïve belief she had in Rand Graham, however, was so very patently Adairia.

"He's kept you here," Julia said sharply. "Has he not?" Because the alternative was that Julia had been suffering with the grief of losing Adairia and the guilt of her inability to save her, while Adairia had been able to come back to her, but had chosen not to.

Adairia hesitated, and for a horrifying moment, Julia believed that Adairia had fallen so far under whatever spell Rand Graham had woven, she'd chosen to remain after all. "He was always going to allow me to leave. But he felt this was safer for me, and I knew you were in the duchess' care, so we were both protected."

He was a master manipulator, was what he was.

But then, everyone in the Dials and St. Giles, and all of East London, for that matter, had always known precisely that about the man who'd replaced Diggory.

It didn't matter. Or it soon wouldn't. After she got Adairia out of here, her sister would forget him, and she'd assume her rightful place with the duchess and the countesses and Harris.

"We are leaving, Adairia." She joined the other woman at the card table where she'd shifted her efforts to tidying up the chips scattered about. "We are leaving now."

Adairia didn't so much as look up. "I can't—"

"You can, and we are. We are both leaving, and if Mr. Graham is as kindly and friendly as you claim he is, then he will, in fact, let you go. He'll let the both of us go."

"But there are men who are attempting to silence those

of us who were lost so that they cannot be made to pay the price. Rand is attempting to lead the London streets in a different way. He's not ruling with a ruthless intent the way Diggory did."

Her stomach turned queasy. This was even worse than Julia had feared. There could be no reasoning with her friend, no swaying her to the truth of who Rand Graham, in fact, was as a person. "That is good," Julia said in placating tones. "But he does not need you to do that."

"She is right, Adairia. I don't."

They both looked to the doorway. At some point, Graham had returned with a stealth that spoke to the ease with which he'd no doubt cut down countless men before they'd been aware of what was coming. "The duchess can provide you the protection I have, and… this obviously wasn't going to be forever."

This wasn't going to be forever. Those words had a thinly veiled double meaning, ones that certainly didn't refer to the arrangement of Adairia being here, but something more.

Adairia's lower lip quivered, and she caught that flesh between her teeth.

Julia at last saw through her own misery to the truth. There was no accounting for who the heart loved. She'd never had a right or place with a man like Harris, and she'd always known as much, but even so, even with his disdain toward her, she loved him still. She always would.

Julia slid closer and placed her hand in Adairia's, lightly squeezing.

Adairia's fingers squeezed hers, and she gave a shaky nod. "V-very well. I thank you for your… protection, Mr.

Graham."

He lifted his head in the slightest inclination that Julia would have missed had she not been watching the ruthless gang leader so very closely.

Graham stepped aside, opening the door for them to pass through, and hand in hand, she and Adairia started forward.

A quiet metallic click split the quiet, followed by another.

"She's not going."

The tall, slightly bearded guard who'd allowed Julia entry managed to train a gaze simultaneously upon Rand Graham, at whom he aimed a pistol, and Adairia.

Graham's eyes narrowed. "You're a fool, Lewis."

Lewis chuckled. "Am I? I'm not the one with a gun trained on me, am I, Graham?"

"I knew you were too loyal to Diggory and his legacy," Rand Graham said tersely.

The equally tall and equally scarred stranger smirked. "You let me in your fold anyway. And that is why you were never the heir apparent to Diggory. You, trying to punish the ones who protected him, trying to lead in a different way." Lewis spat, the spittle landing on Graham's immaculate, gleaming, black leather boots. "There was only one way. There is only one way. And if you think you're taking down the men and women who faithfully served, then you are a damned fool. People pay to bury Diggory and their secr—"

With the alacrity of a cat, Graham moved. Kicking a leg up, he caught the other man's left wrist, dislodging that gun.

And with that, everything happened in a blur, with time alternating between a dizzying slowness and a swift rapidity.

Julia turned quickly, shielding Adairia just as another loud report echoed.

Julia's entire body jolted as a sharp pain ripped through her, and then a surprising numbness followed on the heels of it.

A heavy thud behind her indicated one of the men had been felled.

"Adairia!" Rand Graham's voice emerged harsh but strong, indicating he'd been the one to emerge triumphant.

Julia's body sagged with relief. Or… weakness?

Adairia cried out.

Oh, God, no. She'd been too late. Once more, she'd failed to protect the woman who'd been her sister through the years. She'd come this close to saving her only to lose her here. A thick fog clouded Julia's brain.

"You're hurt," she whispered to Adairia.

Except, wait, that hadn't been her whispering. It'd been Adairia. Speaking to Julia.

Julia pressed a hand to her side, and her fingers came away slicked with a wetness. Blinking slowly, she glanced down at her palms. Not just a wetness.

A crimson wetness.

She slid to her knees, the floor rushing up quickly, the jolt to her knees a surprisingly more jarring pain than the numb place in her side.

A buzzing filled her ears, and as if from a distance, she was aware of Adairia wrapping an arm about her waist and weeping as she guided Julia down onto her back. Julia went because she was tired, and it was increasingly hard to focus.

"Adairia," she whispered, her voice distant to her own

ears.

A figure leaned over her. Only, it wasn't Adairia's precious visage. It was another's.

Harris.

She'd conjured him. "You're here," she whispered. Her mouth moved, but her ears failed to detect even a threadbare hint of sound.

She briefly closed her eyes.

"Don't close your eyes," Harris demanded, his voice clear and sharp and as commanding as he'd always been. And angry. He was that, too. But then, he'd always been angry. He yanked off his jacket.

"You're angry." Her heart hurt.

Or was that her side?

She rather thought it was both. Either way, everything hurt.

"Furious," he said. "Furious that you would put yourself in harm's way."

There came a tearing sound, of fabric ripping, and then he lifted her ever so slightly and wrapped something tight around her.

Julia gasped, pinpricks of stars dotting her vision as a burning sensation at her side sent pain radiating throughout her whole body.

Suddenly, the clarity faded along with his deep, mellifluous baritone, which took on a faraway quality. His words faded in and out, blending with a cacophony of sound. Men shouting. Adairia crying. She closed her eyes, attempting to pull Harris' voice forward, back into focus. Because if she focused on him and being with him, then it meant she was still alive and that he was here, and that surely meant, in some small way, he cared.

"Julia… Julia!" She felt hands on her. Hands she knew so very well. So very tender in their touch. And they shook upon her. "Stay with me… I forbid you to… Do you hear me? I forbid…"

What was he forbidding her to do? That was surely an important order, and yet, all she could focus on was just one part: Harris wanted her to stay with him. What did that even mean? In this moment? Or forever? Except, that of course didn't make any sense. There was too much between them, too much resentment and lies for him to forgive. But surely, with the worry wreathing his words, he cared in some small way.

Mixed in with those words came Adairia's weeping, and Julia wanted to open her eyes and tell her sister to stop crying. To remind her that her life was going to be the glorious, happy one she'd always dreamed of.

She just wished she could have been there to see Adairia find all the joy she'd sought.

And she wished she could have spent the rest of her days with Harris.

With those silent yearnings dancing around her clouded brain, Julia remembered no more.

Chapter 21

There had been no love between Harris and his late wife. She'd been largely a stranger to him.

And yet, he would forever remember the day her babe had been coming. Her delivery had stretched from the early-morn hours all the way into the afternoon and then deep on into the night until a new morn had fallen.

Through it all, as she'd fought to give life to her lover's child, she'd refused Harris entry. He had honored that request, having known that day hadn't been about what he wanted or making him feel some comfort, but rather, her and what she'd been attempting to do.

Then there'd been the moment her chambers had gone silent, the sounds of her screams having faded to nothing, and he'd known death had claimed her and her babe.

He'd not believed there could have been anything more agonizing than sitting as a silent witness to someone's final moments. Now, he sat in a different woman's chambers, cloaked in that same thick, heavy silence, and found how very wrong he'd been.

This was more agonizing.

Being hopelessly and helplessly in love with a woman who now fought a different battle for survival.

Only, she wasn't dead. Not yet.

Seated at the side of her bed, Harris rested his elbows on his knees and studied her, just as he'd been studying her. He took in a shuddery breath.

Not ever.

That voice silently raged inside his mind.

Harris dropped his head into his hands, his fingers tangling in his hair, and he tugged lightly to keep from going mad.

It had been three days since she'd taken that bullet, three days since she'd closed her eyes.

While they'd carted Rand Graham off for questioning, along with the other brute, the room had dissolved into chaos, and Harris remembered none of it beyond binding Julia and then carrying her to a carriage.

Through it all, she'd been still and silent. As still and silent as she was now and had been since that day.

She'd placed herself between Adairia and a bullet. She'd offered up her life for another. It had been the ultimate sacrifice, the greatest one a person could make. And he'd never known a person like her, or even that people could be so selfless. Aside from the duchess and her friends, the men and women with whom he kept company were all as self-absorbed as Harris had always been, focused solely on their own comforts and pleasures. All along, there'd been someone like Julia. A woman who'd known struggle and who'd thought only of surviving and caring about the young woman she'd taken under her wing to protect.

And I shamed her at every turn, questioned her honor. Questioned her motives.

All along, she'd been fueled not only by fear, but also by the deep, abiding love she had for Adairia.

He sucked in a shaky breath, his gaze fixed on that slight rise and fall of her chest indicating that she still lived. That she was here with him still. She'd made him realize that life wasn't the black-and-white world he'd taken it for. That there were so very many shades in between. Just as there were layers to people.

Harris, however? He'd been so blinded by his own past hurts and his own feelings that he'd never considered what had driven her. And having had so much time these past days alone to reflect in silence, he'd at last given thought to what compelled his late wife.

He hated that she'd trapped him. He hated that she'd stolen his right to choose his future and his fate and instead tied them together in a loveless, empty marriage. But he could also appreciate now the lack of control she'd certainly felt with her lot in life, as a woman.

Clarisse had been a desperate woman. She'd committed an act born of that desperation. He knew that now. He saw that now. Fear compelled people in different ways, made a person make decisions they wouldn't ordinarily make. Just as Julia had fled those streets and come to his godmother's household, seeking refuge.

Only, she'd withheld the truth only from Harris. Because she'd known he'd respond precisely as he had.

Attempting once more to get a painful breath through his lungs, Harris caught one of Julia's hands in his. Her skin proved pale against his, her fingers lifeless.

And he, who'd believed his heart couldn't ache anymore,

convulsed under the agony of it. "I'm a damned fool," he said into the quiet, needing to hear something, some sound of life, even if it was just his own voice. Because if he was engaged in discourse with her, then she was still with him and not… what the doctor had told him and the duchess to expect as an outcome. "But then, you knew that, didn't you, love?" he murmured, his gaze on her beloved face.

There was no hint of movement or indication that she'd heard. She was so still, her auburn lashes lying upon her pale cheeks.

"I'm so s-sorry," he whispered, his voice breaking. "I'm a damned fool. Stubborn and arrogant, and you deserve better than me." That didn't stop him from wanting that future with her still. With a long, shaky sigh, Harris leaned forward and rested his head on the mattress, facing her. "I've thought about… you… us… these past days," he murmured into the quiet. "I've thought about when it was that I knew I was so very much in love with you. And it was the pelicans." He closed his eyes briefly, recalling that bright spring day when she'd raced off. Harris opened his eyes and smiled. "You just jumped down from the carriage before it had even stopped, and I'd no idea where you were going, and you were just so excited, and I'd never known a person could feel unfettered joy about anything, and I was… captivated."

The floorboards groaned, and he quickly sat up.

The duchess' niece lingered at the entrance of the room, clad in her nightshift and wrapper. "Forgive me," she said softly, and perhaps on another day and at another time, he'd have felt embarrassed by what the young lady had heard, by having voiced aloud feelings so intimate and personal. Not anymore. "I could not sleep. I… wanted to see Julia."

Releasing Julia's hand, Harris remembered to take to his feet. "Of course," he said quickly as she joined him at the other side of the bed.

He should leave. He should allow the young woman her time alone with Julia, as she'd not had a single moment of it since her… their arrival. But he was a selfish bastard in so many ways, and he couldn't bring himself to quit his spot. Dread gripped him at the possibility that when he did, she'd leave him. As long as he was here, she was here, and they were together. He slid into the chair he'd occupied these past days as Adairia found the seat at the opposite end of the bed that she'd made hers at various points throughout the days.

"She is so still," Adairia said. "So very weak. I have never seen her so." A wistful smile danced on the young woman's lips. "She was always so very strong. So much stronger than me. She never thought anything of going toe-to-toe with grown men or more powerful women. Or anyone who thought to try to hurt me."

With every word spoken, Adairia revealed a greater glimpse into the woman he knew Julia to be. And he took in the tales, silently urging the young lady to continue in her telling.

"One time, a gentleman attempted to take me away, but Julia felled him. She was just ten." Pride lit Adairia's eyes. "She took down a grown man and saved me, she did." Drawing her legs up, the young woman tucked her knees in and rested her chin atop them. She had a younger look to her that defied the experiences she spoke of. "Never remember her crying. She was always so busy looking after me and taking care of me."

Oh, God. He wasn't going to survive this. Knowing how she'd struggled. How she'd lived. How she'd suffered.

Tears glistened in Adairia's eyes. "No one ever looked after her, though," she whispered, and Harris was certain if he touched a hand to his chest, he'd find blood where it had broken open and his heart had bled on through. "I never thought about that until the day I came in here to see her sleeping. I never thought about the fact that I'd never worried after her the way she did me. Even when I'd been… taken to speak with Mr. Graham, and I was there, I didn't properly think about her as I should. Until now, I'd not appreciated how no one, not even her mum, properly cared for her."

A fresh wave of agony cleaved away at his chest. "Julia wouldn't want you to think like that," he said hoarsely, knowing that implicitly.

The young woman seated across from Julia's still form offered a sad smile. "Yes, but isn't that my very point? She never has put herself first. Ever."

He took in a shuddery breath.

She hadn't.

But I want to be that person for Julia. He wanted to be the man who would keep her safe and make her laugh. He wanted to be the person she could cry with, and then he wanted to wipe her tears and devote himself to keeping her from any and all hurt that he could.

Even as he'd no right to her. Even as he'd hurt her and made her feel as though she could not turn to him with her fears, he wanted to spend his life making up for those mistakes. Harris slid his gaze across the room to the fire raging in the hearth. He studied those crimson flames as they danced and twisted about, casting ominous shadows that portended death, shadows he fought desperately to keep at bay.

Then Adairia began to sing. Her voice, hauntingly beautiful, filled the air, soft and lyrical and mesmerizing.

Oh fare thee well, I must be gone
And leave you for a while
Wherever I go, I will return
If I go ten thousand miles, my dear
If I go ten thousand miles
Ten thousand miles it is so far
To leave me here alone
Well, I may lie, lament and cry

And you will not hear me mourn, my dear
You will not hear me mourn
As you sail away to distant lands
Along for you I'll yearn
My heart you'll hold in your strong hands
While I wait for your return.

Suddenly, abruptly, Adairia's song came to a stop.

"Julia," the young lady cried and then began to weep.

His heart froze and then fell. Harris squeezed his eyes shut as a piteous groan worked its way up from his chest.

She was gone.

Harris couldn't open his eyes, unable to view her, still in

death, as Clarisse had once been, a sight that would ravage him and haunt him forever. And yet, he also needed to see her. Needed to share every moment, even this final, darkest, most aching one.

Harris forced himself to open his eyes and then went stock-still, his gaze locking not on closed or lifeless eyes, but rather, exhausted ones, bloodshot but alive.

Then Julia's hand came up to stroke the top of Adairia's bent head. Her pale fingers trembled slightly as she, unselfish as she'd proven to be, as unselfish as he'd failed to see, conferred support and love to that sobbing young woman.

His heart resumed beating, a quick, galloping rhythm, each beat fueled by joy and relief so strong they threatened to take him down.

Storming to his feet, Harris flew across the room, shouting for the doctor.

Julia lived.

Chapter 22

With the aid of the cane given to her by the Countess of Cowpen, Julia followed after Adairia, the duchess, and the duchess' dearest friends. Julia moved slowly along the graveled path, slightly out of breath. The exertion it had taken to get from the carriage to this part of the park had left her embarrassingly weak.

The ten days she'd spent abed had managed to sap her energy in ways worse than the bullet she'd taken to the side. She paused, sweat beading on her brow, and leaned over the head of the cane.

As one, the four ladies accompanying her stopped.

Quitting the older matrons' side, Adairia rushed back and looped her arm through Julia's spare one. They moved at a slower pace after them. Since Julia had come to, it was as though Adairia had gone out of her way to avoid Julia. Even with Adairia's days filled with fittings and appointments as they were, Julia didn't doubt for a moment the real reason for that distance.

"We have not spoken of Rand Graham," she said as gently as she could, given the man she spoke of.

Adairia's mouth went hard in ways it had never before. "I've told you there's nothing to say. He was not behind your attack that day."

"Just your kidnapping," Julia pointed out.

"In fact, he saved you, Julia. Why, Mr. Connor Steele himself indicated that it was others, resentful of Rand's position of power and seeking to displace him, who were responsible."

Julia opened her mouth to speak, but Adairia interrupted. "There's nothing else to say."

Which, in short, meant there was nothing more Adairia intended to say about Rand Graham or her time with him. It was also the first time Adairia had not spoken freely to her, the first time she'd erected a barrier and kept it up. But then, neither had Julia shared any part of what she'd known and shared with Harris.

Julia stopped. "Go on ahead," she said softly.

Worry instantly filled Adairia's eyes.

"Perhaps this was too soon." Adairia wrung her hands. "We can return."

The duchess marched over. "But Julia has already come this far. To abandon our visit now would mean all of this was for naught."

"I don't want you to leave," Julia said to Adairia. And she didn't. She wanted her friend to see London and the world the way Julia had in the previous weeks. With Harris. She felt her facial muscles spasm. Perhaps if Adairia did, she could forget the time she'd spent with Rand Graham.

As though you can forget the time you knew with Harris?

"I knew we should not have come," Lady Cowpen whispered, her voice wreathed in worry.

The lady's sister sent an elbow flying into the other

woman's side. "No, you didn't. You were the one who insisted she'd be fine as long as she had a cane, because canes cure all problems."

Lady Cowpen's eyes lit. "You have to admit the girl does look debonair with the cane."

The lady's sister rolled her eyes. "Ladies aren't debonair. They are… They are…"

"Why can't they be debonair?" the other matron insisted indignantly.

As the eccentric pair bickered and Adairia watched on, giggling, the duchess moved closer to Julia. "Are you certain you're all right to be here, my dear?"

"Absolutely so. I would not spoil Adairia's outing," she said, her gaze on the bright-eyed girl playing referee between the quarreling countesses.

Her Grace's features immediately dissolved into a scowl. "I'm not worried about Adairia's outing. She has her entire life to experience the joy of London and life. I'm worried about you."

It had been so very long since anyone had ever worried about her. Had anyone ever? Had her own mother, even truly? The times Julia had been a small girl who'd fallen ill, or when London had nearly frozen with an unlikely winter chill, there'd not been words about Julia's well-being, but rather, how they could not afford to lose the support that Julia's efforts as a flower peddler provided.

Shifting her weight once more over the head of the cane, she carefully folded an arm about the duchess' shoulders. "Thank you."

A blush filled Her Grace's cheeks. "Whatever are you

thanking me for?"

"For caring about me."

As Adairia and the countesses continued on ahead, Julia and the duchess moved at a slower, more measured pace. "I'm not the only one, you know."

Julia looked off to the other women, Adairia still laughing and the older women on either side of her still arguing. "No, I do know that."

The duchess grunted. "I wasn't talking about those ladies." She paused. "Though they do, of course, care about you."

Julia cocked her head.

With an exasperated sound, Her Grace tossed her arms up. "I'm talking about Harris."

Harris.

Julia's heart sped up. Just the mention of his name would always have that effect upon her.

"I've never seen a soul worry about a person the way Harris fretted over you."

The duchess' words sent Julia's heart soaring before she recalled his anger and his absence these past days. "Indeed?" she said sadly. Because, really, what else was there to say? There was so much between them. Too many lies to overcome. Certainly for a proud man like Harris, who'd been wronged once before by another woman.

"If you were feeling more yourself, I'd give you a gentle cuff for that sad little look you're wearing," Her Grace chided. "That boy never left your side. From the moment he carried you in, to when the doctor arrived, and then when you finally awakened, he was there. I never saw him as heartsick and fearful as I did while he waited for you to come to."

He… was? Surely that meant something.

The duchess took Julia lightly by the arm and helped her up over the slight rise. "I… had no idea."

"I'm sure there's a reason he's not come around."

Except, his absence no doubt meant… more. Knowing the honorable man Harris was, he'd have felt guilt, a sense of obligation and responsibility for her leaving and everything that had transpired after at Rand Graham's.

They came to a stop. Overhead, the trees danced in a soft spring breeze. As those emerald-green leaves swayed, they allowed a streak of sunlight through, and those warm rays set a glimmer upon the lightly rolling river.

Julia bit her lower lip as she registered the place where the duchess had taken her.

Of course, knowing the story Harris had shared, it made sense. This was a place where the duchess and her friends had taken him when he'd been a boy. And as such, it would be a place the duchess would take Adairia to, too. But being here again, now… with the memories of that day.

"Julia! Auntie!! Come!" Adairia called from where she and the countesses stood, observing the pink pelicans. The young woman waved her arms with a girlish exuberance.

The duchess made to leave, but then, seeing Julia remained where she was, she stopped and gave her a questioning look.

"If it is all the same to you, I am going to rest for a bit."

"You're certain you are well, girl?"

"I'm fine," Julia hurriedly assured her.

Her Grace assessed her for a moment longer, as though considering the veracity of that claim. And then, with a little nod, she continued after Adairia.

Julia remained there, borrowing support from the cane, and stared on as the duchess joined her niece. Laughter from that pair, one lilting, the other slightly rusty, melded. There had been the reunion Adairia had always longed for. And yet, so many years had been lost between the two of them. Adairia had never got to have that same reunion with her parents. Even with those great and tragic losses, they'd forgiven Julia for her mother's sins… and her father's. It was a forgiveness she was undeserving of. And yet, selfishly, she'd found a home here. Far greater than the one she'd ever known with the woman who'd birthed her or the father whom she'd never even met. In short, she'd found… a family in Adairia's. It was the most wondrous of gifts, and perhaps she shared her father's soul after all. Because this… all of this should have been enough.

Adairia.

The duchess.

The countesses.

Four women who loved her as their own, and the security and safety they'd granted Julia by taking her in.

But, God forgive her, it wasn't enough. She wanted more.

She wanted him.

Julia briefly closed her eyes. *Harris.*

The wind stirred, and the leaves rustled once more, an echo of his name contained within that gentle swishing.

Opening her eyes, Julia turned and ventured into the

slight clearing of trees, limping slowly over to that private copse that she and Harris had made theirs, and stopped.

She blinked slowly.

For surely he'd always exist as he was in this place he was now, because her memories of that morning would forever prove strong. And yet, no matter how long she stood there, no matter how many times she lowered and lifted her lashes, the sight remained. He remained.

Seated atop a boulder, he tossed something at the water.

From the corner of her eye, it glimmered before landing with a *plunk* and sending a wave of ripples fanning out upon the Serpentine.

"Harris?" she whispered.

He stilled, so silent and motionless she expected she had imagined him being here with her.

But then he spoke.

"Do you know, I have come here for the past seven days, Julia," he murmured.

Befuddled by his presence, and the fact he was here even now speaking to her, Julia shook her head before remembering that he wasn't looking at her. "No," she said. "I did not know that." Because she'd not known where he'd been. Only that he'd not been with her and that her heart had hurt from missing him.

Slowly, he stood and faced her.

Stripped of his jacket and cravat, in nothing but his white shirtsleeves, breeches, and boots, he had an endearingly rumpled quality, and Julia drank in the sight of him. Devouring him with her eyes.

Before she recalled…

How they'd last parted.

Before he'd taken up a place at her bed, as the duchess had shared. Driven there by guilt? Or the caring that Her Grace had spoken of?

His eyes lingered on her face, his opaque gaze revealing nothing, and then he moved his search lower, until his focus landed on her cane.

She reflexively tightened her hold upon the top of it. The gold-etched orchid carved into the piece bit into the thin fabric of her leather glove.

"Are you well?" he asked quietly.

"Prodigiously so," she said on a rush.

They remained there, he beside that boulder he'd made his seat, and she at the opening of the copse, hardly daring to enter, wanting it so very badly that her selfishness proved stronger, and she ventured over to him.

In that moment, they were strangers. *But then, isn't that what you always were to each other?* a voice silently taunted. Jeered.

And yet, they hadn't been. She'd shared parts of him and had wanted to share… all. *And I should have.* "Harris," she began on a rush. "I am so sorr—"

"As I was saying," he cut her off. "I came here every morn for the past seven days." He shifted his focus out to the now-smooth, serene surface. "And I thought about the last time I came here… with you."

She stiffened.

"I thought about us that day, and all the days we were together… and every day, Julia," he said quietly, his gaze still out on those waters. "I would come and wish as we did that day." He motioned with an open palm, and she followed that gesture to the small pile of coins resting on the boulder, ones she'd previously not noted until now. "Do you know what I wished for?" he asked, turning back.

Wordlessly, she shook her head, and he moved closer, his long legs carrying him the remaining way, erasing that distance between them, until he stopped. Just a hairbreadth away. He brought a palm up and cupped her cheek.

Warmth radiated through her, a heat greater than the sun, so soothing and splendorous it brought her eyes closed as she leaned into Harris' touch. "You shouldn't," she said hoarsely. "Someone once told me that if one shares one's wish that it will not come true."

"That is true," he murmured. "But I wished for you to be here," he continued, and her eyes flew open. "I wished to turn and find you standing there, and here you are, Julia."

Her heart leaped. "What…?"

"I wished that you could love me and forgive me."

Julia's breath drew on a quick, audible intake, the cane slipping through her fingers, but he was there, stabilizing her at the uninjured side of her waist, keeping her upright. What was he saying? Her mind tried to make sense of it. All of it. Scarcely daring to believe the words he'd spoken, the ones she so desperately wished to be true and real and not merely the stuff of dreams she'd carried these past weeks.

Harris leaned close, placing his lips beside her ear, his breath, a soft, gentle sough upon her skin, more tender and soothing than the late spring breeze. "And do you know what I realized, Julia?"

She managed to shake her head. That slight movement

brought his lips into contact with the shell of her ear in a fleeting kiss.

"What I wanted most weren't gifts that I would or should wish for, because then they'd be unearned. Having the right to love you and earning your forgiveness are actions that I want to desperately commit myself to."

A little sob escaped her, and Harris brushed the pad of his thumb along her lower lip. Crouching lower, he rested his forehead against hers. "I wanted to ask you if you'd do me the honor of spending every single day with me so that I can make you happy and be there for you, and we can fight whatever monsters exist, together."

A tear slid down her cheek, and he smoothed it away, but there was another to replace it and another.

"Harris," she said achingly. "I don't blame you for your anger." She lifted her eyes to his. "I lied to you."

"I don't care about that," he said pleadingly. "Not anymore."

"You should." With the same tenderness he caressed her, she stretched a palm up and stroked his cheek. He immediately captured her wrist and pressed a kiss against it. "There can be no relationship with lies." She grimaced. "That is, not a healthy relationship, and so much has happened…"

His features froze, forming a perfect mask, and then that mask slipped. "You don't want to marry me."

"I do," she said on a rush. And then she stopped as his statement cut through her racing thoughts. "You want to marry me?" she repeated breathlessly.

"Of course I do, love," he said with an aching tenderness. "I want every day with you. I want children with you, so many daughters with your spirit and strength and courage." His words all rolled together, each one infusing a greater warmth into her breast. "That is, if you want them."

"I do," she said, her voice breaking on a half laugh, half sob. "And a son with your charm and goodness."

"I don't want to rely on wishing anymore, Julia," Harris whispered. "I want us to make our own future and shape our life, and I want us to do it together. If you'll have me. If you want to spend every single day with me, as I do y—"

"Yes," she cried, ignoring the stitch in her side as she pressed herself against him. Leaning up, she lifted her mouth for his kiss. "I want all of that, Harris."

A smile teased the corners of his lips. "Then you shall have that, love. That and more." Lowering his head, he moved to claim her lips once more.

With a laugh born of happiness, she took his kiss and embraced their promise to each other.

The End

If you enjoyed *My Fair Marchioness*, be sure and order the next installment of the *Scandalous Affairs* series, *It Happened One Winter*, which is out December 10th!

Official Blurb

Mr. Martin Phippen, a highly successful London builder, is forced by a business partner's foolish decision, to take on a project in the wretchedly scenic wilds of Yorkshire. Three little scamps have made his work site their private playground, and Martin is determined that their mischief be curtailed before somebody gets badly hurt.

Widowhood means Mrs. Christina Thacker has her hands full with her children, while her exchequer is distressingly empty. To remedy her lack of funds, she focuses on making a match at her sister's upcoming house party. When Christina's energies should be fixed on finding security for her family, she is instead powerfully drawn to the blunt, irascible Londoner with callused hands, sharp wit... and also, an intrinsic honor.

As passions flare between Christina and Martin, she must choose between a future defined by predictable security, or one built—with Martin—on a foundation of love.

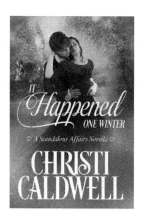

Scandalous Affairs
A Groom of Her Own
Taming of the Beast
My Fair Marchioness

Want to know the stories of the Lost Lords of London:

Lost Lords of London
In Bed with the Earl
In the Dark with the Duke
Undressed with the Marquess

Want to know the story of Claire's brother Tristan, the Earl of Bolingbroke and his wife, Poppy?
Courting Poppy Tidemore

Biography

Christi Caldwell is the bestselling author of historical romance novels set in the Regency era. Christi blames Judith McNaught's "Whitney, My Love," for luring her into the world of historical romance. While sitting in her graduate school apartment at the University of Connecticut, Christi decided to set aside her notes and try her hand at writing romance. She believes the most perfect heroes and heroines have imperfections and rather enjoys tormenting them before crafting a well-deserved happily ever after!

When Christi isn't writing the stories of flawed heroes and heroines, she can be found in her Southern Connecticut home with her courageous son, and caring for twin princesses-in-training!

Visit www.christicaldwellauthor.com to learn more about what Christi is working on, or join her on Facebook at Christi Caldwell Author, and Twitter @ChristiCaldwell!

Printed in Great Britain
by Amazon

80546555R00174